# A Kiss to Die For

*Mae Strack*

Copyright © 2023

All Rights Reserved

ISBN: 978-1-916770-20-1

# Dedication

I lovingly dedicate this book to my life partner Rory – my best friend and soul mate. I love you beyond measure and am eternally grateful for all of your unconditional support throughout the decades. Your ongoing encouragement and belief in me serve as the catalyst to pursuing my passions. Through our journey together, I've been blessed to have lived within the true essence of love, and I cannot imagine a life without you.

# Acknowledgment

First and foremost, to my husband Rory – my rock and greatest source of encouragement, patience, and love.

To my sister Linda – my inspiration for resilience and strength; my sister Jude who left us far too soon – you epitomize sensuality (yes, your bratty little sister did read your diary), with a loving soul – I miss you for eternity; my little sister Pam for your love, patience, wisdom, and support; my sister by marriage Judy – you have been a source of inspiration and a rock for me – thank you!

To my four children and partners, and three grandbabies who may not wish their names forever associated with a steamy romance from their matriarch – you are my world. My love for you is eternal and unconditional. To my nieces and nephews and extended family – I am so blessed!

To my soul friends – you know who you are – without your love and encouragement, this book would not be in print. Thanks to those who took the time to read the draft and offer suggestions and feedback.

# Table of Contents

| | |
|---|---|
| Dedication | iii |
| Acknowledgment | iv |
| About the Author | vii |
| Chapter One | 1 |
| Chapter Two | 11 |
| Chapter Three | 17 |
| Chapter Four | 25 |
| Chapter Five | 39 |
| Chapter Six | 47 |
| Chapter Seven | 57 |
| Chapter Eight | 63 |
| Chapter Nine | 71 |
| Chapter Ten | 81 |
| Chapter Eleven | 91 |
| Chapter Twelve | 97 |
| Chapter Thirteen | 109 |
| Chapter Fourteen | 117 |
| Chapter Fifteen | 123 |
| Chapter Sixteen | 131 |
| Chapter Seventeen | 139 |
| Chapter Eighteen | 149 |
| Chapter Nineteen | 159 |

| | |
|---|---|
| Chapter Twenty | 167 |
| Chapter Twenty-One | 171 |
| Chapter Twenty-Two | 177 |
| Chapter Twenty-Three | 183 |
| Chapter Twenty-Four | 189 |
| Chapter Twenty-Five | 197 |
| Chapter Twenty-Six | 205 |
| Chapter Twenty-Seven | 213 |
| Chapter Twenty-Eight | 225 |
| Chapter Twenty-Nine | 233 |
| Epilogue | 245 |

# About the Author

Mae Strack is a devoted wife, mother, and grandmother. She loves her serene life on an acreage in central western Canada. Her passions include writing and editing, as well as spending time with her family and among nature - mountains, birds, bees, and flowers. Mae has always embraced the gift of literature - crafting stories, songs, and poetry. She has honed her literary skills in various career endeavors within diverse educational, professional, and freelance writing and editing undertakings. An incurable romantic, Mae contends that a little spicy romantic fantasy is healthy for all women, no matter the season of life.

# Chapter One

Marianna tore open the envelope with ill-disguised impatience. Amidst a deep, calming breath, she gingerly unfolded the letter - had not anticipated a quick reply. Truth be known, she had not expected a response at all. Chewing her lip in nervous procrastination, she hesitated. It looked so formal – final.

*"Dear Mrs. Jacobs: We thank you for your recent submission,"* - now for the impending "but," she contemplated skeptically.

Still, her pretty blue eyes shone with hopeful anticipation. It had been a long shot, really – the chance for any serious interest on their part was remote, she realized. Yet they had written, at least.

*"The band members have unanimously agreed to enter copyright negotiations, and therefore we request that you contact our office at your earliest convenience to arrange a mutually suitable appointment. All travel expenses will be covered by the agency on behalf of RedRock. We look forward to your early response."*

Marianna stood paralyzed, unable to digest the significance of the words on the paper glaring boldly up at her. The letter slid to the ground as her hands flew up to her mouth – disbelief clouded her senses. Surely, they weren't serious! They must have contacted the wrong person - that was it! There had to be thousands of wannabe songwriters vying for their attention. Good grief, she hadn't even written the melody – had no musical training whatsoever, other than a knack for coming up with darned good lyrics. How hard was that, really?

Oh man, Mari, what have you gotten yourself in for? Whatever had possessed her to enter that silly contest? Nothing saying she had to respond, right? It wasn't as if they would give a rip. The shrill ringing of the phone interrupted her emotional seizure…

"Hello?" Marianna cradled the phone on her shoulder, still dazed, bending to retrieve the letter, and brushing back thick, shiny auburn tresses as she slowly stood up.

"Mari! How's it going?" With her usual bubbling enthusiasm, Tess sounded like she'd just run a marathon. Marianna knew instantly that something was up.

"Hey, Tess, everything OK?"

Smoothing the letter absentmindedly, she wondered just what mischief Tess was up to this time. Her best friend since Grade 2, Tess was a mainstay in Marianna's life. Although her antics and theatrics often threatened to drive Marianna to stark raving lunacy, she couldn't resist her friend's infectious impish energy and charm. Besides, Tess served to provide a splash of color to Marianna's otherwise humdrum existence. Not that she felt any cause to complain. She was totally content with her secure lot as a single mom to her young son and daughter, who, as a matter of great relevance, thoroughly adored their Auntie Tess.

"OK, before you say anything, just hear me out!" Tess paused to ensure she'd enlisted Marianna's full attention.

"I have tickets to the Hardrock tonight, and just listen!"

Marianna bit back the negative mechanical response that instantly sprang to her lips, determined to allow Tess to vent her enthusiasm. This too, afforded her some time to build a strong case, which she knew was a vital component to getting out of this one.

"The Blues Kings are playing – you know they are your very favorite band – well, locally anyhow…by the way, have you heard anything from RedRock yet?"

Marianna visibly cringed. She knew that Tess was absolutely convinced that the classic rock band would instantly adopt her as their chief songwriter, from this point forward, regardless of the fact that their two frontmen had already secured fame and fortune during the last twenty-five years, doing exactly that.

"Well," she began.

"I know, I know - you'll let me know when and if you hear anything." Under considerable duress from Marianna, Tess had given her solemn vow to refrain from harping on this delicate issue.

"Mari, you must come this time - you know you need to get out, and you promised me! Besides, when you hear what I have to say, you won't regret it - trust me." At the lack of usual emphatic protests, Tess hesitated, "Mari? You OK?"

"Yes, of course, I'm just tired." Marianna wasn't exactly sure what she was, but it certainly wasn't far off the mark.

"Alright, girl, something is not right here. Cough it up." Tess was a pit bull with a beef bone, and Marianna knew better than to try to fluff her over on this one.

"OK, I have received a letter, but I'm sure it's just a standard reply." She winced inwardly at this little white whopper, but she simply wasn't up for Tess's well-meaning words of advice that were sure to follow, if the full extent of the possibilities evident between the lines of that letter were revealed. Within mere minutes, Tess would have her flight booked and personally supervise the writing of at least 10 more songs she would insist Marianna take along with her.

"I knew it!!" Tess giggled with glee. "I can't believe you haven't opened it yet!" Tess squeaked dramatically. "Come on. This could be your dream come true!"

"I will, Tess - I promise. I've just been too busy." She detested lying to her best friend but wasn't up for the confrontation. "Don't worry. You'll be the first to know."

"Great, you can tell me all about it when we pick you up tonight." It was an appointment, apparently. "And dress casual. We thought we'd grab a burger right there and save time - get good seats."

"Whoa, Tess, I haven't said I'm going anywhere yet, and by we, I assume you mean Dennis?"

In Marianna's opinion, Tess's current love interest was a really nice guy. The poor man was totally besotted with the vivacious Tessalina Jones, and Marianna had squarely hinted on more than one occasion that Tess would do well to consider him a long-term prospect. She wished with all her heart, that her friend would settle down and stop passing up the nice guys, in favor of more dangerous, emotionally unavailable men, who tended to satiate Tess's passion for adventure and craziness – seeming to be an integral part of her make-up.

Sometimes, Marianna acknowledged meekly, she wished she were more like Tess – intent on taking every pleasure from life with full abandon and no regrets. Not that she'd ever admit as much to her. Oh no, that would be courting disaster! Besides, she had her children to consider and couldn't afford to traipse around the countryside with a quest for good times as her major priority. As if on cue, Tess continued.

"Well, I insist, Mari, it's just what you need, and you know Jen will sit for you - the kids will be hyped."

Tess held a formidable play card there. It was true. Denny and Katrina absolutely loved it when their neighbor, Jen, came over to sit, which wasn't often enough for their liking.

"Besides, Dennis's friend is in town for the weekend and is craving scenery beyond his four hotel room walls. Now, I know what you're going to say," Tess gave her no chance to sputter an objection, "And Tom already has a girlfriend back home, so you're safe. Come on, Mari; I'm not letting you off this time."

The pleading determination in her good friend's voice rubbed Marianna's conscience, and she heaved a sigh of resignation. All she had really wanted to do tonight, was curl up and watch movies with the kids, and perhaps get a little more writing in after they went to bed. She said as much now to Tess, though it sounded flimsy and drab, even to her own sensible ears.

"You have all weekend for that. Now hurry off your duff. We're coming at 7:30."

Normally, Marianna would have staunchly stood her ground. Still, in truth, the letter had left her with a healthy dose of restless energy, and, at this moment, she couldn't imagine how she'd manage to sit still through a movie anyhow.

"All right, all right, I'll be ready, but no arguments when I want to leave, deal?" Tess would have saucily stuck out her tongue at the determined no-nonsense expression firmly plastered on Marianna's attractive face.

"Really? You'll come? We'll have a great time, you'll see."

Marianna smiled tenderly as Tess rang off. She usually did end up enjoying their outings – Tess really was a hoot, and the night out would do her good, she knew. She'd been putting in extra hours in the late evenings for her small business, bringing work home from her office so as not to compromise her children's entitlement to her time.

Suddenly she remembered the letter, still clutched in her hand. What on earth was she going to do about it? What crazy notion had spurred her to submit those haunting lyrics? But in truth, she knew the answer. Writing had been second nature since she was a very little girl. As far back as memory allowed, she'd had her nose glued to the little desk in her tiny bedroom, composing poems and singing songs she'd loved to make up on the spot. Her mother had affectionately dubbed her "*Little Singing Scribe.*"

By the time she'd hit High School, it was apparent that Marianna had some real talent, and a handful of teachers had encouraged her to consider post-secondary education to enhance her skills. While she toyed with the idea, she was a realist and knew that very few writers were good enough to earn a living at it. Deep down, she really didn't deem she had it in her, and was content to engage in writing as an enjoyable pastime - purely recreational.

Soon after graduating at nineteen, her father suddenly passed away from a massive heart attack, leaving her mother, herself, and her younger sister, Tammy, to carry on. Marianna had already ventured out on her own by this time, and was sharing an apartment with a co-worker at a local bank, where she had recently secured a teller position.

She had tackled her career with dogged determination, in a fierce effort to maintain her independence and sense of accomplishment, firmly resolving never to be left vulnerable like her mother, who had been forced to struggle through life on a meager pension income - trapped in a frugal existence in an older mobile home.

As if in eerie affirmation, the year following her father's death, her mother developed bronchial pneumonia and passed away suddenly, from complications. Her kid sister promptly moved in with her boyfriend and became pregnant, sealing her own fate in the bargain. Marianna was devastated, and became steadfast in her determination to make something of her life.

A few short years later, she had climbed the corporate ladder to branch management for one of the country's largest financial institutions, albeit with many political bumps and bruises. Her career left her little time for outside pursuits, and her writing aspirations became a distant pleasant memory.

Her personal life took a back seat, in her relentless quest for success. She had dated periodically over the years, but had never found any man she was inclined to get serious with. While this was a source of disappointment, it was easily overshadowed by the rigorous workload that her career demanded.

Looking back, she mused affectionately, if not for Tess's firm resolve to secure her friend's happiness, Marianna would not have been blessed with her two beautiful children.

One balmy summer day, she'd accompanied Tess to the lake for a barbecue and beach party with a group of old college friends. The day prior had been Marianna's thirty-first birthday, and Tess wanted to celebrate. Marianna had vehemently protested, but Tess had worn down her resolve.

Her eyes softened at the vivid recollection - the moment she had first laid eyes on Jeff; tall, dark blonde, lanky, and sinfully hot. What immediately struck home was the manner in which Jeff's warm smile reached his eyes, softening his rugged male features, making her feel as though nothing else mattered to him at that moment, except being with her. They had immediately hit it off and, within three months, were married. Marianna was pregnant almost at once, and when Denny was born, she thought herself the luckiest woman on the planet.

Three years later, Katrina arrived with enormous, gorgeous blue eyes, so like her mother's. Jeff had insisted that Marianna's gaze did things to his insides, and he'd nicknamed her *"Pretty Eyes."* He'd even programmed it on her cell phone. Life was idyllic. Marianna had quit her job at the bank shortly after Denny was born and had ventured out on her own as a part-time financial consultant. It was a perfect situation, as she could work as much or as little as she pleased from her home. Jeff provided a decent income as a County Fire Safety Marshall, which afforded them a small but cozy acreage home, just fifteen minutes west of Edmonton. Their life together was truly peaceful and secure.

On the day of Katrina's first birthday party Jeff had uncharacteristically broken his promise to spend it at home, insisting he needed to go and check on a mock warehouse fire set up as part of a training program. He was not altogether confident in the new Deputy-Chief and wanted to ensure the project was operating as planned. Jeff had promised to be home in plenty of time for the party. Marianna was not especially alarmed when he failed to show, as this was very often the nature of his work.

At 5:00 p.m., the last of the parents were leaving with their sleepy tots, when a police cruiser pulled into the driveway. Her heart had vaulted immediately in her throat, as she'd motioned for the kids to stay in the yard with Tess while she'd forced herself forward to meet the policeman walking slowly toward her. When he reluctantly took his hat off, she knew. She hadn't wanted to hear what he had to say - she wanted to scream at him to leave her property. With a sickening certainty, she'd become aware that her world was about to come crashing to a horrific halt.

Later, cradled in Tess's embrace, she'd sobbed uncontrollably as they'd watched in agony, the terrible news footage of the huge warehouse fire that had claimed the lives of three firefighters and the County Fire Safety Marshall. Tess had swiftly switched off the T.V. before the announcer could begin naming the victims. Then…the long agonizing months of grieving, when Marianna had thought she would surely die from missing Jeff with a desperation that shook her to the core of her soul. If it weren't for the kids – and Tess…

"Mommy, Mommy!" Marianna's painful reverie was blessedly shattered as four-year-old Katrina came bounding into the living room, gasping for breath, excitement sparkling in her enormous sapphire blue eyes. Her shiny blond hair, secured in a ponytail, bounced behind her. Jeff's hair.

"Come quick. You have to look at Den's frog pond!" She smiled indulgently at her little girl. "Mommy, it has *tagpoles* in it!" Marianna laughed at the sweet, innocent mispronunciation.

"Kat, Honey, that's tadpoles, and please tell me you put the cover back on the tank." She shuddered at the memory of the slippery green amphibian that had leaped for sweet freedom, making a direct beeline for her bedroom, the week prior. It had taken the three of them the entire evening to catch the little croaker.

"Of course, I did, Mommy." Katrina stared at her mom condescendingly as if she were a silly goose to consider otherwise. "Come on!" Marianna sighed and dutifully followed her daughter upstairs to Denny's room. "See, Mommy, aren't they cute?" Katrina carefully lifted the lid off of the tank. Marianna bent down for a closer inspection of the murky green water.

Sure enough, what seemed like hundreds of tiny tadpoles, were swimming around energetically amongst the slimy plant life and rocks that formed part of Denny's pond-life study. Marianna had reluctantly agreed to allow Denny to convert his recently deceased turtle's home, in an effort to duplicate his grade two classroom project. The three of them had gone to a local swamp, aptly christened "The Beaver Pond," and had collected gallons of the cloudy water. Marianna had been appallingly amazed at the amount of insect and who-knows-what unknown plant and animal life teeming in the algae-filled mire. She wasn't altogether sure she wished to be further enlightened.

"OK, Sweet Pie, time to close this up now. Denny will be home soon, and I have a surprise for you." She gathered the little girl into her arms and gently planted a kiss on her rosy cheek, which smelled suspiciously of strawberry lime gummy bears.

"Oh, what is it, Mommy? Is it a treat?" Marianna grinned at the expression of innocent joy and adoration on the tiny cherub's face.

"Well, not the kind you can eat, Sweetie, but you'll love it just the same."

The welcome chug-chug of the aging school bus escalated Katrina's excitement as the back door slammed. "Let's go find Denny, and I'll tell you."

# Chapter Two

At precisely 7:15 p.m., Jen strolled through the front door and was promptly bombarded by two squealing children. She laughed delightfully and immediately initiated the infamous tickle monster game that marked much of her popularity with Marianna's offspring.

"Thanks for coming on such short notice, Jen. I shouldn't be too late," Marianna gathered up her purse and threw her reflection in the mirror the once over.

"Oh, don't worry, Mrs. Jacobs, I brought my overnight stuff, just in case I decide to crash."

Predictably, Jen had been eager to come over and sit with the children. Sometimes Marianna worried that the enthusiastic seventeen-year-old did not pursue a more active social life befitting a young girl of her age. Shouldn't she have been otherwise engaged on a Friday evening? Just thank your lucky stars, Marianna checked herself and tapped her little wooden nook. She didn't even want to ponder life without Jen.

"It's fine, Mom. Stay out as long as you like. We don't mind," Denny assured her.

She gazed affectionately at her seven-year-old son and marveled at his maturity for one so young. Jeff's sudden death had contributed significantly, and she knew that Denny quite seriously believed himself obligated to fill the role of the man in the family. A twinge of guilt assailed Marianna as she wondered if, perhaps, she was making a tragic mistake by not actively pursuing a father figure for her children during their impressionable growing years. Shaking off her reverie, she ruffled Denny's auburn mop, that was currently sticking out every which way from the top of his head, and knelt down to gaze warmly into his hazel eyes.

"Thank you, Den, for granting your permission," she teased and kissed both kids before heading out the door.

~~~

The foursome arrived at the Hardrock precisely at 8:00. Marianna had ridden in the back seat of the immaculate 1965 convertible Mustang that had endured months of painstaking restoration under Dennis's watchful eye. She chatted easily with Tom, who sprawled totally relaxed beside her and found him to be a very attractive man, blessed with a dynamite smile. He possessed a full head of gorgeous red hair with a light sprinkling of freckles and hazel/brown eyes to complement.

It soon became apparent that Tess's information on Tom was dated, as he frankly informed her that his girlfriend had recently dumped him unmercifully for another man. Her heart went out to him, and she ruefully acknowledged that, before Jeff, she could easily have fallen for a man like Tom. It was one risk, however, that Marianna Jacobs was no longer willing to take. Never would she allow herself to be so vulnerable to such a harsh loss.

Moreover, she knew that what she and Jeff had shared was rare – a once-in-a-lifetime ticket, and she just didn't think she could settle for anything less. It wouldn't be fair to another man to continually measure him against the best. She was content to pour her complete love and energy into raising her beautiful children.

Now, stealing a glance at Tom, she found it difficult to lay blame on Tess for placing her in this position. The man was clearly a phenomenal catch. Still, she vowed passionately that she would strangle her best friend at the first available opportunity.

With burgers and fries now demolished, they watched the band set up on the stage, and Tess quickly seized the chance to corner Marianna. Gazing in open admiration, as their hunky male companions sauntered over to check out some Collection Edition motorcycles set up by the bar, Tess wasted no time getting to the point.

"OK, spill it! I know you've opened the letter – what did they say?" Tess's determined expression promised Marianna that there was no delaying this conversation.

"They want me to go down to L.A. to sign a contract." The words sounded foreign on her own lips, as if she were discussing someone else altogether – a stage performer or a character in a juicy romance novel. The casual manner with which she had spoken belied her inner tremors. Perhaps if she feigned nonchalance, she could take her friend's assured enthusiasm in stride and keep her own hopes from rocketing skyward. Good plan, Mari.

"Omigod, Mari, that's awesome!" Tess was predictably elated. "When do you go?" So much for calm realism.

"I'm supposed to call them to arrange a time."

Marianna's beautiful features took on a troubled expression. This only served to enhance her natural, sultry beauty - the high cheekbones and voluptuous lips. Her eyes were so deeply blue they appeared violet at times – she had often been told she likened Elizabeth Taylor to the actress's younger years. Long auburn tresses fell in shiny gentle waves down past her shoulders to caress her lower back. Jeff had begged that Marianna never cut it – he had loved to run his fingers through the silky locks and had often insisted on washing and brushing it out himself until it shone like polished copper.

God, how she missed the feel of his big, gentle hands massaging her scalp - washing away all of her cares. Tonight, her pensive musing lent an aura of vulnerability to her loveliness that took the breath of more than one gentleman admiring her from a distance in the crowded nightclub.

"So, call." Tess paused, trying to assess Marianna's frame of mind. "What's bothering you?"

"God, Tess, I haven't the foggiest idea what I'm doing." Marianna abandoned her struggle to remain aloof from the situation. "I don't know what constitutes a good contract or whether they are even aware that I haven't written the music to go with the lyrics," Marianna bit her lip in anxious agitation. "I can't do this, Tess."

"Of course, you can, Mari! What have you got to lose? You merely fly your cute little tush on down there and find out precisely what it is you are expected to do. Tell them you will require that your lawyer peruse the contract before you sign it." Tess gave Marianna a gentle, encouraging hug. "Honey, you can't let this go - it's your dream! And besides, if they'd wanted the sheet music, I'm sure they'd have asked for it. Promise me you'll at least phone and find out."

Marianna smiled at the caring concern evident in Tess's encouraging smile and let out her breath, relaxing a little for the first time since she'd opened the letter. It felt good to vent with her best friend – lightened it all somehow. Could this really work out to be something? She promised Tess she'd place the call first thing in the morning.

"Meanwhile, what do you think of Tom?" Tess was ogling the men shamelessly as they made their way back to the table through the throng of revelers.

"He's very nice, Tess, but you know damned well I'm not interested in dating anyone," the unyielding tone brooked no argument.

"And I'm trusting you were completely unaware of his recent split with his girlfriend?"

Despite her frustration with the entire issue, Marianna was hard-pressed to maintain the murderous glare she had fastened upon Tess, and her face softened.

"I swear I had no idea until Dennis showed up at the door with him!" Tess threw up her hands in a defensive gesture.

"But you can be friends, for heaven's sake, can't you?" Tess tried to reason with her.

Marianna had to admit that she found it very comfortable being in Tom's company, as if she'd known him all her life. But friends it would remain - she was determined not to veer off that pathway. Her children deserve all of her energy for now.

The remainder of the evening proved relaxing and enjoyable - Tom was the perfect gentleman, and Tess was apparently content to leave Cupid to rest for now. They parted ways sometime after 1:00 a.m.

# Chapter Three

The tantalizing aroma of sizzling bacon and richly brewed coffee aroused Marianna's senses the next morning. She stretched languorously, rolled over, and reluctantly opened one eye to peek at the clock. She bolted straight up in alarm. How on earth had she slept until 9:00? She tumbled gracelessly out of bed and quickly sprinted into the bathroom to splash water on her sleep-flushed face. After scrutinizing her reflection, she ran a brush through her unruly mane and headed downstairs in search of her children.

She discovered them in the kitchen, dutifully cleaning the breakfast dishes and chatting incessantly with Jen, who was just heaping a healthy portion of bacon, eggs, hash browns, and toast onto a plate.

"Good morning, Sleepyhead," teased Jen, her green eyes twinkling with mirth. "Sit down. Your breakfast is served."

The cheeky teen bowed dramatically, and Marianna secured her housecoat in place and offered a grateful smile as she accepted a steaming cup of coffee.

"Oh, Jen, I'm so sorry – you really shouldn't have gone to this trouble. Why didn't you wake me when the kids got up?" She fixed a reproachful stare upon her children, who were altogether too pleased with themselves at this delightful situation.

"It was no problem, and to be honest, the kids haven't been up very long either – we were watching old Bugs Bunny reruns last night. I hope you don't mind." Jen gave her a sheepish grin.

"You know that I trust you implicitly, Jen - whatever you do is fine by me. But how do you manage to get my munchkins to work so well for you?" Marianna gazed in affectionate fascination at Denny and Katrina, toiling harmoniously together as if it were an everyday occurrence. Ha – wishful thinking! "I have to pull teeth to get them to do dishes without starting a world war," she muttered with more than a little envy.

Sitting down at the table, Marianna found that she was quite ravenous and eagerly lent her full attention to devouring every last morsel of the tempting feast. With much gratitude, Marianna sent Jen on her way, thanking her lucky stars that she had found someone so sweet and trustworthy to watch over her children. Settling Denny and Katrina into their chores, she plunked down warily at the little phone nook in her kitchen. The letter glared at her ominously, daring her to pick up the receiver. What on earth was she going to do? One thing for sure, she knew Tess was right; it would haunt her forever if she didn't follow this through. She took a deep breath in an effort to still the trembling, which threatened to render her fingers useless.

It wasn't an issue of scheduling. Jeff had left her moderately comfortable financially. For the past three years, she had been fortunate to spend her time alternating between volunteering at the school and staying at home with Katrina.

It was only recently that she'd begun to pick up her business ventures again, spending the hours while Katrina attended play school, pouring over business plans and financial statements. It took only ten minutes to drive to the small office space she had rented at a strip mall in a bedroom community not far from their home. An unnecessary expense, she was aware, but it granted some exposure in the professional world and served to provide a healthy tax write-off.

Above all, she loved the luxury of watching her children grow, of always being available for them. The hours at home also afforded her the opportunity to write again. Her passion was really for children's literature, and she had several projects on the go. So far, the only published pieces were in magazines and short stories - all had paid a pittance. The goal was not for monetary gain - no illusions there.

Just two months ago, she'd been scouring her archives for fresh ideas and had stumbled across a rumpled folder of old song lyrics she had written as a teenager. One, in particular, had pulled at her heart. Marianna could still recall the very day she'd sat down to pen it. At that tender age, she'd developed a deep passion for the music by RedRock, a hot new rock band, who were taking the charts by storm. Their genre was a unique blend of country and rock and roll - hence the term "country rock" emerged. The music inspired her, and she fantasized about herself on stage, singing with the band – belting out all their lyrics she so intensely identified with.

Then she'd written that first song - the day after her best friend's boyfriend had been killed in a car accident. It was a dark time. Tess had been devastated, and the boy had been highly intoxicated. It was a blessing that he had taken no one else with him – a single-vehicle crash, wrapping his beloved 1967 Corvette around a tree. He had died instantly. From that moment on, Marianna had vowed never to drink and drive and to do whatever was within her power to prevent friends from doing so. It was a tall order – the police tended to overlook it too often back in the day.

On the very day that she'd retrieved the archived files from storage, Denny had been at a friend's home, and Katrina with Jen on a trek for garage sale toys. Marianna was grateful that they had not been there to witness her emotional reaction to the vivid memories that would always accompany those poignant lyrics.

Gratitude had flooded her heart - Jen was a level-headed girl and very active in S.A.D.D - Students Against Drunk Driving. at her high school.

It had been just a week prior, that Marianna had purchased the reunion concert DVD of RedRock – she had been thrilled when they had decided to do a tour and couldn't believe her good fortune in securing tickets for their date in Edmonton. It was a dream come true - the concert of a lifetime, and the memory of that night, with the entire coliseum rocking along with the band, still evoked delicious goose bumps tap-dancing across her skin.

There had been a booth set up, and despite the throng of bodies swarming the building, she'd managed her way over to purchase a T-shirt, accepting the accompanying entry form for an upcoming contest with mild interest. She supposed she must have experienced some sort of subconscious drive to revive the creative urge that had been so powerful all those years ago, and surely it was pure divine intervention that had possessed her to submit her lyrics to the agency. She hadn't even been sure they'd read it, much less respond. If not for Tess, she'd have forgotten all about it.

All right, old girl, you can do this! Marianna snapped her attention back to the present. With any luck, their office is closed on Saturdays. She gathered what strands of courage she could muster, held her breath, and dialed. She heard vaguely, in the background, the children playing peacefully in Denny's bedroom. It was reassuring somehow - a lifeline, and Jen would be back any moment now to take them for their promised treat. Marianna couldn't fathom why this thought was somewhat discomforting.

"Limelight Productions, Vic here," the deep male voice brought a fresh round of butterflies churning in her stomach, and she was suddenly speechless, the silence dragging on until Marianna was sure one or the other of them would hang up at any second.

"Hello?"

"Yes, my name is Marianna Jacobs, and I received a letter from you recently." Complete silence reigned.

"I sent a sample of song lyrics to your office to be considered by the group RedRock," she continued. Yeah, along with four million others, most likely, she assumed. Geesh, I sound like a dimwit. Marianna silently berated herself.

At his continued silence, she forged ahead – all or nothing, "I was at their concert here in Edmonton and entered a contest. The winner was to be considered for a contract…" Marianna trailed off, feeling like an idiot, certain that this had been one huge mistake.

"Yeah, yeah, I remember now. Sorry, we get a load of mail through this office for many different musicians. How can I help you?" He certainly wasn't making this any easier.

"I was directed in a letter to call your office to arrange a mutually acceptable meeting time." Another pregnant pause.

Marianna suddenly wondered what kind of outfit this was – and just how many people had gotten letters exactly like hers?

"For contract negotiations?" She didn't know what more she could tell him. Lordy, should she just hang up?

"Oh sure, that's right – here it is. The band is in the studio for the week and a bit, and then they're going on a break for a month or so – hectic schedule of late. Beyond that, I couldn't tell you for sure what's available. Can you make it next week?"

"Oh, then I have to meet with the band members in person?" Marianna stammered dumbly, feeling panic rising within. She had assumed that the agency would handle all the red tape. Then again, what did she know about the music industry? *Oh, Mari, you donkey, you are in way over your head.* She was about to tell him she'd have to think about it when he continued.

"RedRock insists on hands-on involvement. They never sign anything without meeting the writers. Actually, they rarely take on new songwriters – had me stumped there for a minute," he chuckled heartily. "That must be quite the number you wrote – they apparently really liked it." Marianna was stunned by this shocking tidbit. "So how 'bout it? Next Thursday, OK?"

"Sure, Thursday would be fine. Where?" Was she insane? Had she really just agreed to this? She felt the sudden urge to slap herself silly and waved absentmindedly to Jen and the kids, who were headed out the door.

"I'll e-mail you with all the travel arrangements, have no fear."

She confirmed her address and rang off as she slumped into a kitchen chair in a pool of nervous exhaustion. Running her hands through her hair, she moved to massage the knotted muscles in her neck - tell-tale tension - and smoothed her denim skirt as she stood up, lost in a jumble of confused thoughts. Jen coming in with Katrina a little while later, escaped her, and she gave a start when the little impish delight pounced on her.

"Hi, Muffin. How was your ice cream treat?" Marianna bestowed a grateful smile on Jen and gave herself a mental shake in a feeble attempt to calm her frayed nerves. "Did you bring one for me?" she feigned a look of hopeful desperation.

Katrina giggled delightfully and pulled out something from behind her back. Sure enough, it was a DQ Dilly Bar, Marianna's favorite cheat.

"Thanks, Little Pumpkin!" surrendering to ice cream heaven, they laughed mischievously in their competition to see who could create the funkiest ice cream mustache, finally agreeing unanimously that Denny had taken the crown for that one, with ice cream up his nose.

~~~

If not for one incredible bundle of energy named Katrina, Marianna would have considered the next several days to be the longest of her life, and it was the second-last week of the school year for Denny. She wavered between disbelief – pinching herself on more than one occasion, as her reality meter worked overtime, and fevered excitement to the possibilities that may lie ahead. Not to mention the fact that she was likely to meet – in person, five of her favorite revered musicians, it was more than a little disconcerting to think that they had actually favored her song lyrics to consider a copyright contract. She couldn't shake the foreboding suspicion that she may very well have bitten off more than she could chew.

Yikes, what was she going to do if they wanted more? Calm down, Mari, she scolded herself – getting yourself all in a tizzy will not help the situation. This was one of the rare occasions she was sorely tempted to drag Tess over and crack open a bottle of bubbly. She needed all the fortitude she could muster.

~~~

"So…what did they say?" Tess was sprawled out on Marianna's big comfy couch with one glitzy sandal dangling off her perfectly manicured toes – a flask of Pinot Noir swaying precariously in her hand.

Marianna took another long sip from her own and sat back with an exhausted sigh.

"I have to fly to L.A. next Thursday. Actually, I think I may have to leave on Wednesday to be there on time for the appointment."

Marianna loved living in the country, nestled in the rolling prairie, just two hours east of the Canadian Rocky Mountains, and would choose nowhere else, but air travel across the border was a bit of a scheduling challenge at times. She peered at Tess apologetically, hating to take advantage by leaving Den and Kat with her for yet another day.

"Don't go getting messed up in that well of guilt, Mari. You'll wreck everything – you can't use that excuse to get out of this!" Tess could read her like a book. "Relax, I've got your back on this end for as long as you need," she assured, "you know your kids adore me. Besides, they need a break from your insufferable seriousness!" Tess teased.

Normally Marianna would have felt a twinge of apprehension at such a remark from her friend, which very well may serve as a prelude to some planned round of mischief. But this time, she was pleasantly surprised at the sense of relief that washed over her and was quite content to let it go. Mari, old girl, perhaps there's hope for you yet. Tess continually chided her on being the world's greatest worry wort. Of course, she considered that this second glass of wine might likely be a factor in her present illusion of languorous well-being.

# Chapter Four

Thursday morning dawned bright and balmy in Los Angeles. The direct flight from Edmonton the previous evening, albeit boring, was relatively uneventful. Marianna was booked for two nights at Shutters on the Beach Hotel in Santa Monica, and she'd been advised that a driver would pick her up promptly at 10:00 a.m.

Her jaw had dropped in sheer astonishment, as she'd inspected the luxury hotel room, complete with a four-poster king-size Victorian bed and a jetted hot tub, sunk divinely into a spacious balcony, overlooking a gorgeous sweep of sand, meeting the Pacific. A soft glow from the pool lights below, reflected off ceiling-to-floor mirrored Spanish-style pillars throughout the 700 square foot tenth-floor suite. It was pure indulgence, and she was determined to savor every delicious second of it.

She had wistfully filled the romantic tub for two, to near spilling over, and promptly sunk into the delectably scented bubbly concoction, allowing the jets to have their way with her - massaging away the knotted tension. Leaning back with a sumptuous sigh, she'd sipped a flute of sinfully expensive champagne that had been tastefully left on ice in honor of her arrival, and she had marveled at the magnificent view – the hotel lights gleaming off the water, vying with the full moon for her attention.

Such lavish pampering was nothing short of heavenly and had sapped every ounce of energy from her bones. Sometime later, Marianna had wrapped herself in a huge fluffy terrycloth complimentary bathrobe, dried her hair, crawled under the goose-down duvet, and promptly fallen fast asleep.

Now, checking her appearance in the fully mirrored foyer, for what must have been the twentieth time, she reflected on the state of her keyed-up nerves and wished that she had not woken so darned early. She had devoured a room-service continental breakfast out on the balcony with the gentle salty ocean breeze stirring her senses - providing calm serenity.

She anxiously ticked off the minutes, quelling the inclination to high tail it back home on the first available flight. She smoothed her peach cotton pencil skirt that subtly hugged her shapely hips and thighs – she had decided to dress for the heat, light and casual, yet elegant with a matching figure forming, but conservative patterned tank top, with vibrant splashes of fuchsia, royal blue, and teal green. The colors matched the natural fiery sparkle in her eyes.

Was the skirt too much? She conceded that she wore it well, but was, after all, turning forty in mere months - no spring chickadee here, that's for sure! Marianna considered her still relatively slim figure. Did she look her age? She supposed so, although Tess always proclaimed that she envied her friend's timeless grace.

Marianna did not think of herself as beautiful and, indeed, could not lay claim to the classic loveliness of runway models. Her mouth was a tad wide, and her nose, she figured, was of the Roman variety, inherent in her Ukrainian roots. Her eyes, by far her best feature, were incredibly expressive, and anyone who knew Marianna could penetrate her inner sentiment – with a quick gaze into those baby blues.

Many a fortunate male had considered himself sensuously seared by a mere glance, though she was ill-aware of it. Just above average height at 5'7", her long, lean, well-shaped limbs caught attention everywhere she went. Though not particularly narrow-waisted, she was reasonably flat and trim. Even Marianna would have to agree that her breasts – just a tad above average size, topped a ten on the scale. In truth, it was difficult to judge her age. With a startling vibrant gaze that reflected a somewhat mysterious yet magnetic personality, wherever Marianna chose to fixate her attention, she commanded considerable interest.

OK, the skirt would do, she figured, but perhaps there was a little too much hint of cleavage? She didn't wish to appear as a groupie, simpering after her favorite rock star. Veritably, her deep reverence for music would never allow her to fall into that mindset.

In younger years, when RedRock was at its peak, she found it difficult to fathom the screaming, fainting female concertgoers, who could not possibly have heard a single note from the band above their own ear-splitting shrieks. Oh, she wouldn't deny the appeal of male virility with at least a couple of the band members. Still, Marianna's appreciation for their musical talent far overrode any hormonal stimulation this eye candy provided. As far as she was concerned, that was just a surface bonus.

Was it a mere coincidence, Marianna mused, that her next novel outline, to be her first in adult non-fiction, was about the impossible feats that celebrities must overcome in order to maintain some quality of life? One of the mothers at Denny's school this past year had recently risen to formidable fame with her newly released Country Music CD, and had shared her anxiety with Marianna over the negative impact she feared stardom might have on her children.

Marianna had pitched the idea for her novel one morning, as the two moms were volunteering on a cultural field trip, and the talented artist had whole-heartedly encouraged her to go for it, promising to provide as much insight as possible.

Glancing at her watch impatiently, she decided to venture down to the lobby to squander the next half hour, anxious to browse the rich collection of artworks adorning the walls. She'd also caught a glimpse of a huge Ming vase encased in glass and wondered what other treasures lay there to behold.

At precisely 10:00, the hotel manager approached to inform her that a car awaited out front. Marianna wondered how on earth he had known where to find her – she'd been anticipating a page over the hotel intercom system. What a country bumpkin, she chided herself. Immediately upon exiting the lobby, she was approached by a man she figured to be approximately her own age.

"Mrs. Jacobs?" At her affirmative nod, he explained that he was the chauffeur sent to pick her up and drive her to the studio. In an attempt to reassure her of his authenticity, she assumed, he dramatically opened his light sport coat to display a brassy black T-shirt, with "RedRock" boldly emblazoned on the front, encircled by a flaming red guitar.

Though verbal utterances were beyond her at the moment, she couldn't resist a grin.

"Nervous?"

His friendly smile of understanding invited instant rapport as he held the rear door of the late- model Cadillac open for her.

"Terrified," she admitted ruefully and offered a tentative smile, wondering just how much this man knew of her situation. Marianna pondered her lack of wariness with this member of the male population, who was a virtual stranger, after all, taxiing her around in a huge city that could probably swallow her up for eternity. As if having read her thoughts, he provided insight, glancing periodically at her through the rear-view mirror as he spoke.

"My name is Benny, and I am the official RedRock chauffeur, along with other duties as assigned," his smile was warm. "I don't often get the opportunity to collect such heart-stopping gorgeous female passengers, though."

Marianna blushed profusely at his teasing wink. This was highly unlike her – modest by nature, and she felt compelled to shake it off, forcing herself now to relax and respond with her usual gaiety.

"Oh, come now, living in L.A. must provide some fair scenery."

Marianna was enjoying the feeling of being back in control, loving the banter - it presented a chance for her to calm down and regain a measure of composure, which she desperately required at this moment. Benny's down-to-earth, light-hearted manner put her instantly at ease.

"Ah, but the old cliché about beauty being only skin deep is true, my fair maiden."

He winked again in the mirror and pulled up to the curb in front of an older brick building that she assumed must house their office. Escorting her into the lobby and onto the elevator, he pushed the fourth-floor button. As the doors slid open, dead straight ahead was a closed door, with "RedRock Productions" embossed on the sign. Suddenly lightheaded, Marianna knew with a certainty that she was way out of her league and fought bravely to squelch her rising panic.

"Come on, it's no big deal. I'll take you in."

Benny's gentle but firm grip on her elbow was slightly reassuring.

"They are all really down-to-earth guys - just be your lovely self, and you'll have them eating out of your hand in no time."

Marianna threw Benny a grateful glance, which he repaid with another one of his trademark blinks. She followed him through the door and down a hallway, devoid of any notable décor, through to a spacious sitting area, clean but sparsely furnished. The warm brick walls, adorned with poster-sized album covers, lent an inviting air. Straight ahead, beyond an entire wall of glass, she spotted the band members, in seeming conference, with instruments in hand.

She had not even pondered, until this very moment, if she would recognize any of them at such close proximity. Benny strolled casually through the glass door, motioning for her to follow. Well, she asked herself contritely, "I've no choice now, have I?"

She was quite unprepared for facing these musical icons in such a venue and had naively assumed that contract negotiations would take place in a stuffy boardroom with a huge table wedged securely between them.

Feeling incredibly inept and vulnerable, Marianna's stomach curled into a thousand knots, and she wasn't altogether sure her legs were going to be of support any longer.

The infamous musicians looked up lazily, in seeming indifference to her presence. Silently, she identified them all - knew their names.

Gary Keller, who shared lead vocals and periodically played drums, quickly resumed his conversation with a legendary guitar player, Jerry Macklin, who paid her no heed, though she knew he'd witnessed her entrance.

Standing across the room, in a separate discussion, were Tim Peters and Rick Jones, bass and lead guitarists, respectively – they also provided formidable vocals of their own accord on certain songs. Another that she did not recognize sat comfortably at the massive set of drums.

Rick offered a welcoming smile now, which she gratefully returned. Oh, sweet mother, what in the world was she doing here? She couldn't squash the uncomfortable feeling of intruding on sacred ground.

For reasons undetected, her attention was suddenly commanded to the far corner, and she knew who he was before she saw him - the other lead vocalist and rhythm guitarist. A breath - robbing gorgeous male specimen, he was the object of many a female swoon and a notorious womanizer, if tabloids were any measure, with a voice that had turned her insides to mush for decades.

Grant Furman's focus was fixed upon her now in a shockingly slow, unapologetic burning appraisal, which sent a strange tingling sensation shooting up her spine. His attention was most likely captured by whatever was resonating through those earphones on his head, she assured herself, but all the same, his steady gaze upon her was unnerving, and Marianna quickly looked away.

Suddenly, Gary came over and offered a hand.

"Hi, Gary Keller. You must be our lady of lyrics."

The firm grip matched his welcoming smile. In spite of her weak-kneed apprehension, Marianna gave him an appraising glance, wondering if his reputation as an egotistical, thoroughly spoiled musical genius - reportedly impossible at times to work with, was well founded.

Another ladies' man, by media standing, and Marianna could easily see why the female population would find it hard to resist his witty charm, not to mention the superb good looks. Gary motioned for the others to follow him through the glass doors. One by one, they all sauntered into the large room she'd earlier passed – a lounge of sorts, she supposed. Not luxurious by any means, but nevertheless comfortable, with huge leather chairs and sofas marking the perimeter of a casual gathering spot. Gary gestured for her to take a seat.

"Can we get you anything to drink?" he headed for the refrigerator behind a small wet bar. She sank slowly into a huge leather chair, feeling uncharacteristically clumsy, and welcomed the immediate sensation of being enfolded within the soft leather's warmth. She pushed away a sudden, fleeting image of herself, hopelessly swallowed up and trapped within its depths, unable to get out and make good her escape.

"A ginger ale would be nice if you have it, thanks."

Marianna didn't dare venture into anything remotely alcoholic at this point. She was already bordering on giddy with raw nerves, and didn't altogether trust herself. It was rather disconcerting, considering she was normally in firm control of her faculties.

"Wow, a girl after my own heart."

Yes, she remembered reading now, that Gary had sworn off substances a few years back – endured quite a bout with the demon alcohol, which had in part destroyed a marriage and delayed his solo career for a time.

He handed her the soda now and introduced the rest of the band, whom she keenly noticed had also avoided spirits. Marianna was touched by the amiable attitude with their warm greetings – obviously doing their best to make her feel at ease. Benny's continued presence lent enormous comfort as well - her ticket back to the hotel, should bravado abandon her.

They chatted easily, inquiring as to the origin of her lyrics. Marianna mustered up the courage to query about the music component and was assured that they would take care of the melody; it was the lyrics that had caught their interest. She sighed audibly with relief, and Jerry Macklin laughed out loud at the obvious jitters that were betrayed by the troubled expression on her pretty face.

"Do you know that your eyes tell a story of a thousand words?" He reached over and patted her hand reassuringly. "Don't worry; we don't bite."

Where had she heard that before? She couldn't resist a glance at Benny and giggled silently at his mock - *I told you so* - visage.

"At least not until midnight."

Marianna joined in the laughter now over this witty pun offered by Tim Peters, in reference to their hit, "Midnight Madness," about a sultry southern country town where *the sun still bites at midnight.*

Once again, her attention was drawn to the man lounging casually in the chair to her immediate left. Grant Furman. What was it about the way he looked at her? It was like the most intimate of caresses - an assault of sorts.

She could detect no hint of outward aggression, and he'd shaken her hand, warm and firm, yet still, she sensed an imminent danger lurking behind his casual façade. A shiver shimmied up her spine, and goose bumps tickled her limbs. She didn't have to ponder that his reputation preceded him. Those steel gray bedroom eyes were for real. She'd wondered about that - sometimes cameras could trick the eye.

Mari, where in the heck is this coming from? But still, she couldn't tear her gaze away – his long, lean, well-muscled legs were sprawled out in front of him, one casual boot lazily crossing the other, arms loosely folded across his broad chest. This was a man in complete control of himself, entirely relaxed and at home in his environment - indeed, any setting, she would wager. And he continued regarding her in that bold, calculating manner – it was thoroughly annoying!

"I think Grant's working his magic again."

Marianna tore her gaze away and jumped guiltily – she could feel the mortifying deep flush of blood flooding her facial features in response to Rick Jones's teasing observation.

"P-pardon me?" Marianna stammered dumbly, in total chagrin, wishing the floor would open up and swallow her whole right then and there. Indignation took hold - it would be a cold day with the devil before she'd ever give Grant Furman another moment of her attention. The man was altogether too assuming for her liking. And more than a little perilous - she reluctantly acknowledged that inner voice.

"We were just wondering if you'd be requiring legal services here, or have you retained a solicitor already?" This is from Gary. Thank goodness, they were getting down to the nitty-gritty now.

"Yes, I have a lawyer who has agreed to look the contract over. Thank you." She was starting to regain some semblance of control now - as long as she didn't look at the man, she warned herself sternly.

"Oh, come on, guys, the little lady has to be feeling overwhelmed by all this hype. Let's give it a break, let Marianna go back to her hotel for a rest, and we'll collect her again for dinner tonight?" Jerry looked inquiringly at Marianna, and she gratefully nodded her assent.

"OK, sounds good to me – Marianna?" Gary addressed her directly. "Tomorrow morning, you will meet with Vic at the agency to go over some contract details, and following that, you'll head back here to the studio to hear a piece of your very own magic put to music," he smiled indulgently and patted her on the back.

"Sounds great!" She turned to Benny, who was jingling the Cadillac keys melodically at the door. With a wink, he headed out, and Marianna smiled graciously in the boys' general direction, avoiding eye contact at all costs. She made a swift beeline after him, not daring to look back. But she could feel the burn from a pair of incredible gray eyes following her out - searing into her back.

She sank gratefully into the leather backseat of the luxury car and sighed heavily, relief flooding every cell of her body. Why had she let the egotistical guy get under her skin so? She'd become nothing short of an expert at foiling male attention since Jeff's death. She couldn't afford to get involved with any man, much less a famous rock star with a body fit for the gods, who could easily vie with the younger men on the scene, as the country's hottest sex symbol.

Even assuming, on a far stretch, he may be remotely interested in her, she didn't want a man in her life. It wouldn't be fair to Denny and Katrina. Besides, she was far too level-headed to allow herself to become another notch on the infamous proverbial belt of the rugged and sexy Grant Furman – however delectable a fling that would be. What the heck was she thinking? Give your head a shake, girl! She scolded herself. You are beginning to sound like some lusty rock groupie for sure now. She flashed Benny a bright smile, quite unaware of the effect upon its recipient.

"I think I'll go up now and take a much-needed nap. Air travel always does me in."

That much was true - Marianna's experience with flying on planes was minimal and confined to her youth. In reality, it was terrifying! It wasn't that she was afraid to die - practical enough to realize that her odds of survival were much greater in the air than on the ground, especially in L.A. No, it was more than that. Marianna could not tolerate being in situations that compromised her control. Large crowds and airplanes posed the greatest challenges, rendering her powerless to exit at her will.

Terrifying, paralyzing panic attacks had plagued her youth, but in recent years, she'd made considerable headway into managing the crippling anxiety.

It had been necessary for the sake of the kids, and Jeff had been instrumental in her success – a perfect antidote of loving patience and understanding. He was the only person in the world who knew of her painful suffering, which had besieged her immediately after her mother's death. Marianna had not even confided the full extent of it to Tess.

But it mattered little now, she thought with confident pride, reflecting on her calm control throughout yesterday's long flight. Still, it had taken all her concentration and energy, and she was fairly well-bushed right now.

Benny regarded her thoughtfully. "Okey dokey, I'll be here at 6:00 sharp to collect you for dinner. Dress casual. We're going to Gary's. Believe it or not, he burns a pretty mean steak on the grill." Marianna laughed out loud at Benny's devilish expression and thanked him sincerely for the amiable company.

~ ~ ~

Feeling renewed and rested after a refreshing nap and leisurely soak, Marianna emerged from the hotel lobby promptly at 6:00. Unbeknownst to her, she invited considerable attention, looking sexy and elegant in a simple black sundress that securely hugged her figure and enhanced her suntanned skin, that had deepened to a golden hue as she'd lounged for an hour and a half at the outdoor pool earlier.

A few invigorating dips had worked away some of the tension in her muscles and left her feeling perky and determined to enjoy her night with the band. They had, after all, been very friendly and seemed like an easy-going group of guys. The one exception she refused to waste any thought on now.

Marianna had no intention of allowing the man to spoil her remaining hours in L.A. After much consideration, while drifting off to slumber earlier, she'd come to the sensible conclusion that it was crazy to allow fear and anxiety to destroy what would probably be her only chance to visit this beautiful iconic city, and hang out with her favorite rock group – she'd be a nutcase to turn that down!

Still, it was purely astonishing that she had landed this surreal opportunity. Besides, where did he get off with his arrogant judgmental appraisal of her? Let the devil take him! If he wasn't the very demon himself, Marianna mused wryly.

Leaning against the gleaming Cadillac at the curb outside the hotel, Benny gave an appreciative low whistle at the enticing picture she presented as she approached.

Marianna's renewed mindset had lent an aura of sparkling self-confidence, and she was oblivious to the powerful seductive effect. She'd run a pick gently through her hair, resulting in a wealth of luxurious bouncing waves flowing down and curling suggestively around her waist. As she moved, her hair provided a teasing glimpse of her slender back, bared from the low-scooped design of the dress. Thankfully, gravity had not yet waged war with her breasts. They were still firm and perky – braless was no issue.

She'd tucked her feet into simple black sling sandals - her toenails meticulously manicured and painted lavender-blue to match the shade of her fingernail polish. She chuckled now at the expression on Benny's face. If she'd had any inkling of how deeply affected he was, by her radiant attractiveness – sparkling blue eyes glowing expressively, reflecting her energy and raw excitement, Marianna would surely have spun clean around and fled into her room, securely bolting the door behind her.

"Quit that. You're making me nervous," Marianna laughed good-naturedly. Benny sighed wistfully and settled her in the back seat of the caddy.

"I couldn't help myself. You are a vision of loveliness, dear lady."

Benny smiled at her in the mirror as he pulled away from the curb. Conversing easily on the way to Gary's, he confirmed the fact that the band very seldom used lyrics that they did not pen themselves. Four of the band members regularly contributed song-writing talent, with Gary and Grant, by far in the lead. Benny seemed unusually silent for the latter half of the ride, and Marianna didn't think it apt to query him.

When they arrived, Gary was busy at the barbecue, set up beside quite the most enormous pool Marianna had ever laid eyes on. She blushed at the appreciative glances, that she couldn't help but notice were aimed in her direction, by the male members of the group gathered on the poolside patio. What was the matter with her? She felt like a babe in the water. Her state of attire was conservative, compared with other females in the crowd, for Pete's sake!

She was completely unprepared for the bold, calculating, lazy inspection from Grant that assaulted her senses from across the pool. Her heart executed a double flip, and she hastily turned her attention to Rick, who gallantly took her hand with a comforting pat and introduced her to the members of their sound and production crew.

Thankfully, tonight, there were other members of her sex in attendance. She began to relax as a vivacious young girl named Heidi took her in hand and gave her a lesson on the key roles that everyone played in the complicated task of producing a top-selling CD - promising Marianna a first-hand demonstration the following morning at the studio.

The two women chose seats at a bright garden table, taking advantage of the shade, that a giant overhead umbrella provided. Marianna was amazed at the blazing power of the sun here, even in its final hours of the day.

Quite beyond her will, her attention strayed to where Grant sat, talking easily with Rick and Jerry across the patio. Suddenly, he laughed out loud at something that was said - a rich, deep, and vibrant sound, and Marianna caught her breath at the miraculous transformation of his features. Gone was the forbidding, brooding restlessness that had fairly much exuded from his pores when he had looked at her. The harsh lines on his handsome face softened with his laughter – good Lord, that killer smile was sinfully dangerous, creating little niggling tingles in the pit of her stomach. His eyes were warm and friendly, and she marveled at the obvious rapport the members of the band shared.

She attempted to ignore the lightening of her spirit at the possibility that Grant Furman may well possess a human heart after all. What did it matter to her, anyhow?

Suddenly, the heat of his gaze was upon her, mesmerizing, as he stared directly into her eyes - the hint of amusement teasing her senses and confusing her thought process. She shifted restlessly in her chair, like a bug under a microscope. Was that perhaps a little mischief in his eyes?

She tore hers away and struggled to focus on something Heidi was saying, but she couldn't deny the man had an uncanny way of setting her nerves on edge. When she next stole a glance, Grant was once again in light conversation with Rick. She looked away quickly before he could catch her gaze and, just at that moment, caught Jerry's speculative look. She really needed to get a grip here.

# Chapter Five

The remainder of the evening passed in a blur, with everyone going out of their way to chat with her, expressing genuine interest in the unique circumstances that had brought her to California.

Another girl, Angela, reassured Marianna that most of the band members themselves had humble roots.

Grant, in particular, had lived in rural Texas most of his young life with abusive, alcoholic parents. He'd left home at the tender age of 15, hanging out with buddies and his worn but beloved guitar, that he'd picked up at a pawn shop for a mere $5.00, jamming with anyone who'd allow him to join in.

Marianna was shocked at the wave of compassion that flooded her senses, at the mental image this portrayed. Five years later, Angela confided, he and Gary had written their first chart-breaker song, "Hot Summer Night." Marianna was touched to learn that he still owned and continued to treasure that guitar. She stole a glance at her watch and was startled to find it was already past 11:00. She looked around in search of Benny, feeling a strange melancholic disappointment that the evening was coming to a close.

"In a hurry to leave?" Marianna jumped at the deep, male voice assaulting her eardrums. She whipped around to find Grant leaning casually against a pillar, arms loosely folded, his dark, rugged frame contrasting wildly against the stark white backdrop. The hooded expression gave no indication of his present mood. What was it about this man that muddled her normally well-tuned sensibility?

"Tomorrow comes early," Marianna returned lightly, relieved that her voice had not betrayed her inner turmoil. Realizing that it was the first time they had spoken to one another, she was assaulted by a shocking familiarity that she couldn't put her finger on - as if in another life, perhaps, they had shared thoughts. It was a feeling that she was not altogether comfortable with. Drawn now to his deeply rich, sensual, and thoroughly male timbre, she felt a sudden light-headedness.

"Surely, at this stage of the game, you don't believe in fairy tales about pumpkins at midnight?" his tone was somehow insinuating.

Late stage? Was he referring to her age, then? Ha! He didn't have much room to talk.

Marianna envied men their fate by managing to season with nothing more intrusive than an enhanced, rugged and distinguished aura. On the other hand, women struggle to retain their femininity, threatened by hormonal changes - consider themselves lucky to avoid sprouting body hairs where hairs should never boldly grow.

Then again, perhaps he imagined her playing a fantasy role, a modern-day Cinderella. Did he view her as a gold digger? Or consider her mere presence an unwelcome intrusion on his precious privacy? Well, whatever crick was in his neck, it was his issue - not hers.

"I do detect an air of innocence about you. Still, I wonder..." Grant bestowed her a slow, thorough examination, leaving no part of her untouched.

Indeed, she felt as if she'd been stripped naked and scorched. She flushed furiously at his bold scrutiny and snapped her gaze away.

"I assure you that I'm a fully independent woman, highly capable of taking care of myself." Now, why had she blurted that silliness out? It's not as if he had been throwing out the offer to do so! She was adamantly determined not to reveal her increasing sense of vulnerability in his presence.

"Oh, I've no doubt about that," Grant returned huskily with that sexy southern drawl that was beginning to do strange things to her insides. "but L.A. is a big town, and somehow, I don't think you've ever played on this ground before."

His direct look and harsh tone of voice brought confusion to Marianna's pretty features. What on earth was the idiotic man going on about? It was as if he suspected she had some ulterior motive for being here. His gaze suddenly altered - searching, as if struggling to make up his mind about something.

"Well, you are right on that score. I am well aware of being quite out of my league here and am frankly worn out. I really need to call it a night."

Breaking their locked gaze, she smoothed back the tendrils of hair from her face. A quick glance told her that his eyes had followed her every move and were now lingering on her hair. Oh, God! She moved away rather shakily.

"If you don't mind, I'm going to find Benny."

With that, she whipped around and turned to leave, but he gripped her elbow with incredibly long fingers that seemed to sear her skin. "Benny's not here," Grant imparted matter-of-factly. "He's otherwise engaged tonight," his dark gaze regarded her thoughtfully.

"But - I saw him just a while ago." Thinking back, she had to admit that Benny had not firmed up a plan to escort her back to the hotel.

"He had to leave unexpectedly," Grant's tone was curt. "Trouble at home."

Marianna was instantly concerned for her newfound friend. Benny had been kind to her and a perfect gentleman – someone she instinctively felt safe with. Hell, a galaxy safer than being in such close proximity to the man standing before her now.

"Oh, is someone ill?" she blurted. Good Lord, what business was that of hers? As if on cue, Grant rejoined.

"My, we are curious, aren't we?" His tone was sullen as he regarded her.

If she didn't know any better, she'd swear the man was jealous. But that was ridiculous! He had all sorts and kinds of females fawning and drooling over him – why would he be concerned with her? He was just naturally crabby, it would seem.

"He lives with his mother and sister, who is, at this very moment, in need of a sound thrashing."

"Oh." As if this explained it all. Why did he make that sound somehow that it was all Marianna's doing? She needed to get away from here now, escape from this man's unsettling gaze and powerful magnetic masculine presence.

There was no denying that Grant Furman was one very attractive, sexy, virile male, and she'd have to be a saint to be indifferent to his charms. He had her at a disadvantage on his own turf in a strange town, and she felt particularly defenseless, with him hovering so close. She could feel his warm breath on her cheek now, like a lover's caress.

Get a grip, Mari! She quickly sprung to action and headed for the house - she would phone a taxi in privacy.

"Wait a minute, not so fast," Grant grabbed her arm and spun her around to face him. "Is there some reason to leave so early?" The inquiry seemed innocent – sincere.

"Yes," It was a squeak, really. Where on earth was her voice, her confidence?

"Come on; I'll drive you."

There was that devastating smile again. Lord, she didn't think she'd survive many more of those tonight. Her eyes were hopelessly riveted on the gorgeous dimples and rugged lines around his mouth.

"Oh, there's no need," she stammered, "I can take a cab."

"While that's probably true, it's no trouble, and I'm thoroughly bored with this party anyhow - I could use a breather."

How in the world was she going to get out of this one?

"You'll be perfectly safe, I promise."

Geesh, that wicked grin again!

"I assure you that I'm not in the habit of forcing women for their favors."

No, she was quite convinced that he must have an entire harem of simpering females, willing to do battle just for a single touch. Her eyes wandered to his hands, big and broad, surprisingly rough in appearance, for a musician. She imagined his touch would be gentle, yet strong – then, she'd already had a taste…her arm still burned where his fingers had been.

No, no, she wasn't going there! Time to get your head together here, girl. All right, so the man was incredibly attractive, not unlike a host of others she'd met. She could handle this one. Deep breath, girl!

"I'm not at all worried about the likes of you," she asserted with a bright confidence that even she had to concede rang false to the ear.

All she needed was to keep her perspective – be mindful of the fact that she was just another female in a deep bountiful fishpond and remain steadfast in her resolve to avoid joining his harem. Her fortitude was challenged at Grant's lingering glance on her long shapely legs as she settled herself in the front seat of his Ford Escape – not the expected racy sports model. She berated herself for donning such a revealing dress and wished she had crawled into the back seat as she did when Benny drove. The thought had crossed her mind but had seemed a ridiculous, cowardly thing to do, being that he'd opened the passenger door for her. There was no way on this green earth she was about to allow Grant to be tipped off to the powerful effect he had on her senses.

With his attention now safely on the road, Marianna inspected the vehicle's comfortable interior, more than a little surprised at his choice of transportation. He likely had a Ferrari or ten, tucked safely away in one of his garages somewhere, she supposed.

"What, did you think - you'd be getting a lift in a hot sports car? Sorry, my common SUV will just have to do," his keen perception unnerved her, but a glance at his mirthful grin assured her he'd been teasing.

"No, this is fine, but I admit that I expected you'd be driving something a tad flashier," she retorted with a sheepish smile.

"Wouldn't most famous musicians go for the expensive, sophisticated look, with affordability not in question?"

"You're assuming money isn't an issue then." His glance was almost challenging. "And yes, I suppose it is a normal guy thing. Although I've known more than a few women to hold similar cravings."

Oh, I'll bet you have, thought Marianna, with more than a little irritation.

What was that about?

Marianna shook it off.

"I apologize if that seemed presumptuous. Your financial status is none of my business. For all I know, this may not even be your vehicle." It was overcompensation, she knew.

"Well, hell no, I frequently resort to felonies to get around in this city."

That sexy southern drawl should be outlawed, and the crooked grin was the topper. She felt a sudden hot flush and rolled down the window for air. The cool evening breeze lifted the fiery auburn tresses from her slender neck, refreshing her skin and soothing her overheated body, returning some of her composure. She leaned her head back against the seat and closed her eyes, enjoying a respite from their interactive banter. Grant said nothing, and she wondered what he was thinking. Mercifully, the car pulled up to the curb, and she reluctantly turned to face him.

The intensity of his gaze sent her blood to boil again. Surely that was illegal, not to mention highly unjust to the female species. His inspection roamed of free will across her face, lingering on her eyes, neck, and dear Lord - breasts, before returning to caress her lips. He wasn't planning to kiss her, was he? She wasn't about to let that happen and hastily grabbed the door handle.

Before she could step out, he was there, holding out a big hand, and it seemed overly rude not to allow his assistance. His touch on her elbow felt like a searing flame, setting every part of her body ablaze. This was ridiculous! She turned around on the ornate hotel lobby steps to face him and murmured her thanks for the ride. She acknowledged reluctantly, surprised and a little disappointed, that he merely imparted a low bow and, with a taunting grin that promised unspoken delights, was gone.

Deep in thought, Marianna slowly approached the elevator and sighed heavily with relief when the door to her suite closed behind her. Gosh, she was exhausted. How on earth was she going to get through another day? Shedding her clothes carelessly, piece by piece, she played a mental briefing of the evening on the way to the shower. She stood under the rejuvenating hot spray of water for a very long time, trying to rinse clear all disturbing thoughts of a certain sexy man with a heart-stopping smile and staggering good looks. It was physical, she knew. There - that was it, she conceded. Her depraved womanhood was simply reacting normally to a very attractive male specimen. It was pure sexual chemistry.

OK, so maybe it could even be termed as volcanic lust, she allowed, although she'd thought herself a little old for that. There were names for ladies her age. She recalled the term cougar and laughed aloud at the thought – nowhere near enough sophistication or experience. She emerged from the shower feeling much more in control, having come to terms with her own involuntary attraction to the man, and honestly, any woman would find him hard to resist. And resist him she would!

Marianna firmly shoved the guy out of her mind and picked up the phone to call Tess and check on the children. God, how she missed them! Tess had insisted it was beneficial for the kids, even if Marianna was fool enough not to appreciate the break. She was eternally relieved that thousands of miles separated them right now, as she knew that Tess would zero in on her mood like a homing pigeon.

As they chatted about the children's antics over the past two days, she resolved to ring Denny and Katrina in the morning before going to the studio - she needed to hear their voices. Thanking Tess profusely, she ended the call. Gratefully collapsing onto the soft bed, she felt secure in the knowledge that nothing had changed, really. Her priorities remained with her children and always would.

But as she slowly drifted off to sleep, a vision of masculine opulence swam in her head - a certain comforting curtain enveloping her, with gentle arms of steel, in a warm fiery embrace.

## Chapter Six

A gentle smile softened Marianna's features after an animated yet tearful chat with Denny and Katrina the following morning. She emerged from the hotel lobby onto the street, alive and glowing with confidence and resolve. Yet there was a hint of vulnerability transparent in her expression. It was a look that often brought out a fierce protective streak in those who knew and cared for her. She stopped short, stunned.

Lounging casually before her against the Ford Escape, Grant was watching her intently as she stood there, paralyzed and unable to move or speak. Arms folded loosely across his broad chest, he wore a faded pair of blue jeans that molded his long muscular limbs like a second skin - a plain black t-shirt fell alarmingly shy of disguising his well-muscled arms and torso. The ebony hair was styled short, and she envied the soft wisps that caressed the nape of his neck. Her gaze fell to the corded strength there, and she wondered what it would be like to place her lips right on that spot - that pulse. She started guiltily as he cleared his throat. She knew her face had just turned three sheets of red.

"Are we ready to go yet?" his tone was exaggerated, and a thick brow lifted, in silent mocking insolence, above steel gray eyes that seemed to flash bolts of fire, with that crooked grin, as if he'd bested her in some kind of cold war.

Resisting the sudden childish compulsion to thrust her tongue out resentfully at the egotistical brute and slap that boorish smirk right off his handsome face, she instead squared her shoulders and hopped into the vehicle, slamming the door soundly – before he had a chance to come around and force his assistance upon her.

Bully! He slid his large frame easily in beside her without a word and immediately pulled away from the curb, a grim expression on his face.

An uncomfortable silence permeated the air. As the minutes ticked by, she sensed a morose cloud hovering over him, a dark gloom shadowing his features, making them appear harsh and forbidding.

Good grief, the man was moody! Arrogant too! Well, she wasn't about to let him spoil her day – she was truly looking forward to experiencing her song recreated within the band's music, and she would just have to accept the fact that in this, he was likely to play a major role.

Her thoughts turned to the day ahead. What would it sound like? She had taped a sample version of the tune that had burned into her brain at the time she'd written the song, and now brought it with her, in case they insisted on a melody to match the lyrics. Once again, Marianna was struck by the enormity of the vault she'd taken. Dwelling on this, however, would get her nowhere, she conceded. If it was meant to be…

"Is this your first time in L.A.?" Interrupting her reverie, the question caught her off guard.

"Yes."

How on earth was this relevant? In fact, he had already insinuated that he knew as much. Apparently, small talk was not his strongest social skill. At least not with her, she deduced, recalling the easy manner with which he had chatted the night before with the other guys.

"You've come a long way."

"Yes." Brilliant vocabulary Mari, she mocked herself. What was it about this man that had her constantly upside down, not knowing what to say or do next?

"I don't often get the opportunity to travel."

"When are you returning?" It was just casual conversation, after all, she decided.

"Tonight. I have a Redeye flight, I'm afraid." Why was she supplying this piece of information, she wondered? And didn't that sound a tad regretful to be leaving? "I really need to get home," she asserted.

"Have you seen Sunset Boulevard yet? Any other tourist hot spots?"

She peered at him now, wondering what he was thinking. She was afraid to answer that question. Would he offer her a tour?

"No, I really haven't had much time." In truth, she wasn't particularly interested in all the bright lights and celebrity haunts. Tess would be horrified to know that Marianna was, in fact, pining for her quiet country home.

"Well, I guess you'll have time this afternoon and evening then."

It was a statement. But why did she get the feeling he was expecting something from her? Oh hell, she was tired of this pussyfooting around! If he had a point to make, he was doing a damn lousy job of it. It was high time she let him know that this small-town girl held not the slightest interest in his ritzy, glitzy world.

"Actually, I plan to spend some time on the beach before I go."

Too much information, Mari! Better if she'd lied and said she planned on sleeping the rest of the day away. She'd really just been dying to shed her sandals, feel the sand between her toes, wade in the warm ocean waters, and take a long walk on the miles of beach that was accessible across the ground of the hotel.

Marianna had only ever visited the ocean a handful of times in her life and always found it to be an exhilarating experience. There was something about the wild frenzy of the waves, the raw power that attracted her like a magnet and captured something deep within her soul. It was spiritual, she supposed. A sudden discomfort loomed with the realization that the ocean reminded her of Grant. But that was ludicrous! Shake it off, Mari. He's just a tempting morsel, nothing more. She scolded herself.

"Would you like some company tonight?" It was a throaty caress.

He had pulled over to the curb in front of the studio and was watching her now, his searching gaze taking the very breath from her lungs. Was he expecting to find an answer somewhere deep in her eyes? All at once, he reached for her hand. The grip was gentle and strong, his large hand covering her smaller one like a protective shield. He ran his thumb idly over the ring she still wore on her left finger. She snatched her hand back as if it had been burned.

"What does your husband think of you traipsing halfway across the continent after a rock band?"

What kind of stupid question was that? She was tempted to tell him that her husband trusted her implicitly, thank you very much, and would throttle one Grant Furman for his presumptuous behavior with her, but it was not in her nature to lie.

"My husband died several years ago," she averted her gaze, not wishing to witness his reaction to her revelation. She jumped at his touch, gentle on her arm.

"I'm sorry, I made an assumption when I saw the ring. Do you have children?"

The hand dropped, leaving an icy, empty feeling at the spot on her arm where it had been.

Why was she still sitting there, entertaining this interrogation? Still, she responded.

"Yes, two," Marianna's face lit up, and her eyes glowed with affection as she thought of them. "They would certainly love to come to L.A," she forgot how annoyed she was supposed to be and smiled warmly, as she glanced through the windows at the scenery around her, in total ignorance of how lovely she looked, with that soft glow radiating from her every pore. She heard Grant's sharp intake of breath and sent an inquiring glance.

"Well, someday you should bring them," he cleared his throat as he opened the car door.

She wondered why, this time, she felt a sense of familiar comfort as she allowed him to help her from the seat – it was all so confusing! He escorted her without preamble to a small office above a corner grocery store, where she was introduced to Vic.

Though the man was not overly well-spoken, he knew his stuff when it came to contract negotiation. There were no obvious concerns on her end, and in a daze, she thanked him and stuffed her copy of the agreement into her handbag. The original, she knew, her lawyer would peruse for finalization at a later date. Grant led her out onto the street once again to the SUV. The remainder of the trip was shrouded in silence, and Marianna was grateful that it lasted only for a few blocks.

They entered the studio together, and she was heatedly aware of Grant's six-foot, three-inch frame towering over her. Strange tingles stimulated every nerve she possessed, and she heaved a giant sigh of relief, when at last, he moved away. Marianna chose a stool in the corner by the door for good vantage – from there, she could observe the entire band at work. For the first hour, she was intrigued by the intensity of their practice session and the creative genius evident, as they collaborated together to make changes. Her own song, it seemed, was not on the agenda for now. Grant and Gary now worked on something together, in rapt concentration.

"Hi, Gorgeous!" Jerry dragged a chair over and plopped unceremoniously down beside her.

His huge boyish grin was infectious, and Marianna could not resist responding in kind. Instinctively, she knew she could trust Jerry, felt safe around him, and immediately relaxed in his company. Much like Benny. Why couldn't it be the same with one other certain tall, dark band member? The object of her thoughts captured her attention momentarily.

She watched the muscles ripple on his forearms, as he picked and manipulated the strings of his guitar, the power of concentration reflected in his eyes. Her gaze strayed to the strands of hair caressing his thickly corded neck and traveled the muscles down to his shoulders and beyond. A lightheaded, giddy feeling overtook her senses. He was, by far, the most ruggedly attractive man she had ever laid eyes on. Almost thirty years ago, when she had first ogled the RedRock record album cover, she'd thought him to be the most appealing, with his brooding, dark sulky stare. Most of her teenage female friends had vied for Gary, whom Marianna had to admit, played a very close second on the scale of sex symbols.

There was no comparison, however, to Grant Furman in the flesh, and she admitted that even nearing fifty, powerful virility fairly oozed from his pores. Suddenly, he caught her gaze, and she looked away quickly, mortified at having been caught staring at the man once again. But not before she had been pierced by that sensuous magnetic gleam in his eyes. Like a challenge - was that what it had been? As if he was all too aware of the power that he held over her, and was quite prepared to use it to his advantage. His trademark crooked smile had been one of victory – she truly needed to take care around this man.

"Quiet today, aren't we?" Marianna glanced at Jerry apologetically, catching his speculative gaze.

What in the world was wrong with her anyway? It wasn't as if Grant Furman would take a serious interest in her, in any case. There was no denying the mutual spark, though, she grudgingly acknowledged. Once again, she solidly vowed to stay out from under the man's spell and turned her full attention to Jerry.

"I'm amazed at the amount of work that goes into your practice." This much was true. The patient team spirit in their song writing and playing was an awesome force to witness. Never again would she doubt the claim that musicians tediously earn their financial rewards.

"Most people would be. I'd love to say we are all rich and pampered, with nothing but time on our hands to go out and dally with beautiful ladies such as yourself, but alas, we are enslaved by our own passions."

Marianna laughed at his teasing grin and recognized the truth of his statement.

"I guess I must have thought you simply jumped up and plucked out your songs, knowing them so well that you needn't practice - you all make it look so easy!"

"Yeah, well, sometimes it flows like magic, and you have to capture those moments," Jerry shrugged casually.

"Grant is like that. When inspiration hits him, there's no holding back, and he never quits until the piece is completed. Like a dog with a bone." She shivered at Jerry's analytical musing, harboring no doubt, that Grant would indeed pursue anything he wanted, with the same tenacity.

She was suddenly grateful that her flight home was booked for tonight and for Jerry's comforting presence beside her.

"He keeps me an honest working man," he continued with a broad smile. "No rest for the wicked, so the cliché goes."

"Perhaps, but I'd say you provide perspective to it all," she offered intuitively.

"You lighten it up when it gets too intense, and I love your zany sense of humor." She smiled at his mock outrage. "Not to mention, you are one of the world's greatest guitar masters."

Marianna was right on the mark there. Any band would kill to claim Jerry as one of theirs. He had begun his career more than thirty years ago as a solo artist and had formed his own band before RedRock got their big break. She knew Jerry to be the oldest of the members, with five or more years on the rest of them. However, he possessed an eternal, youthful boyishness that was entirely captivating and belied his years.

"I do believe the lady is trying to flatter me." Jerry bowed in his chair. "I accept - it's nourishment for my fragile ego." He regarded her thoughtfully. "You're wondering when we're going to play your song."

"Actually, I'm just thrilled to have the opportunity to sit and watch you play anything," Marianna replied truthfully. "But I do admit, the thought of hearing my own song played by RedRock, is a tad over the edge of exciting for me."

The thought struck her that she was indeed extremely fortunate to have the opportunity to witness their musical ingenuity. She knew instinctively that very few people were privy to these sessions in the studio and couldn't quite fathom her good fate.

"So, what lucky man awaits your arrival home this evening?"

The question took her off guard. Was he flirting with her? She hoped not, as she had thought to have found a safe friend in him.

"An eight-year-old handsome young man by the name of Denny, and his delightful younger sister, Katrina," Marianna's beautiful eyes softened with thoughts of her children.

"Do you miss him very much?" Marianna started at his keen perception. A search into Jerry's eyes revealed nothing beyond genuine interest.

"Their father, you mean?" At his affirmative nod, she sighed. "My husband – late husband, Jeff, was killed three years ago in a fire." The vulnerable ache was back in her eyes. At once, she gave him a wistful soft smile and found herself pouring out the entire story – right back from her teenage adoration of the band to Jeff's death and the painful years of recovery since. Jerry had leaned toward her, face in hand with his elbow propped onto the arm of the chair, listening intently, with gentle patience and empathy.

"You are an amazing lady with all your accomplishments, and now here you are – about to enjoy the fruits of your labor."

"Oh, I don't think I've done any different than most would in my situation." Marianna truly didn't believe herself to have achieved any great strides. However, she had to admit that this present endeavor, if successful, would constitute a formidable accomplishment in her world.

"Let's break for lunch."

Grant's abrupt statement grabbed everyone's attention, and Marianna's heart skipped a beat as his solemn gaze stopped her in her tracks. He looked furious, and once again, she was confused. What on earth had she done to deserve this attitude from Grant? For reasons she didn't care to analyze, it was hurtful, and she felt the sting of tears threatening to spill.

Well, this is absurd – she had to get a grip on reality here!

"Seems we've earned the wrath of Grant. Now that's interesting indeed," Jerry stated simply, as he casually took her elbow and guided her through the door into their lounge area, apparently not the least bit intimidated.

They plopped down on the comfortable leather and came to a consensus that pizza sounded like good fare. Marianna chatted easily with Jerry for a minute more, all the while wondering what exactly one did to earn the wrath of Grant. Suddenly, the foyer door opened, and in walked Benny, escorting a vivacious little redhead, who she assumed to be his sister, judging by the striking similarity.

"Hi, guys!" Benny glanced around the room. "Oh, and the lovely Marianna. Great that you're still here! I was afraid I'd missed you before you left." Benny's appreciative gaze caught the eye of his observant companion. "I'd like you to meet my sister, Shauna."

They exchanged pleasantries, and she couldn't help but notice the gleaming assessment in Shauna's stare. Genuine pleasure shone from Marianna's eyes at seeing Benny again.

In her peripheral vision, she noticed Grant abruptly stand and storm from the room, slamming the door to the studio behind him. Benny followed him, and despite her valiant attempt, Marianna could not keep her gaze from straying through the glass wall to the two men, locked in avid conversation. Grant looked as though he'd cheerfully like to murder someone.

She'd have to be in a catatonic state, not to take note of the impotent fury that was clearly boiling underneath the sexy redhead's skin, as her fiery gaze stabbed the two men who were paying absolutely no attention to her at present. Marianna was also keenly aware of the remainder of the male population, pointedly ignoring the entire drama. She wondered if perhaps this were a regular occurrence, and, for the zillionth time, it seemed, thanked her lucky stars that very soon, she'd be on a plane home to sanity.

# Chapter Seven

The conversation in the lounge was subdued, and soon after the group had voraciously wolfed down the pizza, they joined Grant and Benny, who apparently had made peace, if their shared laughter was any indication. Marianna had felt Shauna's critical eye pinned on her the entire time and could quite honestly not remember an occasion in her life when she'd felt more self-conscious, while indulging in the simple matter of eating.

It was a piece of pizza, for cripes sake!

"Marianna, can we see you for a moment?" Gary inquired with a friendly smile.

A tad breathless, she walked over to where he and Grant now sat, perched on the edge of a small platform. Her knees threatened to buckle. Had they changed their minds then? Was something wrong? Perhaps it had all been too good to be true. She reflected wryly that this might indeed be her saving grace.

"Did you have a tune in mind when you wrote the lyrics?" Gary inquired.

Grant sat back and folded his arms, watching her intently.

OK, brace yourself, girl. Here comes the catch.

"Well, yes, but I confess that I have no ability to write the accompanying music." At Gary's thoughtful gaze, she nervously pondered just what was on his mind. She guessed correctly that she'd soon find out.

"Can you sing it for us?"

Her mouth gaped in total horror. No, they wouldn't possibly expect her to do that, would they?

At Gary's inquisitive glance, she knew she had to say something quickly! "Actually, I thought that was your job," she countered with feeble humor.

Well, hysteria was more like it, Marianna mused grimly. She started, as Gary suddenly laughed heartily. The man was insane, she decided.

"A lady of substance, beauty, and wit."

Marianna struggled to grasp a wisp of courage, or to be struck down where she stood, praying for a way out of this predicament. Well, it was time to play her last card before throwing in the towel and getting the heck out of Dodge!

"I did bring a tape with me. Would you like me to get it?" She had placed it in her purse that was presently stuffed under the stool she'd been sitting at earlier.

"Yes," Grant replied, "It'll do for now, anyway."

What did he mean by that? Surely once they'd heard the tape, they didn't expect her to still sing it, did they? She quickly retrieved the recording and fairly threw it into Grant's outstretched hand so as to avoid bodily contact. His look of derisive amusement told her he understood quite well what she was about.

He and Gary headed over to a maze of recording equipment and plugged the tape into a machine in the far corner, making some adjustments to the switches. At once, the surreal sound of her own voice filled the room, soft - melodically slow and sad, yet beautiful – even she had to admit.

Still, Marianna was more than a little embarrassed. While she loved to sing and did so often in the presence of her children and friends, who had all encouraged her on numerous occasions to pursue a like career, this was a colossal stretch. She took note of every flaw and suddenly regretted having brought the tape along with her. These men were professionals - accomplished musicians and vocalists, and she couldn't even begin to compare! Never before had she felt so insignificant among a group of people – she did not belong here. The singing stopped abruptly, along with her hope for the song.

The look on their faces revealed nothing of their thoughts. Both men sat, seemingly in deep contemplation. Occasionally, one would say something to the other. Marianna had reclaimed her position on the stool and could not hear what was spoken, thinking that this was what Judgment Day would be like. Jerry perched in the same chair as before, picking a gentle tune on his guitar. It took a moment for Marianna to register the harmony to her own melody.

The beauty in his creation took her breath away - touched her soul. Never in a million years would she have dreamed of such music to accompany the lyrics she'd written. He smiled indulgently in her direction.

"Marianna," Gary claimed her attention. "We will make a few minor changes to the melody – I hope you can live with that."

Live with it? God, she had expected them to choose the melody – if it even came to that.

"Of course," she said, recovering her composure somewhat. "You are the experts here, and it is, in fact, your song."

She glanced at Grant and was taken aback at the gentle smile he bestowed upon her.

"You need to understand something," Gary continued patiently, "There is a striking depth and passion to the lyrics, that come through, in the tune you've chosen. We don't often take on new writers because it's difficult to capture it, and frankly, we are damn good songwriters ourselves. It's much easier to work with a creation that is born from passion. And Lady, you are full of it. Your song pretty much reaches out and grabs the heart, and that's special. It's what immediately caught our interest, even without the music, and frankly, why you are here."

Marianna didn't know what to say except to thank them gracefully.

"It is we who are grateful, Marianna – perhaps someday you'll share the inspiration with us," Gary invited candidly.

"What made you decide to send it to us?" Grant gave her a thoughtful look.

God, why was the man so freaking handsome?

"You could have recorded it yourself," he observed.

"Truthfully, I wouldn't know the first thing about that. Also, assuming that I could ever hope to achieve success as an artist, I could never adopt the lifestyle - I'm a single mom and need to be there for my children."

"Oh, and you suppose we are not?" Gary asked with a raised brow.

Marianna was horrified at the implication she'd made – that successful musicians neglect their families. She was about to utter a profuse apology, when Grant spoke up.

"She's right. We all know that."

It was a matter-of-fact statement, not one of judgment. Still, there was a calculating gleam in his eye as he watched her, and she was beginning to feel extremely squirmy.

"Besides," she fled to safer ground, "It was you who inspired the writing of the lyrics in the first place."

Their rapt attention encouraged enlightenment.

"Your first album had just come out, and I was hopelessly smitten." She went on to explain Brian's death and the senseless loss that inspired the song. "At the time, even though it was my own creation, I could clearly hear RedRock in my mind, playing that song. Does that seem silly?"

Grant and Gary exchanged a knowing look. Marianna slid back to that moment in time and felt a shiver race through her body at the realization that she was about to hear the poignant tune brought to life in reality, not just in her mind.

"Not at all." Gary picked up his guitar. "Sit back and listen to your song take shape."

Marianna did just that and, for the next hour, was rooted in rapt concentration - fascinated, as they worked out the chords and harmony to accompany the lyrics. She was in awe, thunderstruck by the beauty of creation - literal genius in motion.

"OK guys, you ready?"

At Gary's cue, Marianna realized that they were about to play the song in its entirety and sat back, knowing without a doubt, that it would be Grant who would grace it with vocals. It was a slow tune, alive and throbbing with emotion. The lump in her throat threatened to consume her, and she fought back the raw emotion.

*He drove through the night*

*A warrior of love*

*His armor well placed*

*No fear to speak of*

*The longer he drove, the faster he flew,*

*Fleeing a ghost that he never knew,*

*Chasing a memory, following through,*

*Searching for someone like you*

Hearing her words come to life through Grant's deep husky crooning - an earthy southern caress, Marianna was transfixed — enthralled and moved beyond any emotion she'd ever experienced before. Another verse and a musical interlude enhanced the stirring sensation.

*Dying with the sunset,*

*Floating with the wind,*

*Sacrificing all he had,*

*Everything he'd been*

*Finding out much too late,*

*There is no compromise,*

*In the final second of his life,*

*He would realize.*

*The love he'd left behind.*

The chorus was repeated much slower, and Marianna could no longer control the tears that were flowing involuntarily down her cheeks. The music ended, and Jerry laid down his guitar, sauntered over, and gave her a gentle hug.

"It's OK sweet girl. That's the way it's supposed to be."

"Thank you, that was incredibly special."

She and Grant locked gazes, and he nodded ever so slightly, presenting another tender smile, tugging at her heartstrings and stirring up emotions she was ill-prepared to deal with. She felt the sudden urge to flee far away from him before it was too late.

Too late for what, she asked herself. Lordy, she was perplexed! A deep dive inward, confirmed that it was much more than this incredibly sentimental musical journey that had her imprisoned on this emotional roller coaster - there was simply no denying, that the root of her turmoil was on account of one Grant Furman, and she had serious doubts as to whether she'd ever be the same again. Rising slowly to her feet, she left the studio, acutely aware of every person in that studio whose eyes followed her out the door. If they only knew…

# Chapter Eight

Marianna was incredibly grateful for Benny's returning presence and relaxed with a contented sigh, as he drove the scenic route to the restaurant they had agreed to dine at tonight - in spite of her lack of interest in glitter and glamour, she had to admit that it was all very impressive. Her mind strayed, reliving a last panicked glance behind her as she'd left the studio - focusing on one stormy redhead, who, if looks could kill, would have stricken Marianna dead on the spot.

"I hope the guys didn't scare you too badly. It would be nice if you'd visit again soon." Benny gave her a searching look. "You'll have to forgive Grant's sour mood. It has nothing to do with you. I'm sure of that."

Drat, would she ever have a moment without that man's invading presence?

"Oh, I'm sure it's none of my business."

Her attempt at foiling the subject was in vain as he carried on.

"Still, he's normally a pretty easy-going dude, you know. I shouldn't have brought Shauna to the studio - it was a stupid move on my part."

In spite of herself, Marianna's curiosity perked up at this, and she tried to affect a casual interest, although every fiber of her being was alert for his next words. Her heart was pounding in her ears, and for some unknown reason, it took considerable concentration to keep her breathing on an even keel.

"Oh, is she a girlfriend of his or something?" Great, now she sounded like the groupie she had just recently vowed never to become. Benny didn't seem to think oddly of her query, though.

"Yeah, they had a thing going, I guess, for a while. I'm not really sure. Neither one of them says too much about it, but I'm certain Shauna would like to think she still is. In any case, something happened, and Grant refuses to even acknowledge her presence most times."

Benny glanced in the rear-view mirror as he changed lanes.

"Shauna most likely blew any chance she may have had with him – she has a tendency to keep more than one guy on a string at a time. It's a weakness with her, a quest for power. And I'm certain that Grant would never tolerate that. Still, it seemed pretty intense for a while."

Benny stopped the car in the restaurant parking lot and smiled at her.

"All I know is I get the privilege of escorting a beautiful woman into one of L.A.'s finest restaurants, and I feel like the cat who caught the canary."

As they entered the luxurious lobby, Marianna couldn't help wondering how she was going to manage to avoid spending the evening in close proximity to Grant. Had she actually agreed to his company tonight? In her muddled state, she couldn't quite remember, but in any case, she was determined to go to her hotel directly after the meal – alone. The voluptuous Shauna would undoubtedly keep him aptly entertained.

But as luck would have it, when they joined the group, the woman was nowhere to be seen. To further reinforce her ill fortune, Grant was seated immediately beside her. Rick and Jerry sat directly across the table, and she pointedly chatted with them throughout the meal at every opportunity. She needn't have worried about Grant – he hadn't paid a moment's attention to her all evening.

Occasionally, a fan would pop over for an autograph, but Jerry informed her that the aging rockers did not receive nearly as much attention as they had in their glory days, which suited them all fine. As they discussed plans to continue socializing at a local blues club, Marianna quickly said her goodbyes and thanked them sincerely for their warm hospitality during her stay.

Benny had offered to drive her back, but she insisted on grabbing a cab, as a very cute little blond girl had joined him at the table, and Marianna had the distinct impression that he really would rather stay with her. She had just reached the curb to hail a taxi, when a hauntingly familiar deep voice stopped her dead. Damn!

"Off so quickly? Flight change, or are you standing me up for our date?"

Date? What a ridiculous notion! Grant was looking deeply into her eyes, his smoldering gaze heating her insides with hot flickers of flame. Hell's bells, don't look at him, Marianna instructed herself, and searched the street frantically for that elusive poor girl's limo. For Pete's sake, they were usually lined up on the curbs - where the hell were they all now when she needed one the most? Her annoyance was overshadowed only by her growing apprehension in Grant's intimidating presence.

"I don't seem to recall that we had a date," she retorted nervously.

Grant captured her chin in his large hand and turned her to face him. He was so close — too close - she could feel his breath, warm on her face, his heady male scent enveloping her senses, making her feel as if she were drowning in a well of molten sensuality. She could not look away as his eyes leisurely traveled her features, caressing her hair, startling wary blue gaze, generous lips, and sleek neck - down the length of her, lingering heatedly on the soft outline of her breasts and back up again to settle on her parted lips.

He was going to kiss her! She knew it - couldn't allow it, and yet was paralyzed, deep in some wicked spell he had managed to mysteriously weave over her.

And there, on a busy L.A. thoroughfare, she registered nothing of the bustling city around her as his lips captured and molded ever so gently over hers, sliding sensuously, arousing a primitive response from deep within her. She was sure he could hear her heart thundering in her chest – she could certainly hear his - feel it.

At her own helpless, sensuous response, he intensified the kiss, slowly and sumptuously exploring the sweetness of her mouth with his tongue - gentle but firm.

A horn blared rudely beside them, and he broke away, releasing her chin with obvious reluctance as he swore under his breath.

God, she was suddenly bereft, as if a soothing, warm blanket had been ruthlessly ripped from her body, leaving her chilled and craving more. He took her elbow firmly and guided her across the street to the parking lot where he'd left the vehicle. She was shaken to the core and could do nothing other than follow his lead. Her mind was spinning, and she sat shaky and pensive, attempting to sort out her feelings.

"I've decided to spend the evening resting in my hotel room before I catch the plane."

It sounded lame, even to her ears, and she avoided his gaze. He said nothing as he pulled out of the parking lot and onto the busy street. Before long, she could see the coast in the distance and the miles of sand that stretched endlessly along the shore. Grant remained silent as he turned into a parking lot in front of a deserted beach.

She whirled to face him, about to demand that he instantly take her to the hotel, but something in his eyes stopped her. He closed them now, concealing his earnest expression.

"Please walk with me awhile. I'm sorry about that kiss - I don't know what came over me. I promise to behave."

His sudden change of demeanor, and pleading, good humor, melted her resolve, and she impulsively nodded her acceptance. Marianna declined to acknowledge the ebbing excitement bubbling within her at the prospect of an evening in Grant's company. Too, she chose to ignore the niggling disappointment over the fact that Grant seemed to regard that languid steamy kiss as a regrettable mistake. Her lips were still tingling delightfully.

"Tell me about yourself."

A quick glance at his softened features assured her that it was not a demand, as it sounded. They ambled amiably beside each other, barefoot in the silky white sand, which was still soothingly warm from the heat of the day. Marianna found herself opening up to him, chatting easily about her life. She didn't want to explore the reasons why she deemed it pertinent to paint him an accurate picture of who she was and the simple life she lived, so far removed from the furious pace of Los Angeles. Her eyes lit up when she talked about her rural home, quiet and serene, and especially when she spoke of her children.

"You are a very unique lady, Mari."

The use of her nickname on his lips was somehow intimate, like the softest caress. It sounded almost like "Marie," but not quite.

It occurred to her that no one had ever spoken her name quite like that, and she knew instinctively that no one ever would again, save this complicated, enigmatic man looming so large beside her.

They were perched on a colossal piece of driftwood, much closer than was safe, in Marianna's opinion - not close enough, the devil on her shoulder taunted. Their thighs rested together, and all of her senses were alive, screaming with the electric stimulation that his husky male voice evoked - his scent, his very presence. Peering at him now, she nearly cried out with delicious alarm at the smoldering look in his eyes as they explored her face. The smoky blue/gray depths held her captive, vibrating with excitement.

"I'm no different than most other women I know." She didn't understand what had given him the impression that she was somehow special unless it was the song, she reasoned. She needed to establish perspective before being completely devoured by the villain from this bizarre fairy tale. He smiled now - that dynamite grin, which had the power to rob her of every ounce of sense she possessed. Thank God he couldn't know that. Oh Lordy, her knees were weak.

"That's the intriguing part - you're quite unaware of it, totally oblivious to your special charm."

Now she was going to faint, she was positive, even though it would be a first in her life. But with Grant, there seemed to be a lot of those. What the heck was he talking about? Her perplexity must have been evident on her face.

"Do you know how long it's been since I've sat down and talked heart-to-heart with a woman? Authentically? About important things - things that matter?"

His face was alive with conviction and something else she couldn't define.

"All the ladies I know are either star-struck, or driven by money, and the glory that hanging out with a famous musician apparently can provide. Either way, they aren't looking at the real me, could care less how I feel."

Marianna's heart went out to him now, suddenly understanding how he would be reluctant to trust women - to trust her. Was that where all the animosity had come from?

"You have it in you to care, Mari. I can feel it - see it in your eyes. You look right through it all, to the core of me, and you have the capacity to listen to my soul - and that's a rare find in my world."

The look he gave her now was heated, so powerfully sensual, she thought she might die from the havoc it was wreaking with her femininity, creating delicious warm bolts of pleasure to her loins. God help her. She had to look away.

"I know. I promised I'd be good."

He took her hand and helped her up. Her limbs were shaking so badly that she seriously doubted her ability to walk. While all her senses cried out for him to continue the sensual assault with his mere gaze – and more, she was immensely relieved to be alleviated from the temptation. She knew with utmost certainty that if he should so much as touch her, she would do anything he asked – make wild, unfettered love all night, right there on the public beach, and to heck with her flight. *You really need to get a hold, lady*, Marianna screamed inwardly.

They didn't talk much on the way back, but Grant maintained his firm grasp on her hand until they reached the SUV. The ride to the hotel took only five minutes, but it seemed the longest of her life. The air was positively charged with sexual energy, and she knew they were both fighting this battle, though his motivations for doing so likely far differed from her own.

On the sidewalk, in front of the hotel, he gently took her face between his hands, the long fingers caressing her eyes and cheeks. She thought he would kiss her then, and her lips involuntarily parted in anticipation. Instead, he took her hands and placed a lingering kiss on her forehead - then backed away slowly, releasing his grasp on her fingers as the distance increased.

It was the most beautiful, romantic moment she had ever experienced. Also, the most miserable, and she grieved the broken contact. At this instant, she realized how very fortunate it was that in just one hour, she would be on that plane, headed for home, to blessed safety and serenity. But oh, she would treasure the memory of this. The tears welled hot in her eyes as she blindly boarded the elevator to her room.

## Chapter Nine

Though she'd believed it impossible, she slept soundly for most of the flight home, exhausted from the emotional turmoil and the crippling stress of this incredible deviation from her familiar, routine lifestyle.

Almost immediately after Marianna walked through the bustling arrival gate, Tess promptly appeared with two very excited kids in tow. Marianna marveled at how good it felt to hold her children close to her breast once again. She'd missed them fiercely - except when she'd been with Grant, she acknowledged with sickening guilt.

More than ever, she was convinced the entire experience had been fleeting, a passing ship in the night cliché. She was free to go back to doing what she loved most - mothering her two incredibly wonderful children, and Grant would go on with his life, a world far removed from her own. Even if there was any measure of substance to their feelings, she knew a future with him could never become a reality. Not worth another thought.

"Mommy, Mommy, Auntie Tess took us to the zoo!"

Katrina's sparkling excitement radiated from her face, and Marianna spent the next thirty minutes listening in rapt attention to her and Denny's report of all the cool things they had done in her absence. Their energy was enviable so early in the morning – she knew they had to have been out of the sack by 5:00 a.m.

"Well, gee, I guess you didn't miss me at all then."

Marianna feigned a formidable pout, which did nothing to fool her children.

"Mom, you're so silly," laughed Denny.

"We're happy you're back, but it's OK if you have to leave again, right, Auntie Tess?"

Marianna threw her best friend a scathing look, sensing that she had somehow set the kids up for this future possibility.

"What?" Tess shrugged her shoulders in seeming ignorance.

Marianna good-naturedly bestowed her friend a monster hug as they all helped to unload her luggage from the car and into the house. She looked around at the familiar surroundings and sighed - she was home. All was right with her world again. With a moan of exhaustion, she sat down at the kitchen table, accepting a coffee from Tess, who now sat perched across from her with that don't keep me waiting expectancy written all over her face.

"OK, OK, I'll tell you all about it. Just let me have a few sips of decent coffee first, huh?" Marianna teased unmercifully and laughed at the expression on Tess's face. The children were upstairs unpacking their overnight bags and had promised Tess they'd watch a movie while she and Mom had a good chat. Marianna dutifully provided Tess a blow-by-blow account of everything that happened during her trip, with the exclusion of Grant. She was afraid to tread that rickety ground, unsure of her muddled feelings and how Tess would interpret the situation.

"Wow, that sounds great!" Tess sat back and stabbed her with a knowing look. "Now, what is it you aren't telling me? Let's see; you've covered all the boys in the band except Grant Furman. I know he was there, sang your song, and has always been your favorite. So, spill the beans! Is he as hunky as you imagined? Is he a boorish snob – a typical jerk?" she fell silent at the sudden radiant blush on Marianna's face.

"Oh my gosh, you've gone and fallen for the guy, haven't you?"

It was meant as a teasing comment, she knew, but Marianna couldn't stop the vehement denial, which in itself, revealed all she was trying to conceal.

"Of course, not. That's insane!"

It came out much sharper than she'd intended, and Tess looked a little taken aback. Marianna was immediately contrite.

"Oh, Tess, I'm sorry. I didn't mean to snap."

For once, her exuberant friend was silent, waiting for Marianna to unload – and unload she did. Not a stone was left unturned, and when she was at last rendered worn-out mute, Tess took hold of one of her hands and bent to look Marianna square in the eye.

"Mari, Honey, that is the most exciting, romantic story I've ever heard – every woman's fantasy, really, and I can see that this has affected you more than you care to admit. Maybe there's hope for you yet."

Marianna just wanted to go to sleep, didn't want to reflect on the truth of Tess's words – the hope. She said as much to her, and Tess insisted on hanging around for the day while Marianna got some much-needed rest. She knew she'd be better equipped to deal with her churning emotions after some rejuvenating shut-eye. But as she drifted off, a pair of smoky gray eyes and the sweet caress of a husky, southern drawl haunted her dreams.

~~~

The next few weeks were blissfully uneventful, with Marianna settling back into her routine, and the illusory trip to L. A. began to seem like a distant memory, almost a vision - someone else's fantasy. Grant was never far from her thoughts, and she firmly resolved to regard him as a romantic daydream, seeing as how the damn guy wouldn't go away. It was perfectly normal after all - she was a single woman, healthy and vibrant, at her sexual peak, so of course, she would deem such a hunky male sampling quite irresistible.

Marianna was determined to maximize the opportunity for quality time with Denny, through the remainder of the summer break. She took him and Katrina often to the local BMX Park in town - just a ten-minute drive, and loved to watch him negotiate those hills, gathering as much speed as possible before careening down the other side – it always made her heart stop. She marveled at how much he'd grown in the past year and giggled, as she watched Katrina, in a hopeless quest to keep up with her brother on her own little bike, which she'd just learned to ride without the training wheels. Today Marianna had allowed her on the course for the first time as it was almost deserted, posing no threat, and Katrina was relishing her newfound freedom.

Settling in with her laptop, intent on completing her current novel by summer's end, she soon surrendered to the hypnotic magic of creativity. Her characters had a will of their own, and Marianna was hard-pressed to force the roles. She simply let it flow - from whence the source, she couldn't say. She remembered hearing Gary Keller once, during an interview on the Oprah Show, speak of his song writing gift. He described it as divine intervention – when it came - there it was, and no matter where he was, he always took it seriously with pen and paper in hand because, by morning, it would undoubtedly be gone. Marianna had similar experiences with her writing inspirations and wondered fleetingly if it was the same for Grant.

Uncomfortable with the direction her thoughts were straying, she glanced at her watch and called to Denny and Katrina.

"Hey, you two, it's almost time for supper!"

She'd prepared it ahead of time - potato salad and meatloaf, a family favorite. The heat was stifling, and she wanted to tackle some weeds in her small vegetable garden and water her flowers before the kids went to bed. Once home, she was about to join the children at the table when the phone rang.

"Hello there," her voice was intentionally throaty and sultry.

She had fully expected it to be Tess, who had promised to call and give her the lowdown on her special date with Dennis, who apparently had something special planned. Marianna was intent on taunting Tess unmercifully - turn the tables, as it were, for all it was worth.

"Hello yourself," her heart vaulted into her throat.

The owner of the smoky, sexy southern drawl, that had haunted her since the moment she'd left L.A., could not be mistaken. Why on earth would he be calling her? It had been the absolute furthest possibility from her mind. Marianna felt a sudden, alarming premonition, though she couldn't quite define it. All she could fathom was that it terrified her. Her heart was now slamming dangerously in her chest. After what seemed like an eternity, she finally reclaimed her voice.

"Hi," she offered. "Where are you?" she inquired dumbly.

Good Lord, what did that have to do with anything? Hadn't she efficiently filed him under F for fantasy? Once again, her world tumbled upside down, and she could scarcely breathe.

"Actually, I'm sitting at the Edmonton International Airport, waiting for fans to mob me for autographs, but so far, not one person has recognized me - I'm feeling a tad sorry for myself, really, and my ego is in sore need of attention."

She laughed nervously at his witty remark. In Edmonton?

Oh my God, what was he doing here? She was sure they didn't have any concert venues – not that she'd been keeping tabs, she assured herself. Had she missed something? Perhaps while she was away...but no, Tess surely would have mentioned it. Marianna scrambled to collect her jumbled thoughts.

"So, I was just contemplating renting a car here and realized that it would be much nicer if I had a personal guide to show me around. I was wondering if you were up for the job."

Marianna groaned inwardly. That voice was surely going to be her undoing. But try as she might, she could not quell the tingling rush of excitement flooding her veins. Damn – *"she was a simpering groupie"!*

"W-what are you doing here in Edmonton?" As if she had a right to ask such a lame question - as if it were any of her business. Still, curiosity won over.

"The truth?" His voice was a silky caress.

"Of course." She held her breath.

"Well," he slowly began, "I had a few days off."

That's right, she remembered now, they had several weeks actually.

He continued, "I'm sorry I didn't call ahead to warn you – it was impulsive, I know – a last- minute decision." His tone was apologetic. "I was intrigued with the captivating description of your calm, laid-back lifestyle and wanted to get a look-see into your world – a glimpse into our new songwriter's life."

She wished fervently that she could see the expression on his face.

"Not to mention touring the world-famous West Edmonton Mall, for which I'm told I'll need a personal guide just to avoid getting hopelessly swallowed up by a shark or two - if not the sheer size of the place."

Marianna burst out laughing at his boyish charm. It was a pleasant change from the stormy, forbidden man she was accustomed to.

"Well, that's not the only thing we are famous for, you know." She was about to mention the years that superstar NHL hockey player Wayne Gretzky had graced their fair city, as well as his teammates, who were icons in their own right.

"Yes, I followed The Great One's hockey career and am frankly quite ticked that he retired, but he did come to L.A. too, you know." Dang, he had read her mind. "I suppose you think if you don't retire, no one can, is that it?" Marianna's laughter rang across the line once more.

"You should do that more often." It was a quiet observation.

"What?" Marianna's momentary confusion made her sound breathless. Hell, she *was* breathless; whom was she trying to kid?

"Laugh!" Grant's husky reply fairly reeked of sensuality, and her stomach did a flip-flop. "It's music to the ears, a balm to the soul. You don't indulge often enough."

And how would he know that, having only spent mere hours in her presence?

"Perhaps you hadn't heard it because I was not exactly in my element when I was in L.A. I'm actually a fun-loving person at heart, you know." Now, why had she felt the need to divulge this to him?

"Nobody is in their element in this industry, Mari. We just go with the flow while the luck is still running, but OK, I'll buy it – with a hint of seriousness in the mix," Grant paused, "So, how about it? Do I have a guide? Or do I get lost forever in the bowels of the giant mall – never to be seen or heard from again?"

Marianna hesitated. How could she agree to this? What would she tell Denny and Katrina? As if on cue, Grant spoke.

"If you're worried about your kids, I've already taken the liberty of securing proper bribe material, not to mention tickets to the local Trappers game tomorrow evening."

Oh, Lordy - Denny would be ecstatic when – if, she reminded herself sternly, he got wind of this. She chewed on her lip in deep consternation.

"I don't know," she wavered. "This is not something I'm accustomed to." Now, there was the understatement of the century.

"My kids have never even seen me with another man since their dad passed."

She trailed off. Now she'd vocalized her assumption that he actually wanted something other than friendship with her – surely, he found that a tad presumptuous.

"Pick me up at the airport, and we can discuss it then. Mari?" His tone was gentle and solemn. "I promise that I harbor no expectations, and if you're feeling uncomfortable, we'll call it a day— I'll go back to my world and leave you be."

Well, that was something. At once, Marianna came to the realization that her growing fear of one Grant Furman was not near as intimidating as her own emotional turmoil whenever she was near the man. Quite out of character, she simply did not trust herself, and this frightening reality was highly disconcerting. Still, he did give her his word - she had the distinct advantage of being on her own turf this time.

"I'll be there as soon as I can."

Just why had she agreed to this madness? She gave herself a solid mental thrashing. It was the most ridiculous, irresponsible, dangerous undertaking she had agreed to in a long while. How pathetic can it get? She'd fairly leaped at it once he'd given his promise, and she now admitted ruefully that it was not him posing the greatest danger here. The Mexican jumping beans bouncing around in her stomach confirmed that it was also the most exhilarating, exciting, and deliciously naughty diversion that she had ever dared contemplate - she could no more have resisted it than cease taking air into her lungs. Her heart was pounding wildly in her ears, and she felt more alive than she had in a very long while. Somehow, she'd work things out. Tess would take Denny and Katrina for a few hours until then. She could handle this, she assured herself, and besides, Tess would stop at nothing short of strangling her if she sent the man packing back to L.A.

"Bring the kids. It will be safer."

Oh boy - smart man, this one. She had to agree that this made good sense; he was certainly a man of forethought.

Then did he feel it too? The rekindling of those sparks fairly flew across the telephone line. She was experienced enough to know that it wasn't all one-sided. But it may well be purely physical on his side - a challenge of sorts.

Well, of course, that's all it is for you too, right - a delightful few days spent with an exceptionally attractive man? Nothing wrong with that, she assured herself. Marianna knew she couldn't risk any serious intimacy with Grant, so she might as well enjoy this while it lasted. She chose to disregard the feeling of pleasure she derived from knowing that Grant had spent considerable contemplation of her children.

After ringing off, Marianna went in search of them and found both hovering intently over Denny's pond. They had already placed the dinnerware in the dishwasher and soaked the pots in the sink as she had taught them to do, and Marianna felt a welling of pride fill her heart.

"Mom, come look!" Denny cried excitedly. "There's more tadpoles."

Marianna groaned inwardly at this news. She was dreading the impending moment when they finally had to abandon the project. It was a point that Marianna had reinforced with Denny several times - tried to make very clear to him. They could not keep the pond study for more than a few months, and the little frogs would have to be returned to their natural environment before the frost came in late September. She sighed, thinking there would be ample time to discuss this later.

"Kids," Marianna began tentatively, "we are going to the airport to pick up a friend."

She didn't exactly know what to tell them. This was not particularly in her usual realm of behavior, and she'd been truthful with Grant - the children had rarely seen her spend any amount of time with a man other than their father. Katrina didn't even remember Jeff, she thought sadly. They both looked up at her now expectantly. She took a deep breath.

"Remember my trip to L.A.?" Both kids nodded.

"Well, the man who's going to be singing my song is coming to visit for a few days."

She searched their faces for any traces of anxiety or dismay and found nothing. Why would there be, though? She had never dated after Jeff died, so she deduced that they had no reason to feel threatened by a male visitor.

"Get your hats on and meet me in the van."

She knew they would perform Olympic somersaults to beat her down there. They couldn't resist a mystery and loved going for a ride because it usually meant a treat for them - either a visit to the park, ice cream, or occasionally both. It was sometimes worrisome that she was overindulgent with them, and she wondered whether Tess could be bang-on with her insistence that the children needed a man in their lives.

Another Jeff would be impossible to find, though, and she'd long ago resigned herself to the fact that she'd had her chance at true love, even though destiny had ruthlessly cut it short. She sighed, wishing for the millionth time that it could have been different and they could know their father's love. There wasn't a man on earth who could fill that gaping chasm, and Marianna had never sought to find one - she wasn't about to start now.

## Chapter Ten

Butterflies threatened to turn her stomach inside out as she pulled into the busy airport parking lot. Thoroughly convinced at this point that she was stumbling into the grandest mistake of her life, Marianna could hardly turn back now. She'd just have to exercise extreme caution. Thank God for her children! Nothing could happen with them around. With that reassuring thought securely in place, she was immensely more relaxed. A twinge of guilt assaulted her, over using them as a barrier, but there was no time to dwell on this presently.

As they entered the arrival area, he was there - standing rugged and tall, staring at her with that sexy crooked grin. As if he was the only passenger in the place, she immediately picked him out of the crowd. Well, the dang man stood out like a beacon, she insisted inwardly, in her own defense! Heaven help her.

He was even more alluring than she'd remembered. How was that possible? It really was purely inequitable - it should be outlawed, at least. Annoyed by the potent force of her reaction to him, she shuffled the kids along and rather abruptly introduced him as Mr. Furman, affording him a remote smile that didn't quite reach her eyes. Then two very inquisitive children, impatiently standing by her side, demanded to know when he was going to sing their mommy's song for them. This efficiently diverted his searching gaze, but she hadn't missed the raised brow.

Marianna flushed furiously, wishing she'd never divulged this piece of information to them. But Grant laughingly assured that they'd hear the song very soon and bent to shake their hands. The flaming red and black guitar that Grant hoisted easily over his shoulder captivated Denny and Katrina's attention. "Why do you suppose I brought this along with me?" He patted the guitar reverently.

"Can you really play that thing?" Denny's wide-eyed innocent curiosity spurred Marianna's smile.

The sudden, rich, lusty timbre of Grant's laughter enslaved all of her senses, rendering her immobile. These were, without question, shaping up to be the longest few days of her life.

"I promise to try my very best. Now, who's in for an ice cream treat?"

Grant had quite effectively won the kids over for life with that simple offering. Eyeing the Big Bad Wolf suspiciously, she wondered just how many other children he'd wooed during his womanizing career. It was a good reminder for her to keep her head and avoid any entanglements with this charismatic man.

Denny and Katrina's whoops of delight surely reverberated throughout the entire airport as they piled into the van and headed for the nearest Dairy Queen. The children chattered incessantly for the duration of the entire trip, and she was shocked by the easy manner in which Grant interacted with them.

In fact, she couldn't quite believe these were her own two flesh and blood offspring, who were normally cautiously reserved with strangers - men in particular. Watching from the corner of her eye, she was certain this was a new-fangled Grant, surely not remotely related to the one she'd encountered in L.A. If she didn't know better, she'd believe him nothing more dangerous than a big kid himself, and in spite of it all, she found herself giggling uncontrollably along with the children at one of Grant's corny knock-knock jokes. Yes, this was a completely different man altogether, beamed up from who knew where in the mysterious universe. Marianna endeavored to ignore the blanket of contentment this reality brought to her fragile demeanor.

Stopped at a red light, he turned to face her with a smoldering gaze, the laughter all but dying in the air. Oh Lord, she thought as he lent his attention back to the children - it was the same Grant, after all. With just one steamy look, he'd sent the blood rushing to her head, her stomach topsy- turvy, and her hormones in a frenzy, bouncing around in her body like flaming darts. A two-second glance. She knew, with absolution at that moment, that she was in deep peril, and her only recourse was to pray for sweet mercy. For the very first time since she and Jeff had built this house, she was truly intimidated to be walking through her own front door.

~~~

Marianna's features screwed up in rapt concentration as she carefully sampled a spoonful of her infamous spaghetti sauce that she'd promised the threesome for dinner - determined to get just the right flavor. Grant's rich, mirthful laughter, along with Denny and Katrina's, floated lightly into the kitchen, apparently on account of their game of "Go Fish" in the adjoining family room. The pasta was bubbling merrily on the stove, and the garlic bread was crisping in the oven. A spinach salad complimented the meal, although she knew she'd have to work to convince the children to sample it, being they'd already had their dinner, earlier.

Wandering to the family room, she stopped and stood unnoticed, observing the three of them. Taking pleasure in the light-hearted banter and teasing, she was struck, awed by the lack of animosity between her two children. Normally by now, she'd be refereeing a formidable battle of wills. They got along well most of the time, thank goodness, but as a general rule, card games were declared open season.

Grant looked up and bestowed, what may quite well have been, the devil's most charming smile upon her, and she caught her breath - an involuntary reaction, the likes of which were beginning to assault her body on a regular basis whenever he was around her.

She'd been rendered motionless a few minutes earlier when Grant had fulfilled his promise to play Marianna's song for them. The deep sultry, southern crooning seemed to reach out and touch her, and she was transfixed by the sensation that she'd been somehow branded for life.

"Dinner is served."

She gathered her wits and bowed ceremoniously to the amusement of her children, ushering them formally to their seats. Before she could take her own place, Grant was there, pulling out her chair. His nearness sent tiny shivers of delight up her back as she breathed in the warm, masculine scent of him. This chivalrous act seemed a dramatic contradiction to the dangerous, fiery glint in his eyes. Marianna visibly relaxed as he moved away and took his own place across the table from her.

She was amused and more than a little pleased as he dove into the meal with relish. They ate in relative silence, listening to the children's animated stories about their summer antics to date, and whenever their eyes met, Marianna quickly averted her gaze. Oh, for Pete's sake, she was a blooming basket case and, for the life of her, could not seem to secure a handle on her emotions! Her confusion was more than a little disturbing, and Grant's effect on her was entirely too intoxicating for comfort.

As she rose to the task of serving warm peach cobbler and cream for dessert, Grant began to clear the table, and she was unable to still the unsettling premonition that he seemed to belong in this setting - in her kitchen, bantering with her two children as if they'd known him all their lives. That was crazy; get a hold, Mari!

She sternly reminded herself that Grant was dallying here for a few days and then would be gone. So why, then, had she introduced him to her children? It seemed an irresponsible thing to do, if not downright dangerous. Though, in her heart of hearts, she knew that Denny and Katrina were in no peril from Grant. Still chewing on her lip, she considered she'd made a grave error in offering him the use of the guest suite on the basement level, which doubled as the family rumpus room. He had accepted immediately, quite to her surprise. What had she been thinking? Where in the world was her common sense? The man could obviously well afford his own accommodations, for heaven's sake. Wouldn't he prefer more luxurious surroundings? The aging hida-bed was not exactly hotel quality.

She stifled a mischievous giggle at the mental image of Grant furiously attempting to pound out with clenched fists a few annoying mattress lumps in a futile quest for comfort.

Her friends would surely surmise that she'd lost her marbles, allowing a strange man to sleep under her roof - except Tess, of course. That was another matter entirely, and Marianna knew she'd have to spill the beans to her good friend before nightfall. Tess had already left two messages on the landline to accompany the numerous texts, while they were out. Marianna wondered what best approach to employ in preparing Grant for that daunting introduction.

~~~

They were settled cozily into plush leather loveseats in the living room, relishing rich, fresh- ground coffee. Grant had taken it upon himself to build a crackling fire in the grate. Marianna glanced pensively around her, avoiding his gaze at all costs and feeling strangely vulnerable in her favorite escape haven - the one room she considered truly her own, with its enveloping warmth and casual elegance. Despite the respectable distance between them now, it seemed disturbingly intimate to be lounging here with him, and she felt strangely violated. Why this was not exactly unpleasant, she couldn't begin to explain and was about to suggest they go somewhere else - anywhere, when Grant spoke.

"I don't wish to make you uncomfortable in your own home," his voice was a soft caress.

Her jaw dropped. Was he psychic? He was studying her intently, and the sincerity evident in his deep voice was melting her insides.

"I can go stay somewhere else, Mari." He searched her face for the answer.

"Hell, I can go stay in one of those fancy theme rooms at the big mall."

The arresting grin was back, but there was a gentle teasing warmth there too. Oh God, she wanted to kiss those dimples.

"Not much fun by myself, though…" The suggestive heat of his gaze fairly reeked with implication and kindled licking flames in her loins.

"No, it's OK, you can stay here. We'll be able to cover more ground that way, and you'll miss the serenity of my country home if you do that."

Mari, you have officially misplaced your brain cells, she scolded herself — why didn't you take the out he so conveniently threw on your plate?

"Besides, the kids would be highly disappointed and likely never forgive me."

Good, now there was no justifiable reason for him to think she actually wanted him to stay in her house to satisfy any private agenda. It was true — the children were positively enraptured by the man, and she couldn't blame them for it. She'd never met anyone quite like him before.

They came to a mutual agreement to take the kids for a walk around the property, with Denny and Katrina insisting they do their customary *bush walk*, which was really nothing more than a sheltered pathway in the trees Jeff had cleared years ago, for the kids to get out into the wooded glory of their country acreage — experience nature at its ultimate.

The children delighted in showing Grant the grand hawk's nest perched high in a majestic spruce tree and the wild raspberry patch that blanketed an entire meadow on the slope, which gradually slanted down to the stagnant beaver pond. They returned in good humor, just in time for Denny and Katrina's baths and bed, and Marianna suggested they relax outside on the back deck with a glass of wine to take advantage of the cooler evening air. She was in sore need of something to soothe her frayed nerves.

*A Kiss to Die For*

To her immense relief, Grant maintained a comfortable distance, and the conversation turned to the band's future plans and her song. After a time, a peaceful silence fell upon them, and they were lulled by whispering evening sounds as the birds flitted above, taking full advantage of the waning heat, to feed. They were treated to the sight of chickadees, goldfinches, nuthatches, and blue jays, all companionably vying for space, descending gracefully upon the six huge feeders mounted on the deck railing, indulging in a last evening meal before darkness ascended.

Her attention was fixed upon a delicate hummingbird - her favorite - drinking daintily from a fuchsia blossom, and the vibrational buzzing from the miraculous speed of its tiny wings. Marianna knew she could never sacrifice this beauty. In the distance, the loons beckoned from a nearby lake, and the underbrush came alive, teeming with bustling nocturnal activity - rodents venturing out tentatively, foraging for seeds and roots that were plentiful still. The gentle humming from the bees feeding upon her many flower baskets was now ebbing as they settled into their nests for the night. Marianna let out a contented sigh.

"Mommy, Mommy," Katrina rushed outside, clad in her favorite girlie nightgown, plastered with dainty pink hearts, her wet hair flying wildly behind her.

"Denny won't give me the comb, and he stole my favorite toothpaste too!" Her little chin quivered with the threat of tears. So much for congeniality, thought Marianna wryly and sighed in resignation.

"OK, Honey, I'll be right there, and I've told you before - the toothpaste is for both of you to share."

She rolled her eyes apologetically at Grant as she rose to follow her daughter, who was, by now, in a clear declaration to her big brother that Mommy was coming to *tell him a thing or two*.

She was rewarded with another of Grant's dynamite smiles, which robbed her of yet another round of precious air. That's what the problem was – oxygen deprivation to her muddled brain, she told herself forcefully as she marched up the stairs after Katrina. Settling the kids into bed, she was dumbstruck when Grant suddenly appeared at the door.

"May I have your permission to read them a bedtime story?"

She couldn't believe that this dynamic giant of a man would actually desire to do such a thing and nearly giggled aloud at the vision of him relating a child's fairy tale. Marianna appealed helplessly to her two children, who were smiling at Grant with blissful adoration – she couldn't wait to see this!

"Of course!"

Would this man never cease to amaze her? As far as she knew, he'd never been married - of course, that didn't necessarily equate to an absence of children, but instinctively, she guessed that there were none, which was a shame, considering how well he got on with her children. As he joined her in the living room afterward, she lent voice to some of her thoughts.

"You sure have a way with my kids. Do you have any of your own?" A little snoopy, perhaps, but curiosity overrode her sense of caution.

"As much as I enjoy your kids and your intoxicating company," as he slowly eased his body down beside her, his look was pure molten, "if I had children of my own, I would be with them right now - not here. Fate had other plans for me, I suppose."

His eyes were hooded, concealing any emotion that might accompany that revelation.

"But I'm a damned good uncle." He bestowed an incredibly sexy smile upon her.

Lord, many more of those, and she'd be packing an oxygen bottle. His expression took on a boyish charm as he related many tales and antics of his nieces and nephews. It was evident that he enjoyed and cherished a close, loving relationship with his two sisters and brother, and he related his plans to visit them all during the next few weeks of his break from the band schedule.

To her surprise, Grant voiced his intention to retire early, reminding her - like a child enamored by a promised treat, of the tour to West Edmonton

Mall the following day. Well, this is a welcome relief - isn't it? Why, then, did she feel such acute disappointment – an aching emptiness at the thought of enduring the remainder of the evening without his company? Shake it off, girl. You've survived the first day relatively unscathed, she told herself, but the words had a niggling ring of untruth, which she steadfastly refused to acknowledge.

# Chapter Eleven

Katrina squealed with glee as Grant hoisted her onto his shoulders for a better vantage point to see the dolphin show on the lower level of the giant shopping mall. Denny had proclaimed proudly that he was big enough now and didn't require a lift any longer. They watched the animal trainers below them, working skillfully and playing with the dolphins, providing food in reward for the many tricks performed by the sleek, intelligent aquatic animals for their captive audience. The presentation ended, and the crowds reluctantly dispersed, moving on to other shopping ventures or perhaps the Water Park, where the four of them were headed for the remainder of the afternoon, before the evening ball game.

They had toured the mall that morning, stopping to lunch on Bourbon Street at a small but elegant Louisiana eatery and continued on to Galaxy Land, an astronomical indoor amusement park, where the kids relentlessly dragged them on all sorts and kinds of rides until Grant finally declared he'd lose his lunch if he stepped foot on one more. The kids accepted this in good nature, but Marianna knew it was only because they loved their next destination – complete with its gigantic indoor wave pool.

Emerging from the ladies' change room now with Katrina, Marianna was thankful she had the good sense to have chosen a conservative one-piece bathing suit, as her bones were pretty much turning to mush at Grant's searing gaze, studying her from head to toe, as any healthy warm-blooded male might do, she reasoned. Thank God Katrina had a hold of her hand, or she may very well have crumpled on the spot, so shaky were her limbs.

For the rest of the afternoon, Grant took obvious delight in barreling down the twisted maze of water slides - the children submersed in there with him, like dirty shirts. Her worried demeanor over her young daughter dissipated somewhat when Grant assured her that he wouldn't let go of the little girl.

Marianna had earlier confessed her fear of water, and though she didn't mind an occasional refreshing dip in the lake or pool – could even dog-paddle short distances, she had to admit that she could barely tread water effectively, let alone swim to save her children. She had put Denny and Katrina in lessons at a very early age, staunchly determined that her children would develop a strong confidence around the water, that she herself sorely lacked. As a result, they both knew how to swim, but still, she remained cautious, accustomed to keeping Katrina with her, and was more than a little apprehensive at her daughter's fearless delight with this newfound liberty.

True to his word, Grant held firmly to Katrina as they plummeted down the most frightful contraptions, plunging with giant splashes into the pools below. Her daughter's rapturous giggles reassured Marianna, and she settled snugly into a beach chair with a good book, allowing the soothing warmth from the sun blazing through the enormous glass roof high above, to envelop her. She felt secure in the knowledge that Grant would watch over the children throughout the massive structures of slides and pools.

"OK, Mom, it's time for burgers and fries." Denny declared matter-of-fact a while later as Grant appeared suddenly at the table behind them with a heaping tray full of food - sufficient for an army, she estimated.

Marianna could not tear her hooded gaze from the masculine perfection the man presented - in nothing but swimming briefs, with water glistening off the generous spray of body hair, adorning most of his torso. She wondered what it would be like to swirl her fingers through the silky mass of curls on that broad chest.

Her eyes flew open, and she snapped her mouth shut in horror, as she recognized the forbidden territory, to where her thoughts were magnetically straying. Thankfully, the children's attention was thoroughly absorbed by the food!

"Grant bought us some poutine too." Denny declared joyfully. He dug enthusiastically into his favorite gooey snack - a mess of French fries smothered with gravy and melted cheese, which she only allowed occasionally.

Marianna swiftly reminded him of his manners and to utilize the little plastic forks provided. She had to suppress an involuntary chortle at the look of mock insolence on Grant's face, insinuating that she was probably the world's worst party pooper. She hadn't realized how ravenous she was, and they cleaned up the entire meal in record time, she was certain.

Lounging around the cobblestone poolside, Marianna and Grant delighted in watching the children cavort merrily along the manmade shore, their faces ablaze with animated delight every time the loud buzzer signaled that enormous waves were about to descend upon them.

Grant leaned over and pointed, drawing her attention to a bungee jumper preparing to leap off a giant rafter at the far end of the pool. Marianna knew that for a mere $100.00, a person could jump off of a platform near the incredibly high roof, suspended 120 feet in the air, to the water below. To her, this seemed ludicrous and a frivolous waste of hard-earned cash, but Grant seemed to get a kick out of the whole thing.

He hadn't moved away, and she could feel the warm, soft caress of his breath on her ear and cheek, creating thousands of tiny tingles along her skin. The effect was hypnotic, and she scrambled up, mumbling a lame excuse that she needed to use the washroom. His sardonic gaze on her retreating figure was calculating, and she knew beyond a doubt that her desperate ploy had not fooled him - not one little bit. Still, it granted a much-needed reprieve.

Lying in bed later that night, sleep eluded her. She tossed and turned for an hour before padding softly down the hall to fill the tub, making as little noise as humanly possible. She was certain that the soothing warmth of the scented water was just the medicine she required to calm her vibrating nerves. With her hair loosely pinned up, she stepped into the steaming hot water, sinking down with a delectable sigh, letting the bubbles embrace her weary body. She closed her eyes and reflected on their very busy day.

The kids had been totally drained of all energy and had fallen fast asleep on the drive home. Grant had helped her huddle them into the house and prep for bed. They were dead to the world before either one of them could even suggest a bedtime story. Though the hour was late, Grant had gently captured her hand and asked huskily that she come and sit outside with him, declaring that he didn't wish to waste a moment of this respite from his normally hectic schedule - adding reasonably, that it was not right, having no one with which to share the beauty of this solace. It had all sounded so perfectly innocent.

Against her better judgment, Marianna had surrendered and was thrilled at the prospect of another heady evening in his tantalizing company. They'd sat in companionable silence for a while, watching the birds nesting in for the night as the darkness descended around them.

"I can't believe how light the sky still is at 10:00 here. In L.A., the city lights illuminate everything for miles around by 8:00." Grant had interrupted her flow of thought, and Marianna had smiled, knowing that he quite well understood the science behind it all and was simply marveling at the experience.

"This reminds me a little of Colorado." She had waited for him to continue. "My sister Terri's place, is like a second home to me. Her and her husband own a spread - about 300 acres of range land, just bordering the foothills of the Rocky Mountains. It's gorgeous but a lot more open than here." The wistful note in his voice had hinted at a deep sadness. "I go there as often as I can, which isn't near enough." He sighed and flashed her a grin. "You are a lucky lady, and the best part about that is that you know and appreciate it."

He'd looked deeply into her eyes then, and she was thankful for the closing darkness surrounding them, for if he'd searched closely enough, he surely couldn't have missed the misty reflection of caring tenderness that had overwhelmed her senses in reaction to his pensive words.

"I didn't expect you to be the type of man who would appreciate all of this." She'd spread her arms wide to encompass their surroundings. Even though the countryside was predominantly flat farmland, with low rolling hills at best, it was heavily forested in places, and Marianna's home was nestled among the towering spruce and poplar trees, reminding her of Sleeping Beauty's Seven Dwarf's cabin - her own private clearing in the forest.

"What exactly did you expect?" He'd sat back deliberately, anticipating her answer, and she'd had difficulty finding the right words.

"Oh, I don't know that I expected anything in particular. It just surprises me, with your permanent home being in L.A." She'd been vaguely aware of the soft glow of the patio lanterns - the twilight having triggered the sensor. She'd quickly averted her gaze, not wanting to go into all the reasons for her previous assumptions about his character. Still, his burning gaze had scorched, searing her like a laser - nailing her to the spot, pinpointing the very core of her thoughts.

"So then, you considered me a city boy - has-been rocker, drinking and drugging away whatever fortune I had left, leaving a trail of broken hearts in my wake?"

In the face of her speechless gape, his eyes had hardened to steel/gray stone, and he'd looked abruptly away. In truth, that was pretty darn close to what she had surmised, at least the part about the women. Surely, not everything in the tabloids could be unfounded, and he'd been the subject of many a juicy article. As if reading her mind, he had continued.

"You shouldn't believe everything you read, Mari, but they all do, don't they?" Though the words were spoken with casual ease, the icy glint in his eyes had betrayed the depth of his anger. "Why should you be any different?" There was a hard bitterness to his tone. "That's why they write it."

A sudden fierce anger had overcome her at this off-handed attempt to stereotype her with all the other females on the planet. She had chosen, at that moment, to ignore the fact that she had indeed done the same, in taking some rumors about him to be gospel, and felt a little miffed at having the injustice slammed home by this arrogant man. How dare he presume to know her innermost thoughts and perception of his character? He hadn't even given her a chance! Crystal fire had sparked from her eyes as her anger simmered into a scorching blaze.

"How dare you assume what I may or may not choose to believe?" Her breasts had heaved in her agitated state, breath coming in shallow gasps, and despite the twilight cover, there was no way he could have missed the startling effect that the stirring frenzy had cast on her beautiful features. The mocking smirk suddenly marking his face, had aggravated her sense of outrage even further.

"And I suppose you think that I'm just another simpering female who'd stop at nothing for a little attention from the likes of your arrogant bones." The scathing glance she'd flung at him caused him to laugh out loud heartily. Exasperated, Marianna leaped from her chair and stormed inside, slamming the door properly in her wake. Let the man stay out there and get hypothermia! For all she cared, he could sleep out there. She'd stifled the strong urge to firmly bolt the doors just to teach him a well-deserved lesson and see how much he appreciated nature then, with a horde of bloodthirsty mosquitoes for his blanket. No, the bully would probably break down the door. Well, she wasn't about to hang around like a good little hostess to say a proper goodnight. She'd been suddenly grateful that Tess had agreed to wait until the next day to meet him.

So enraged, she'd missed the raw hunger in Grant's gaze as he'd silently watched her retreating figure from the doorway that had softly sprung open seconds earlier.

# Chapter Twelve

Now shrouded in mist and completely mortified at her extreme outburst earlier, she attempted to melt away the imprisoning tension in the steaming hot, foamy bath water and wondered just how on earth she was going to deal with the intense pressure of survival under the same roof with the brute. Tess would undoubtedly insist on taking the kids for the day and night, leaving her alone with him. Never in her life had she felt so inept at dealing with a man. One minute, she wanted to wrap her arms securely around him in comfort, and the next, she wanted to rigorously strangle him. But she was horrified at the sensuous realization that the thing she wanted most was to rip off both of their clothes and melt into his strong embrace - lose herself in the rugged male essence of him. In total dismay at the direction of her wayward thoughts, she sprang up like a cannonball in the bathtub, spewing water and soap bubbles in every direction.

How had she let this happen? With a troubled sigh, she bit her lip and conceded that it was no use to deny she was irreversibly, insanely attracted to the man. Hell, she was crazy about him! Good Lord, she must ensure that he never become privy to it. She could only begin to imagine the tortuous means he'd employ to manipulate things to his own favor.

Absentmindedly huffing an effervescent cloud of bubbles from her nose, she admitted ruefully that if she were completely honest with herself, Grant had never said or done anything to suggest that he was seriously lusting after her body, much less in pursuit of a wild passionate fling with her. Damn, she was the one who was ravenously mooning after him! She groaned aloud and threw the sponge at the wall.

Cowering miserably now in the bathtub, any remote semblance of relaxation she may have achieved, promptly drowned in the steamy depths of the water. She conceded, once again, that she truly didn't trust herself around the man. He had kissed her only once, and for all she was aware, he may have found that wanting. After all, he'd never tried it again, had he? Yet that solitary kiss was burned in her memory, into her very soul. She could still feel its electrifying seductive heat, and she wanted, oh, so much more.

This just wasn't like her - something was definitely awry, she decided, more than a little panicked, as she furiously finished scrubbing her hair. Perhaps there was some substance to the recent hype she'd read about women hitting their sexual prime, transforming into hormonal-crazed nymphomaniacs. This must be it! She had certainly never felt this way before about anyone, including Jeff, her soul mate, whom she'd loved beyond measure. They had enjoyed a passionate sex life, and she had thought it could never get any better. But this was beyond mere passion - some sort of insatiable craving that she feared was about to totally consume her and was unnervingly quite beyond her control.

Somehow tomorrow, she must convince Tess to stay within sight, every moment, every nanosecond. The worrisome thing about that was that her own and Tess's ideas of what constituted a dangerous situation were, in all likelihood, to be totally out of tune. Nevertheless, now that she'd come to terms with her own pathetic fallibility, there was no way Marianna could risk being alone with the man again, and she desperately needed safe ground. Her very future depended upon it, not to mention her sanity.

She rinsed her hair viciously and hurdled out of the tub as if trying to escape the Loch Ness monster and, in her haste, hit the slippery, sudsy tiles precariously off balance. Her feet flew out wildly from under her, and she ungraciously met the floor on her backside, with a resounding thud, arms and legs flailing in every direction. She cried out in sharp pain as her elbow made brutal contact with the hard porcelain and then lay there, stunned, gulping to catch her breath while assessing the damage. A sudden pounding on the door brought instant paralysis. Please let that be one of the kids!

"Mari, are you OK in there?" At her shocked silence, Grant crashed through the door, the concern evident in his dark gray eyes as he took in her ungraceful position on the flood-ravaged floor.

The sudden realization that she was sprawled stark naked in front of him, sent her in a wild scramble for the towel, but Grant was already wrapping it gently around her shoulders while she lay there – mouth agape and speechless.

It was simply more than she could bear, and to her utter dismay, she burst into a stream of humiliating tears, sniffling and snorting, in quite the weak female fashion that she abhorred. He gathered her gently into his arms, murmuring reassurances into her hair, and this tender, caring side of Grant was nearly her undoing. Marianna wasn't sure which was worse - this compassionate giant or the sensuous rogue. She found herself melting into his hard strength, gaining comfort she had never imagined she would ever need - being of normally sturdier stuff, and came to understand miserably, that this uncontrollable sobbing had very little to do with her fall on the bathroom floor.

Grant released her slowly, assisting her up with infinite care, checking her over gingerly and satisfying himself that no lasting injuries were present. He escorted her gallantly to her bedroom, leaving with strict instructions to call him immediately if she needed anything.

Though the urge to surrender to the bliss of his powerful masculine strength and large comforting presence almost overwhelmed her, she knew this to be a whim - an indulgent fantasy that would end the moment

Grant boarded that plane back to L.A - it was one luxury she could never allow. Dead exhaustion swept her entire body as she crawled beneath the sheets, not bothering to put any night clothing on. Still, she lay awake, her head hidden wretchedly under the covers, wondering how she could face the morning in the company of this dynamic man. Eventually, she drifted off to sleep to the distant sound of a coyote's mournful call.

A sharp rap on the door had her shooting straight up in bed, frantically scooping the comforter tightly up under her chin. Please, God, she hadn't called out for him in her sleep, had she? Blinking in her confusion, she tried to assess what time of day or night it was.

"Wakey, wakey!" Tess's all too cheerful greeting careened off the bedroom walls as she bustled in and began searching the closet, presumably in an attempt to help dress her – but Marianna was far too relieved, to be properly upset with Tess for this bold intrusion. She'd fully expected it was Grant barging through the door, checking to ensure she'd survived the night. Of course, she was not at all disappointed that it wasn't now, was she? Her brow furrowed in puzzlement, and she groaned inwardly.

"What are you doing here, Tess? Where are the kids? Did Grant let you in?" Marianna shook her head to clear the web of muddled bewilderment strangling her waning sensibility. Tess threw up her hands to ward off the barrage of questions, yanking a pastel green knit sundress out of Marianna's closet and throwing it sleekly on the bed. It was undoubtedly one of her sexiest summer outfits. She hadn't worn it since Jeff died, although she laundered all of her clothing on a regular basis. Now she was becoming thoroughly annoyed. She opened her mouth to forcefully voice her objection, but Tess beat her to the punch.

"I'm here to take the kids off your hands."

Surprise, surprise.

"And they are, as we speak, packing for a blistering fun-filled day at the beach. Yes, I did pack the sunscreen, and yes. I did meet your hunky celebrity." With a conspiring smile, she winked at Marianna knowingly. "Now I understand why you have fallen completely head over heels for the guy."

If she only knew just how uncomfortably accurate she had come, to the truth, with that remark, Marianna contemplated miserably.

"And I won't take no for an answer, so don't even bother trying to argue." Tess continued to yank clothing from the drawers, critically surveying a lacy strapless bra for effect. "By the way, what on earth happened to your bathroom door?" At Marianna's miserable telltale blush, Tess's keen observant eyes took on a sparkle of Cupid's delight.

Oh Lord – she was trapped in a nightmare!

"I can dress myself, thank you very much!" Marianna snapped grouchily.

She flew out of bed and stomped into the adjoining ensuite in a determined, but futile effort to avoid this ridiculous line of questioning, driving the toothbrush into her mouth in a furious frenzy, as if trying to scrub the memory of that one sensuous kiss out of the recesses of her soul. One kiss – what was the matter with her? Tess sauntered over slowly and leaned on the door, watching her friend with growing interest, not in the least intimidated by the tirade.

"OK, Mari. What's going on here? You can't hide from me - we're soul sisters."

She offered a gentle smile, and Marianna threw the toothbrush down with a deep, troubled sigh. It was true, they shared absolutely everything sooner or later, and she truly did trust Tess with her very life - it wasn't Tess she was fearfully wary of.

"Tess, I don't know what's happening to me - my life feels like it's been turned upside down, and there's not a damned thing I can do about it." Marianna ran a hand through her disheveled hair in agitation, and the look of misery in her eyes brought an instant motherly comforting hug from Tess.

"I'm a flipping mess!" Again, the tears flowed, hot and heavy, spilling out frustration, confusion, and rage at her dreadful impotence - but underneath it all was the paralyzing grip of peril invading the very depths of her soul. Spent, she wiped her eyes, bestowing a grateful smile upon

Tess, who had stood there saying nothing, offering her silent support through the entire torrent.

Suddenly it dawned on Marianna that she'd have to face Grant, and the last thing she wanted was for him to bear witness to any physical evidence of her distress. She knew him well enough by now to realize that he would stop at nothing to get to the bottom of her despair, and she could not, under any circumstances, reveal the nature or depth of her turmoil to Grant Furman.

"Where is he? You said you met him." She drew heavily on the well of self-discipline that had been her stronghold throughout her life and forced the mustering of her wits. What was that saying? Fake it 'till you make it? She could handle this. Marianna fanned her eyes vigorously to erase the evidence of her anguish.

"He was headed out for a morning jog when I came up the walk - said he'd be back in half an hour. God, Mari, he really is a gorgeous man." Tess sobered instantly at the warning look in Marianna's eyes. "O.K., I'll shut up about that for now."

It was a reluctant retreat, and Marianna grasped at once, how ungrateful she had been to her best friend. It was truly out of character, and she knew that Tess had to be somewhat confused and concerned about it all.

"Tess, forgive me. I promise we'll talk about it, but for now, please don't leave." The desperate plea must have hit some chord with Tess as she firmly shoved Mari into the shower with the assurance that she wasn't going anywhere until they'd had a chance to talk.

With immeasurable gratitude, Marianna emerged ten minutes later, revitalized and feeling much more like herself. She could deal with this - it was simply a matter of perspective, she assured herself. She needed to cease placing so much weight on the whole affair. Well, that was certainly an ill-chosen pun, she giggled inwardly. See, wasn't that better? Yes, she must promptly ditch this solemn gloominess. God knows, he probably hadn't given serious thought to that casual kiss. And that's all it was, she told herself firmly - a casual acquaintance, albeit a rather stimulating one.

A little voice in her head squeaked that if that kiss had been casual, what would a proper one feel like?

The murmur of voices and gleeful squeals from her beloved children brought her back to the task at hand, and she knew it was time to face the music. Giving herself a mental shake, she joined them in the kitchen, gratefully accepting a steaming cup of coffee - breathing in deeply the tantalizing aroma, while skillfully avoiding Grant's searching gaze.

"What are you two up to today?" Tess's seemingly innocent question hung in the air like a bad odor. Marianna pinned her with a glare that would have rendered a more sensible person quaking in their boots. Tess surely didn't possess a sagacious bone in her body, as she unflinchingly ignored Marianna's scathing look and continued breezily.

"The kids and I will be gone for a long time," she drew the word out suggestively, and Marianna felt the rush of blood from the tip of her well-manicured toes to the crown of her glorious hair.

"I suppose that's up to you, Mari." Grant's challenging gaze pinned her in place, the satirical lift of his eyebrow partnering that lazy lopsided grin, which sparked a strange little tingling along her raw nerves. "You are my tour guide, after all."

She promptly looked away and valiantly geared up to inform him that the entire lot of them were going to the beach - to heck with his damned sight-seeing, and little miss matchmaker over there.

"First, I thought I'd steal Mari for an hour or so," the matchmaker declared. "I have something that really needs her attention. Would you be OK with the kids for a bit, Grant?"

Marianna's eyes popped open wide - she couldn't believe the audacity of Tess, boldly presuming that Grant should play babysitter for her kids - and that whopper of a lie that accompanied it! The woman was truly shameless – she had to give her that.

Staring in fascination from one to the other, she gaped in startled disbelief at Grant's easy acceptance of the situation. What was the matter with him? Was he daft? The man was a rock star, not a childcare worker! Was everyone in her world losing all the common sense they were born with? Worse yet, why was she dutifully following Tess into whatever diabolical scheme the treacherous woman had dreamed up this time?

~~

"My God, Tess, I can't leave Denny and Katrina alone with him! I hardly know him!" All of her pent-up frustrated anger was now firmly directed at Tess, who wasn't the least bit daunted, as she pointedly opened the car door and unceremoniously shoved Marianna in the passenger seat.

"Oh, for Heaven's sake, Mari, take a pill! The kids love him, and he obviously adores them - they'll be fine for an hour or so. Besides, you do know where to find him," Tess rationalized, as if this was a perfectly normal justification, as she backed the car efficiently out of the gravel driveway onto the paved subdivision road, pointedly ignoring Marianna's heated glare. "The suspect axe murderer is staying with you, and I think you've gotten to know your hunky musician a tad more intimately than you're letting on."

Trying to disregard the knowing twinkle in Tess's eye, Marianna pondered that intuitive statement and recognized the truth within it, although Tess could never have known. In the short time she had spent with Grant, she'd come to embrace a deep trust in him, at least when it came to her children.

There was little that concerned her in that corner except perhaps a conspiracy between the three of them, and she was more than a little baffled at the way in which the children's adoration, which had always been unequivocally bestowed upon her, was now solidly bequeathed to Grant. Though she admitted to feeling a juvenile sense of betrayal by her own kids, she recognized the source, stemming from her own insecurities. Truth be known, her sense of pleasure in their acceptance of Grant's affections far overrode this – which was ultimately the source of her rising panic.

"Where are we going?" A pointless question, she supposed, but curiosity got the better of her.

"I have an insane craving for Slapjacks that can't be denied." It was their favorite brunch spot, affordable enough to take the kids now and again.

Marianna grinned, in spite of her morose mood, envisioning the mountains of pancakes Tess was capable of consuming single-handedly, in one serving. She envied Tess this luxury, wishing she didn't have to watch her calorie intake so closely. She had packed on some pounds after Jeff's death - hanging out with her grief and finding solace and safety in comfort food. Tess had gently but firmly reminded her that there were two precious children who needed her around until they at least grew into responsible, self-sufficient adults, so she had to mind her health.

It had taken Marianna almost a year of rigidly following a strict diet and exercise program to drop the weight, and she felt infinitely better for it. Her food choices were far more flexible now, and she could eat pretty much anything in moderation, but not quite like Tess, who had the metabolism of a Tasmanian devil, she was sure. She sighed, granting her friend a tender smile as she watched her devour a mammoth plate of pancakes, eggs, and sausages. Dang! Another reason to be grateful.

"Spill it, girl." Tess was never one to beat around the bush.

Marianna knew that no matter how tough and assertive she may come across, Tess would really listen and validate her feelings - even if she maddeningly disagreed. She was probably the only person in the world, save for Jeff, who could lay claim to this virtuous unconditional support, and Marianna was eternally beholden.

"Nothing has happened, if that's what you're thinking," Marianna wanted to get that fact well established at the onset, "but the man sends me over the edge. I'm completely powerless in his presence, it seems, and he really hasn't even made any moves on me to speak of." Tess listened patiently, watching the emotional play of confusion, anger, hurt, and frustration on Marianna's pretty face as she poured out her feelings. Marianna earnestly confessed her fears and the way in which her orderly, safe existence suddenly seemed threatened by one tall, dark stranger who was really not a stranger at all. She'd been close to him most of her life, at least from the intimate distance of a musical recording.

"It's crazy, Tess - I hardly know him, yet there's something so earthy and familiar." As much as she wanted to believe that he was a complete cad, she couldn't ignore the sense of rock-solid integrity in his character and knew instinctively that Grant had not lied to her about anything he'd told her, thus far. This grated on her, because that acknowledgment brought a ray of hope into the equation, which in turn, spelled danger. She was no longer able to lean on her mistrust of the man to help her keep a safe distance. On the other hand, he'd never offered any insight into his feelings either, at least not where she was concerned - but that wasn't an issue, was it? Hell, no! He was a temporary acquaintance at best. She shifted in her seat uneasily, at the blanket of lonely depression brought on by that nagging reality.

"Mari Honey, it sounds to me like you've got it bad for our Grant Furman." It wasn't a warning, but a statement, and Tess didn't seem remotely concerned with this reality. In fact, Marianna surmised suspiciously, there was almost a conspiring gleam in her friend's eye.

"It's not love, that's for sure." Marianna was adamant in her declaration. "It's nothing like what I had with Jeff - couldn't even compare."

"Now, how could you begin to know that?" Tess prodded gently as she sat forward, "Until you've given it half a chance? There's no universal law that says you can only have one true love in your life, Mari. You have to go with your heart and know that it will necessarily not look or feel the same. He's not the same person, and you will never be able, nor desire, to replace Jeff."

That was for sure. Jeff had been dependable and affectionate, adoring and sweet - a hunk in his own right. No, there simply was no comparison.

"It's not really an issue anyhow. Grant's never given me any indication that he is the least bit interested in me." Marianna provided. Tess raised her eyebrows sardonically, the expression telling Marianna that she didn't believe a word of it.

"Oh, I've seen the way he looks at you, Mari - it's positively electric."

"No," Marianna interrupted emphatically, "it's pure testosterone, is all, and surely you haven't forgotten his staggering reputation with the ladies."

"It's all hearsay and at least ten years in the gossip grave. You, of all people, should know that." Tess was making reference, Marianna knew, to her research on her celebrity book. "Besides," Tess continued with that gleam in her eye, "he's here, isn't he? There must be hundreds of women he could have chosen to while away these few days with."

Although Marianna couldn't deny the logic in that statement, she steadfastly refused to allow her thoughts to venture down that perilous stretch of road.

## Chapter Thirteen

Much to Marianna's chagrin, Tess refused to be cajoled into any promises to stay within close proximity for the remainder of the afternoon, beyond agreeing reluctantly, she'd suggest to the children, that five at the beach may be more fun than three. As the two women entered the front foyer, Denny and Katrina each grabbed one of Tess's hands, their beach towels rolled up under their free arms, and sunscreen lathered all over their little bodies. Apparently, Grant had been busy. Marianna's wide-eyed troubled expression softened as she smiled at the innocent excitement and expectancy on their cherubic faces.

"We have to go now, Mommy," Katrina stated matter-of-factly, "and you'd better thank Mr. Grant for fixing the bathroom door," her daughter instructed her. Katrina and Denny had compromised between Marianna's insistence that they address him formally as Mr. Furman and Grant's casual, light-hearted preference to letting them call him by his first name.

Marianna couldn't stop the rush of color on her cheeks at the innocent reminder of the previous evening's events. Oh Lordy, he'd seen her naked! She refused to acknowledge Tess's inquisitive raised brow.

"And I helped him," Denny's chest puffed out with pride. "I showed him where all the tools were and told him which ones that I knew he would need." Marianna suppressed a chuckle at the serious expression on the face of her little son, whom she once again realized was growing up all too quickly.

Now, surveying the expert repair job, she looked up gratefully at Grant, who was ruffling Denny's hair affectionately. A little voice niggled her that Denny needed that male role model in his life. Marianna had agonized over whether or not to keep the small acreage, with most of her friends urging her to move into town. But something held her back. This was their dream property - her and Jeff's, and she wanted the kids to grow up knowing the land their father had been so passionate about. If it weren't for a very angelic neighbor or two, she'd have sold out within the first year, but now she couldn't imagine living anywhere else, and she knew the kids were happy.

"Well, thank you." Marianna didn't know what else to say. "I appreciate your looking after the kids while we were gone, too."

"My pleasure." Grant was leaning casually against the door frame, powerful arms folded across his chest, flashing that famous grin - his eyes exploring her face, creating delicious tingles everywhere they touched. They held a teasing sparkle, which made her want to giggle with excitement, and to her horror, she found herself smiling back, quite beyond her control. Lord, was she an idiot?

"Well, we are off to the beach," Tess declared too brightly, breaking the spell. "Are you two coming with us?" She was already heading out the door, the lecherous traitor!

"Yes, of course…" Marianna began.

"Not this time - Marianna promised to take me along the Chickakoo Lake trails today." Grant interrupted congenially.

Oh, nuts, she'd completely forgotten all about that ridiculous commitment! How was she going to get out of this one? Why could she not manage to keep one step ahead of the wily man, or at least match paces?

"Surely you'd rather lay on the beach and relax, this being your vacation time," Marianna trailed off weakly, hopeful that he'd observe some sense in that lame excuse.

"Not at all. A good hike is one my favorite ways to unwind." He gave her a seemingly innocent and yes, - a heated glance as if to say, come with me, and I'll show you some other ones - *wink, wink, nudge, nudge.* Her stomach flip-flopped. "Anyway, you told me there were small beaches on the lakes there."

Well, she had, hadn't she? Silly girl! Darn - she talked altogether too much! But the alternative was infinitely more frightening when she was even remotely near to this man.

"Well, that's it then. See you two later, and don't wait for supper for us. The kids and I are going to chow down on some greasy burgers and fries there."

Marianna stabbed the now triumphant Tess, who was fanning herself suggestively, with a murderous glare. The children's enthusiastic shrieks allowed no illusions about winning any further ground, however. At once, they were gone, and she stared stonily at the closed door, wishing some alien ship would come along and beam her up at that moment, finding this a far less fearful prospect, than to face the charismatic man, whose very presence had her heart pounding wildly in her breast and her limbs wobbling like rubber bands.

She smoothed her hair in a nervous gesture and swung around to face him, determined to get a firm grasp on herself and figure out some way to keep a measure of distance between them. Her breath caught in her throat at the naked desire, that was unmistakable, in Grant's eyes.

Good Lord, she had to get away. Mumbling something unintelligible, she moved to escape upstairs to her bedroom - anywhere, but with lightning speed, Grant grabbed her arm and pulled her back firmly against the hard length of him.

She closed her eyes, trying desperately to control the dizzying, conflicting emotions warring within, and felt lightheaded - drugged by the clean, masculine aroma assaulting her nostrils, causing them to flare in stimulation. The faint odor of his aftershave only enhanced the intoxicating effect the man was having on her body. He shook her gently now and turned her to face him.

"Why are you so afraid of me?"

Her eyes snapped open, and she was not sure she trusted herself to answer that question. Because I want to rip off your clothes and jump your bones? Because you do things to my loins that no man has ever managed before? She couldn't say any of this to him - couldn't allow him that leverage.

He was looking at her now, those molten bedroom eyes still aglow with passion, searing her skin - first her hair, eyes, nose, lips, chin, then down to the swell of her breasts - she watched in fascination as he swallowed thickly. At once, he narrowed his gaze, let her go, and turned his back to her.

Marianna stood there, unable to move or think. When he finally turned to face her, a mask of iron self-control had stolen over his features. His struggle was visual and ironically gave her a heady feeling of power. The fact that she had affected him so deeply was more erotic than any potion she could imagine ingesting. In spite of the screaming alarms clamoring in her brain, her eyes strayed to the thick muscles of his upper arms and torso, and she battled an overwhelming urge to slip her hands under his t-shirt, over his chest and shoulders - to explore, slowly and exquisitely, exposing his body for her thorough inspection. It was obvious the man honored an exercise routine to keep himself in shape.

Her eyes were heavy with passion, and her lips were swollen and parted. She knew that if he were to kiss her now, the battle would be done. She no longer held the strength, nor the desire, to resist him, and she could only pray for mercy - that was the last thing she wanted at this moment, her entire being aroused and aflame.

"For God's sake, stop looking at me that way unless you want me to carry you straight upstairs to your bedroom and deliver just what it is you're inviting!" His voice was hoarse and shaky. He had turned away now and was gazing thoughtfully out the window, his battle for control still in play. But not before she had witnessed, with flames of excitement licking her body, the evidence of his arousal straining against his denim jeans.

"I'm not going to hurt you, Mari," Grant murmured softly. "I won't deny my desire, which I'm finding increasingly difficult to temper, especially when it's obviously reciprocated." He turned to face her, glancing hotly at the tell-tale outline of her erect nipples, boldly betraying her passion.

The distance now between them was a lifeline barrier, and she seized it like a drowning person, wildly snatching the chance to steady her ragged breathing. She was humiliated by her own transparent lack of self-control and tormented by the burning fire in the center of her womanhood - the hot, silky moist evidence between her thighs. There she was - not for the first time with this man, acting wantonly like the pathetic rock groupie she had sworn never to become. At this moment, she was concentrating all of her energies on taking maximum advantage of the space he'd provided her. She could manage nothing beyond it.

"I have to return tomorrow."

His tone was soft - regretful, and she was shocked at the acute pain of abandonment this brought, serving to fire her defenses. And why not? A little dally with the girl at the port would be a tempting interlude that any man in his position would be loath to miss out on. She welcomed the diverting anger. Well, it couldn't come too quickly for her liking. The sooner her life was restored to normal, the better. She clung fiercely to that admonition.

"Show me the trails? I promise I'll behave."

That boyish charm again. He reached for her hand, and she eyed him warily - how could she tell him that it really wasn't his resolve she was worried about? It was out of the question, and so she allowed him to lead her, once more, into what may well be the destruction of her very soul. This solitary man yielded a power over her that was far beyond fathoming and frightening to the core. For the life of her, since Jeff had died, she could not bring forth his beloved image to her mind's eye. And that scared the hell out of her.

~ ~ ~

Marianna and Grant, each lost in private thought, strolled in companionable silence along the miniature natural beach, surrounding one of the small bodies of water that collectively made up the Chickakoo Lake recreation park. The pristine ponds were on Crown land, and therefore, protected from environmental spoilage, through government regulations. The ecosystem was virtually untouched by human development, and the park was far enough off the beaten track to qualify as the area's best-kept secret.

True to his word, Grant's behavior was above reproach, treating her more like a best buddy than an attractive woman - one he'd claimed to so desire, and had set on fire less than an hour ago. If this disappointed her, she was at least grateful for the opportunity to relax with him. They'd declared a silent truce of sorts, both making an effort to honor a pact, though Marianna suspected that their reasons for doing so were entirely at odds.

Still, the electric sexual energy smoldered on low heat, and they both took care to respect its power. Grant seemed to have less difficulty with this, so she avoided looking at him too often, as they spoke, or delving too deeply into his eyes when she was compelled to do so. For the reflection staring back at her, was that of a woman in need - not love, she was sure of that, but certainly a deep caring that she no longer could deny, and of course, there was his breathtaking male beauty - the rugged square masculine jaw and the mesmerizing lines around his mouth. His eyes were dark and brooding at times and at others, smoky and sensual, or piercing gray ice chips when he was provoked. Bedroom eyes, she'd always known they would be, though she had only ever seen two-dimensional photographs of Grant. But she'd known.

Now, Grant took her hand and gently pulled her down with him onto the fine, clean sand at the edge of the small lake and pointed to a family of ducks, swimming lazily, ever vigilant, yet not overly concerned about their human audience.

"It's so damned peaceful here," Grant murmured and took a deep, cleansing breath. "L.A. seems a lifetime away right now."

Marianna could relate to that - exactly how she'd felt about her home when she had been in L.A. She gazed in awe at the brilliant colors sparkling like rare jewels in the rippling wake left behind the paddling ducks, her arms hugging her long graceful limbs and her chin perched thoughtfully upon them. No matter how often she came here, the natural beauty never failed to touch her soul – she could never imagine living anywhere else. She glanced at Grant to find him watching her closely.

"I have something for you." He reached into his shirt pocket and handed her a small package.

At her look of astonishment, Grant chuckled. "Go ahead, open it. It won't bite."

Marianna unwrapped the gift slowly - warily, wondering what on earth it could be. Her face brightened with joy as, in her hand, rested a compact disc labeled, "Love Left Behind – live studio recording," and in small print, "RedRock, vocals by Grant Furman, Written by Mari Jacobs." He laughed at her innocent pleasure in the small token.

"I figured you wouldn't mind using the shortened version of your name."

Marianna was choked up with emotion and could only nod enthusiastically as she gazed down at the magic in the palm of her hand. Grant squeezed her arm in congratulations and praise.

"We did O.K., Kid."

She looked up at him, tears of gratitude shining in her eyes.

"You are so welcome."

Grant saved her from the effort of speech that wouldn't come at that moment, and the genuine earnestness in his voice nearly rendered those tears into a cascading torrent.

"So, keep this in a safe place because there are limited copies, and the public ear will never violate this version – it's yours. We are recording the song for the C.D. when I get back tomorrow. A little break in my break." Grant smiled, obviously pleased with his witty attempt to lighten the moment.

"It's very special. Thank you so much."

"You're very special," Grant whispered huskily, as his gaze gently caressed every feature on her radiant face, as if trying to memorize it for future retrieval. "We need to go now, Mari."

She shivered at the thick, raspy tone of his voice as he helped her to her feet. He reached to take her hand in a gentle clasp, stroking her fingers with his large, calloused thumb in a feather- light caress, each stroke sending sensual shock waves through her entire body. She knew she should pull her hand away, but on his part, it was an innocent gesture, she was sure. How could he possibly know of the raging inferno that fired her blood, the throbbing ache in her loins, just from his mere touch? When she was sure she couldn't stand another second of this pleasurable torture, Grant released her hand to reach for the keys that were suspended in her other one.

The five-minute trip home was endured in awkward silence, with a sense of inevitable expectancy hanging in the air between them. Marianna was thankful when they pulled into the driveway, and she hastily escaped to the safety of her shower as soon as they entered the house. She desperately needed time to think. Perhaps she could call Tess, see if they're back yet, meet them somewhere - anything but stay here alone with Grant.

The mere thought was terrifying as hell. She knew she should be taking solace in the fact that he was leaving the next day. Why this was not serving to strengthen that firm resolve, she had so meticulously constructed only yesterday, was too frightening for contemplation. It felt like a lifetime since there had been no Grant Furman in her world, and the thought of any existence without him now, seemed infinitely depressing.

## Chapter Fourteen

An hour later, she descended the stairs in nervous anticipation, feeling slightly ashamed at having passed out on the bed while pondering her dilemma - she hadn't intended to, but the emotional exhaustion was taking its toll on her frayed nerves.

She had to admit that the catnap had provided renewed strength and perspective. Lying there, she'd come to the realization that it wasn't fair to Denny and Katrina - her hiding behind them, like a frightened child or a deer caught in the headlights. She was a full-grown woman, for crying out loud, and needed to get a lid on her emotions - or die with the ecstasy of losing all control, something whispered inside her head. Lord, that was exactly the sort of irresponsible thinking that was getting her into all this trouble. She firmly straightened her back and conjured a bright smile. Grant was in the kitchen, preparing fried ham and eggs for their supper. It smelled ravenously delicious.

"Hope you don't mind. It's just the two of us." He grinned down at her roguishly, taking in her freshened features - the luxurious length of her auburn hair cascading gracefully down past her delicate shoulders. Her face was devoid of makeup and glowing with the pleasure that being in his company, once again, evoked.

He was like a drug - her fix. Well, tomorrow, she was getting off it, cold turkey! This solemn pledge lent her renewed courage to endure these last few hours with him. Yes, she was a big girl and could do this! No, she *would* do this!

His searching gaze was beginning to create havoc with her knees, and so, to avoid making a complete idiot of herself - perhaps swooning ridiculously on the floor at his feet, she busied herself putting plates and cutlery on the table in preparation for the tantalizing meal Grant was beginning to dish up for them.

Noticing the refreshing jug of iced tea that he had made, she reached for some drinking glasses in a cupboard near the stove, where Grant was standing. In her cautious effort to avoid the deadly peril of brushing body parts with his, she twisted sideways and lost her hold on one of the glasses, which promptly smashed to pieces on the floor at her bare feet. Immediately, strong, steadying arms around her waist held her in place.

"Don't move. There's glass everywhere."

He was gone, presumably in search of a broom, and was back in an instant, setting himself to the task of sweeping up the spray of gleaming shards, confirming her assumption that, of course, he would know his way around her kitchen - just another piece of her life that the children had so trustingly shared with him in her absence.

So, what of it? He'd seen her broom closet, for God's sake! That and much more, ho ho! So why did it bother her so? It was only that the man seemed so damned comfortable in her home - fit in like a glove, more accurately, and that irritated the hell out of her. She jumped in alarm as he made a firm but gentle grab for her ankle.

"Hold still. There's a piece of glass embedded in your toe," he ordered brusquely.

Upon closer inspection, she could see a tiny sparkle protruding from her big toe, gleaming like a diamond, she thought. She fought near hysteria, attempting in vain to endure the burning caress of his fingers, but the telltale inferno in her loins spoke of her body's betrayal, and she closed her eyes, swaying slightly, putting her hand on his shoulder for merciful balance. Too late, the electric shock of the contact with his broad, muscular body sent warning bells clanging in her head.

She opened her eyes to find his fervent heated gaze upon her, searing her flesh and sending a blazing trail of fire along every nerve in her body. His eyes held hers as he produced the offensive object that was the catalyst of this sweet torment - bright crimson with her blood. She hadn't even felt him remove it, so gentle had been his administration.

"Th-thank you," she stammered and withdrew her foot hastily from his hold, as if a menacing viper had locked her in its possession. Perhaps that wasn't far from the truth, she mused, biting her lip in nervous agitation. She straightened, swept her hair behind her ears, and smoothed an imaginary wrinkle from her denim shorts, all the while acutely aware of his gaze on her.

"I love that about you."

What had she gone and done now?

"The way you run your hands over your body like that, making me wish it were my privilege to do so."

Hot flames scorched her senses anew at his husky words. He tore his gaze away and finished plating.

They ate the meal in silence, each lost in their own thoughts. Marianna dared not look at him, as she knew that the aching desire, that was greedily consuming her, would flare from her eyes, and she needed only to get through this one evening, to find blessed, safe ground once again. She could feel his eyes boring into her and would have sold her soul, in that instant, to be privy to his thoughts. She jumped at the ring of the telephone and rushed into the office to answer it, blessing fate for providing this timely distraction.

"Mari, how's it going, girl?" Tess's voice was muffled by a loud background noise.

"Where on earth are you?" Marianna barked with unreasonable annoyance, as she had dearly hoped they would be on their way home by now. "How are the kids?"

"They're fine. I'm taking them to see Johnny Depp." Marianna knew that the kids would run laps to see "Pirates of the Caribbean" for the zillionth time, and she figured Tess herself must have already watched it at least a dozen. Johnny Depp was her all-time favorite screen hottie - but when would they be home?

"They want to stay over - I told them it was OK."

She should have seen this one coming, and her heart lodged in her throat. Tess had a bedroom decorated exclusively for them, and they loved sleeping over with their favorite auntie, who engaged in boisterous pillow fights with them and sinfully allowed them to eat buttery popcorn in her own colossal king-sized bed. Marianna stifled the growing panic, with the implication this new development brought.

"Tess, I'd really rather they come home tonight." Come on, girl, think up a good reason, quick! "They're really rather tired and may give you trouble." It was feeble, at best.

"Den and Kat could never be trouble, you silly goose." Tess laughed. "Besides, it's better they are out of your hair for tonight." Marianna knew exactly what she was up to and could just imagine the wicked gleam in her eyes.

"Tess, nothing is going to happen here, so please just bring them home after the movie." Marianna was beginning to feel ill under the strain of trying to gain some semblance of control over a situation that was increasingly eluding her grasp. "And besides, Grant has to leave in the morning."

"Mari, it will be too late, and I'm not letting you off this easy. Enjoy your evening, and for heaven's sake, relax - the guy's not asking you to marry him! Just enjoy the moment with him. Don't be such a chicken! You never know where Cupid's arrows may meander. Also, you won't have to take the kids to the airport with you when you give him a proper farewell."

Oh, if it were only that particular moment she had to worry about, she might - just possibly, emerge unscathed.

"I'm not a chicken. I'm just adhering to my better judgment, which tells me that I can't afford any casual flings right now."

Marianna looked up to see Grant watching her from the doorway and knew instinctively, from the scathing, sardonic expression on his face, that her last comment had not gone unregistered. She didn't even notice Tess ring off and stared dumbly at the phone in her hand, her mind reeling in confusion, as Grant turned abruptly and left the room. God, she ached to run after him and tell him that it could never be anything casual with him, at least not on her part.

And there lay the crux of the matter, she reasoned, biting her lip in agitation. She had no idea what his thoughts or feelings were. if any at all. Her eyes sparkled with growing outrage at the predicament she ascertained he had placed her in. For the love of Pete, what kind of a guy just stalks off without stating the reasons for his ire? Did he think she was a mind reader? Well, it was better this way, she assured herself firmly, listening to his quiet movements in the guest room below. Was he coming back up, then? Or had he decided that spending time with her now would be an infinite waste - now that he knew she wasn't ripe for a cheap sexual fling? What else could it amount to, after all? He had admitted that he wanted her, true, but they had shared nothing beyond that physical level. It was pure lust on his end - she was under no illusions there.

Marianna wandered slowly into the kitchen to find that Grant had cleaned up completely from their meal, leaving no trace of evidence that they had shared such domestic intimacy. Tomorrow, he would leave her behind without any discernable sign of his intrusion on her normally sedate life. Perhaps then, she would be able to regard this entire experience as a dream, a distant, fleeting moment in her existence. One day, she may even pen a story about it. That ought to be a good one, kiddo! She grinned in spite of herself as she climbed the stairs to her room.

Deep in thought, she lay in her bed after a long hot shower, wondering how to assuage the pent-up restless energy that was plaguing her. She could hear the haunting strains of his guitar, seeking her out through the floorboards of her home. Grant had informed her that he never left home without it, and she really couldn't imagine him that way either.

Surely, she'd never before heard any melody so beautifully sad, so moving. She didn't recognize the song, but it somehow seemed to call out to her in a mournful serenade, and although she knew in her heart, that the song was not of her inspiration, she felt a strange ownership - a personal aching connection. Unable to bear the poignant chords any longer, Marianna wrapped a thick, soft comforter around her ears to block out its unmerciful beckoning. Hours later, after crying herself to deep exhaustion, Marianna finally succumbed to a disturbing slumber.

# Chapter Fifteen

A dismal gray cloud cover hung heavy over the morning, like a foreboding prophecy, acutely matching Marianna's dreary state of mind, reminding her that she was forever altered by a power far beyond her. In the hours she had lain awake the previous night, she had recognized the painful longing within, at the reality of Grant's departure, to be more than a wistful regret for a lost opportunity for love play. Grant had touched something deep inside of her, like no other man before, not even Jeff. Pursuing it further was out of the question, she knew, even if there was a remote possibility that he felt anything similar. No, it was something she'd keep for herself - a treasure she could cherish, take out, and reflect upon in safer moments.

The ride to the airport was endured in weighty silence - the air stagnant with unspoken thoughts, and Marianna wasn't sure how much more of the oppressive quiet she could endure.

"Give me your hand."

They were at a stoplight, and Grant reached out to her. She felt lost and bereft, watching her small hand, so seemingly insignificant, disappear into his larger, powerful one - melting into his warmth. She could feel the comforting beat of his heart on the tip of his thumb, which was now caressing her hand slowly, in a very disturbing fashion.

"You are cold."

Ho, ho, if he only knew! Her hands were about the only part of her anatomy that were not completely afire at his touch. The light turned green, and she snatched her hand away, offering gratitude for small mercies.

"I want to thank you for a wonderful time, Mari."

It was a verbal caress - her name on his lips. If she lived a thousand years, she knew she'd never forget that throaty, seductive sound. She felt a ridiculous regret that she hadn't the benefit of recording it - to capture forever.

"Being with you here has brought such a refreshing change of perspective to my life," he continued. "You can't know how much it's meant to me."

He was, of course, referring to the peaceful break in his hectic schedule. She could well understand his appreciation for the opportunity and certainly couldn't argue against the immense peace and tranquility that her country acreage offered.

"It's been wonderful to have you here," she offered graciously, "The kids will miss you terribly." She didn't dare look at him now and was grateful for the distraction of driving - just one look into those sexy gray eyes, and she'd be toast, reduced to begging him for even just a casual fling. She was assaulted by a fleeting alarming visual of throwing herself at his feet - a complete submission to him, in sweet surrender. Lord, he'd probably hop out of the van and achieve an Olympic sprint to the airport in his frantic haste to escape.

"Yes, but what of their mother?" It was a loaded question that she wasn't quite sure how to answer. "Mari, I want to apologize for walking out on you last night - I thought it best under the circumstances."

What did he mean by that? What circumstances? She glanced his way and caught her breath at the smoldering sparks flickering in his eyes. God, the man was pure sensuality. While the injustice of this sent her blood to boiling, she found that she truly couldn't fault him for his track record with the ladies. He surely couldn't be accountable for the dynamic effect he had on women, any more than they could resist his magnetic charisma.

And not for the first time since she'd met him, Marianna found herself wondering about his relationship with the spunky redhead, Benny's sister. What was her name again? Shauna, that was it. Was she the reason he had not pursued their physical attraction more aggressively these past few days? As he had so candidly inserted, her own response was hideously transparent, and neither one of them could deny the intense chemistry - not that he had tried. It was only Marianna who seemed to be in some all-out battle for sanity - only she who was in danger of sacrificing all common sense. Contrarily, Grant had been in complete control - the epitome of confidence and strength, the entire time. She would be thanking her lucky stars to the end of eternity for his departure, if she weren't so damned depressed about it.

Marianna parked the car and reluctantly accepted his large hand, urging her to accompany him into the terminal. She watched sulkily as he checked his bags and returned to her with a gentle smile, that softened the rugged male features, eliciting a sharp pang somewhere in her heart. He pulled her down to sit beside him on a nearby bench.

As he put his arm around her and gently drew her to snuggle into his side, for the life of her, though she knew she should resist, she was powerless to deny herself this sweet pleasure. The pressure of his guitar, cradled protectively in his other arm, somehow deepened the intimacy - it was so much a part of him. Surely there was no harm in this final bittersweet indulgence. She breathed deeply the scent of his male essence and gloried in his warm, gentle strength.

Oddly, their sexual tension seemed set aside in favor of the moment. However, Marianna knew it to be smoldering dangerously just below the surface. At this instant, she knew instinctively that he, too, was bent on honoring this pure magic - for reasons known only to him. It didn't matter. It was enough for her now - all she had left. Perhaps it was his parting gift to her - he was not a monster, after all. Only the devil himself, a little voice whispered.

~~~

"Mommy, mommy! You promised we'd go today!" Katrina was shaking her none too gently from an exhausted slumber. "Come on. We have to get ready!"

Marianna shook her head, attempting to clear the ensnaring cobwebs from her mind. Painful memories of Grant's parting the previous day flooded her consciousness, and a depressing gloom threatened to settle over her.

"OK, Kat, Sweetie, slow down and give me a chance to wake up." She fumbled for the clock and heaved a sigh of relief. Lately, it seemed she'd been making a habit of sleeping later than usual, but this morning, Katrina had jumped the gun.

"Listen, little lady, it's only 7:00 a.m., and we'll not be leaving for at least two hours. Now go get dressed." She sat up slowly, gave her daughter a giant hug before pushing her gently toward her room, and sauntered into the shower. It was the remedy she needed to perk up her lagging spirits.

A half-hour later, Marianna prepared breakfast, feeling decidedly brighter, with renewed determination to get on with the business of settling back into her old, familiar routine. Tess would be here any minute - they had all decided to go to the zoo and then, later, for a picnic at the park. Tess had promised the kids she'd take them on a bumper boat ride, and they were more than a little excited, especially by the trivial fact that the boats were equipped with water guns.

"Knock knock!" Tess announced cheerily as she entered the kitchen. "Are we ready to go on a jungle trek today?" Marianna laughed at the safari attire Tess had chosen specifically for the occasion. Always the drama queen!

"How are we this morning?" Marianna smiled brightly at Tess's probing gaze, knowing the question was aimed precisely in her direction.

"Fine, it's a wonderful day. Here, help me load the picnic basket." Marianna's upbeat façade sounded forced even to her own ears. They stocked the basket with apples, bananas, peaches, carrots, celery, and the sandwiches Tess had brought with her. Marianna knew she'd put Tess off only momentarily and that her friend would not rest until she'd been given a blow-by-blow account of every juicy, minute detail of Grant's departure.

When she'd picked up the kids the previous morning, after coming back from the airport, they hadn't had time for talk, as Dennis was collecting Tess for an afternoon of boating on the lake. Marianna had to smile at that - the glamorous Tessalina Jones, lounging precariously on the edge of Dennis's fishing boat. Presently, they loaded the kids in the car and set out for what promised to be a glorious outing.

It wasn't until mid-morning, when they decided to stop for a coffee and let the kids loose in the Kidzone Jungle - a confusing, gigantic maze of tubes, ladders, and slides, that an opportunity for a private chat arose.

"How'd it go? What did he say?"

Marianna knew that Tess was fairly bursting with curiosity and decided she couldn't torture her friend any longer. She took a deep breath and chewed on her lip thoughtfully as Tess waited eagerly.

"It was no big deal, really. I drove him to the airport, and he left." What more could she tell her, really? It was true - nothing actually eventful had occurred – except her broken heart.

"That's it?" Tess squeaked. "Not even one little kiss?" Tess was an incurable romantic and believed anything was possible, such as a famous rock star sweeping a small-town girl off her feet and whisking her off into the sunset to live happily ever after with him in his luxurious palace. At what point did reality enter into that kind of reasoning?

"Actually, he did give me one kiss, but it was just a friendly farewell." Even as she said it, Marianna heard the bogus ring to those casually uttered words.

Rooted in fact, the kiss was not passionate by any sexual definition and didn't even involve touching lips. Even so, the slow, feathery caress of his lips, placed so gently on her forehead, had branded her for all time. He had looked deeply into her eyes, his magic hands framing her burning face, and she'd been certain he was going to properly kiss her.

For a split second, she had gazed in fascination, at the warring emotions across his face – he'd released her slowly then, leaving her with face upturned, head swimming, and lips still parted slightly in fevered anticipation. In a farewell gesture, he'd brushed the knuckles of his hand in a lingering, light caress up the side of her cheek, and off he'd gone.

She'd watched him disappear through the gate, into the throng of passengers, caressing the tingling spot where his lips had touched, and had felt an aching, forsaken loss. Not a word - not even, it's *been swell*, don't call me, I'll call you, or *thanks for the boner*. Well, what had she expected after all? It was exactly what she wanted, wasn't it? Why, then, was she so utterly despondent?

"Well, hell, Mari, why didn't you kiss *him*? It's acceptable in this day and age, you know." Tess regarded Marianna in sudden alarm at the pallor that had just washed over her complexion. "What's wrong?" She shook Marianna gently.

"Oh, it's nothing." Marianna forced her attention on Tess. "Oh, Lord, it's the music. They're playing his music." It was useless to try to pull the wool over Tess's eyes - she was far too astute for that. Misery oozed from Marianna's pores.

"Okay." Tess listened to the background music, recognizing the rich tones of Grant's crooning voice filling the air around them, and paused, trying to assess the shape of her friend's state of mind. "You're missing the hell out of him." The gentle warmth in her eyes was a healing touch.

"Sinfully." Marianna sighed sorrowfully. "I don't understand why - a fantasy that got away from me, I suppose." She glanced over at the kids to ensure their safety and proceeded to pour out all of her confusion and sadness to her good friend - it was time for that now.

"Wow, Mari, this sounds to be a whole lot more than just a fleeting physical attraction." Tess reached out and lovingly smoothed an errant auburn tendril off Marianna's cheek with her perfectly manicured hand.

"Well, not on his part. That's pretty obvious." Marianna looked at Tess with her heart in her eyes. Tess didn't look convinced.

"Nothing happened beyond that first kiss in L.A. - not even a second helping, unless you count the farewell peck." She shook her head in confusion. "There were times - I felt I could see his soul in those bedroom eyes, as if he were teetering on the verge of sharing some deep dark secret, judging whether or not I could be trusted with it. Then, he'd give me that infuriating smug - the all-knowing once over, and I'd write it off to my overactive imagination."

Marianna was horrified at the threat of tears, and her head ached with the effort to avoid an all-out crying jag right there in the Kid's Jungle. Tess rubbed her arm in a gesture of comfort and support.

"I've given up trying to determine what's real or fantasy. Anyway, it's all water under the bridge now." Marianna shook her head in resignation, throwing her hair back off her face, and offered her friend a shaky but determined smile.

"Well, the reality is about to pounce on us now," Tess warned as Denny and Katrina came bounding excitedly over to them through the mob of energetic children. Both women laughed out loud at their infectious exuberance.

They decided to head to the park for lunch then, and as they munched merrily on their picnic feast, Marianna locked eyes with Tess over the children's heads and silently mouthed a thank you. What would she do without her dear friend? Now that was something worth fighting for!

# Chapter Sixteen

Marianna spent the next several days focusing all her energy on preparation for Tess's fortieth birthday celebration. She had enlisted Dennis' collaboration in what Marianna believed to be a perfectly ingenious plan. Tess was the ultimate organizer and a hard act to follow. She had, in fact, arranged for Marianna to sing with a local band on Marianna's thirty-ninth milestone, and though she had wanted to strangle Tess at the onset, she'd thoroughly enjoyed the experience - the exhilaration of the entire undertaking, far outweighing her stage fright.

Now, grinning like a Cheshire cat, Marianna was certain she'd finally scoop the upper edge on her friend. It was all set up. Dennis had driven Tess to work that morning and was scheduled to pick her up directly afterward, under the guise of them meeting Marianna at the airport.

The story they'd concocted, was that Marianna had been called back to L. A. on short notice to straighten out some details on the contract, and needed Tess to take the kids overnight. Dennis had dreamed up some legal beagle explanation for the necessity of Marianna's presence there in L.A. She knew that Tess would leap enthusiastically at the opportunity, as she stubbornly harbored a romantic belief that Marianna and Grant were fated to meet again.

Marianna was also aware that her friend's feelings for Dennis had deepened considerably in the past month, or at least, Tess was finally acknowledging the fact that she had fallen head over heels for the guy – it was the real deal. Marianna could not have been happier for any two people. Dennis adored Tess, and Marianna knew that if given the opportunity, Tess would love to have children of her own. Her success in real estate over the past several years afforded her the financial freedom to raise a family without monetary stress.

Hence, when Marianna approached Dennis with her brain-storm for him to whisk Tess away on an exotic holiday, he came up with the ideal plan to complement the scheme. Once at the airport, Dennis would ask Tess to take Marianna's van home, as the neighbor had agreed to come over and check out a suspicious noise under the hood. Meanwhile, Marianna planned to beat them to the airport and arrange for Tess to receive an intercom page, directing her to board a particular flight under the pretext of retrieving an important personal message from Marianna, who was already on the plane, as far as Tess would know.

Dramatic as all get out, she knew, but Marianna was certain Tess would fall for it. Upon reaching the seat, Tess would find Dennis to greet her with the news that he was taking her on an exotic two-week cruise and insist she sit her cute little fanny down and buckle up. Once he had her safely seconded on the ship, Dennis had arranged for a crewmember to videotape a thoroughly romantic marriage proposal.

Oh, it was diabolically clever! Marianna was thoroughly pleased with herself and so disregarded the niggling feelings of guilt over the little white lies, in honor of all the evil stunts Tess had played on her. She knew Tess would be properly shocked and speechless - if that were remotely possible, to learn that her normally straightforward, practical friend, would be a party to such a devious deception. Marianna would give anything to see the look on her face. She giggled gleefully to herself.

Now, returning from the airport, she felt confident it would go off without a hitch. Dennis had graciously offered paying for the entire holiday, but Marianna had insisted on covering Tess's fare, as it was to be a joint birthday and wedding present. There was no doubt in her mind that Tess would be overcome with joy, to accept Dennis's proposal. She sighed wistfully, dreading the lonely two weeks ahead, devoid of the distraction who was Tess, and mentally reviewed a list of things she wanted to accomplish with the kids before the school year began, to keep herself busy and her mind firmly on track.

The following morning dawned bright, with a hint of autumn in the air as the final days of August loomed. The nights were already significantly cooler, and Marianna had called the technician to clean the furnace in preparation for the colder weather. Today, however, the three of them were beach bound, as the Weather Channel forecast was for "hot and sunny." The kids were busy gathering their toys and debating heatedly over who would get to use the dolphin beach towel. Marianna had already packed the lunch cooler and was just loading it into the van when the phone rang. She nearly tripped over the hose in her rush to get it, praying that nothing had gone awry with Tess and Dennis's vacation plans.

"Hello." She collapsed into the office chair in a breathless heap.

"Hello yourself."

Every nerve in her body buzzed in reaction to that low, husky drawl. The blood pounded in her ears, and a draining weakness permeated her limbs. She couldn't imagine why he'd be calling her now. She knew she'd never survive another unannounced visit from Grant.

"Oh, how are you?" That was intelligent - she chided herself.

"Great, now that I've heard your voice."

Smooth operator for sure, she told herself, but her heart sang an entirely different tune at his appreciative words. Marianna sat in dumb silence, not having the foggiest idea of how to respond.

"We need you to come back to L.A. Mari."

Her mind reeled at this news. Was this some dumb trick of fate? Payback for deceiving Tess?

"I thought it would be quicker to call you personally, rather than go through the agency," Grant continued.

So that was the reason he'd called her then. The desperate ache of disappointment, that invaded her gut, shocked her with its intensity.

"What is it that needs my attention?" Her heart slammed in her ears, but she managed to keep her voice cool and impersonal in an effort to focus on business and take the edge off her rising anxiety. If he noticed, he didn't let on.

"Mari, we need a couple more songs for the CD, and we'd like to see what you have."

If only the voice weren't so darned sensuous, she could remain aloof and handle this professionally. This was completely unjust, she determined.

"I told you that I have no other completed work." She had declined showing her assortment of scribbled lyrics to him one evening when he'd asked to see her songs. At the time, she had felt self-conscious and incredibly shy at the prospect of sharing such an intimate part of herself with him.

"That's not a problem. We can work it out together."

For a moment, she imagined he was talking about something else altogether, but no. The songs, Mari, the songs, she chided herself.

"My kids start school in two weeks, and Tess isn't here to watch over them. Can't we do this by e-mail?" She was desperate to avoid facing him in the flesh again, but another part of her was teeming with excitement at the prospect. She knew she had to gain control over that treacherous side of herself right quickly!

"Mari," he paused, effectively silencing her protests. "I want you to bring Denny and Katrina along, and they can stay with my sister on the ranch. They'll love it, and her kids are about the same age."

"Oh, I don't think so," Marianna began.

"We need you to be here. You have seen how great music comes together. Mari, you understand that - long distance just doesn't cut it."

A thousand thoughts were racing through her head - she needed to grasp onto some sane, sensible alternative. Anything to save her from traveling back to L.A.

"We need the band together for this one, Mari, and you have to be here."

Grant's tone was insistent. She felt like a caged animal, backed into a deep dark corner.

"But that's ridiculous - you are all highly talented songwriters. Why do you need me?" Marianna was truly astonished at his resolve, and wondered what more could be underneath it all. Surely competent musicians would not resort to such lengths to collaborate with their songwriters.

"We liked the breath of fresh air your song provided to our mix, and we need a couple more like it to achieve some balance. Come on, Mari, if you're worried about money…"

"Of course not." She cut him off short. Marianna knew that if she sold the rights to another song, money would not be an issue – she figured he was well aware of that too. She'd been astounded at the hefty sum she'd soon be receiving for the first one - much more than she had ever dreamed.

"Well, expenses are covered, in any case." Grant fell silent, waiting for her reply. If she ever needed divine intervention, this would be the defining moment.

"How long would I have to stay?" Now why had she asked that? Unless she had just agreed to this ridiculous suggestion - well, in truth, it was more of an order, wasn't it? One that she was certainly under no obligation to follow, she reminded herself. You are the one in control here, Mari. Ha - the little voice mocked her. Marianna suddenly felt bullied by the arrogant beast on the other end of the line, but he responded before she could sputter an objection.

"As long as it takes, but I promise, you'll be back in plenty of time for school."

Was there just a hint of a plea in his tone? No, that was wishful thinking, and she knew by now just how persistent he could be when he wanted something to go his way. Besides, in truth, she had absolutely no idea how musicians normally conducted this kind of business. For all she knew, these things happened every day. A thought hit her - could this affect her present contract if she didn't go? Why hadn't she asked him that yet?

"I'm sure you can work out some other arrangement, Grant," Marianna pitched a final, feeble protest.

"Mari, please," Grant cut into her defenses with that simple appeal.

Something in his voice…

"Perhaps I can make arrangements for a few days at most, but I really do not feel right about leaving my children with your sister." She had never left the kids with anyone other than Jen or Tess and was not at all comfortable with Grant's proposed arrangement.

"You'll be with them most of the time, as Terri lives within commuting distance, and you can spend the first few days out at the ranch. That way, if you are still not comfortable with the arrangement, we'll come up with Plan B, or" Grant offered reasonably, "you can fly home, no strings attached."

Marianna's hesitation was highly out of character for her, when it concerned the welfare of her children. So why was she giving this an ounce of consideration? She knew the answer to that one - she trusted Grant implicitly with matters concerning her children. He genuinely cared about them and would never jeopardize their safety - of that, she was certain.

"Would you please e-mail me with the travel arrangements then?" What on earth was she getting herself in for? She hadn't the slightest notion of which songs to consider. The band certainly seemed to have a heap more faith in her than she did herself. The deciding factor was her future financial comfort – post-secondary education for Denny and Kat, she assured herself.

"You can bet on it. I'll see you in a day or two."

What? That quickly? Was he insane? She needed at least a week to psyche herself up for confronting him again. She opened her mouth to protest, but with a resounding click, he was gone. It was her that had relinquished sanity, and, in all honesty, she knew it had flown the coop from the first moment she'd laid eyes on the roguish, sexy hunk of a man. And there was little left to do now but pray to the Cupid gods for mercy.

The next few days left her scarce time for anything other than frantic travel preparations. Denny and Katrina had been predictably ecstatic when they learned of their unexpected holiday destination.

"A real ranch?" Denny demanded to know everything about it. "With real horses and real cowboys? Will they herd cattle? Can I help them?"

"Whoa, Denny!" Marianna chuckled, hauling her son onto her lap. "I don't know the answers to any of your questions yet; we will just have to wait and see." She tweaked his freckled nose and hugged him fiercely. "Mr. Grant assures me you are going to love it, and there will be children there who are your age."

"Can I bring my new Barbie?" Katrina looked up solemnly from her coloring project, as though this may make or break her willingness to join them. Marianna knew that her daughter was already organizing preparations for the trip, in her little head. Where does a four-year-old learn such skills? She supposed she had herself to blame, always making sure everything was in perfect order in their world.

"Of course, Sweet Pie," Marianna assured. "You can even bring Buster if you wish." Buster was Katrina's most prized stuffed toy that she cuddled with almost every night. Katrina's blue eyes lit up with this imparted good news. It seemed that her children were far less anxious than she, at the prospect of spending the remainder of their summer in the company of a certain Grant Furman.

# Chapter Seventeen

Marianna made a concerted effort to relax as Grant maneuvered the SUV expertly along the winding scenic secondary highway, leading to Terri's ranch home. She was more than a little nervous at meeting the sister of this dynamic man, whose mere presence beside her was creating strange havoc with her insides. Grant had been waiting for them at the airport, and she'd been profoundly consumed with a burning elation at first sight of him, drinking in every feature that had been permanently etched into her mind's eye. Despite the accompanying misgivings, she felt new life singing through her veins.

It was a beautiful day, pleasantly mild, and Marianna sighed with pleasure at the picturesque countryside whizzing by - rolling pastures and high fluffy cumulous clouds kissing the mountain peaks in the distance. Gosh, it was gorgeous here - she could certainly see herself retiring in a place such as this. They had been on the road for a little over an hour now, and still, Grant had not spoken directly to her. Of course, she had to admit, it was tough to get a word in edgewise, between the excited chatter of her two children, who were bent on divulging every detail of their very first plane ride to Grant. She laughingly admonished them, assuring them that Mr. Grant had ridden on many planes himself.

"Actually, planes scare the pants off me."

All three of them were speechless at his easy confession - she couldn't believe that this sturdy, confident man would have any such qualms.

"Wow, I guess I'm pretty brave then, huh?" Denny was flabbergasted that this giant of a man should be afraid to travel in the very airplane that he, himself, had just spent several hours inside, suspended high above the clouds. They had changed planes in Seattle, and Grant had met them at the airport in Denver to avoid the long drive from L.A.

"You sure are, Buddy." Grant winked warmly at him in the rear-view mirror.

"You must have had some pretty stressful moments when you were touring over the years." She was curious as to the inner workings of this man who effortlessly had complete power over all of her senses.

"Oh, I did a lot of driving, we all did, actually – bought an old Greyhound bus and traversed the entire country."

The quick heated smile that he directed at her, promptly melted all the defenses she'd worked so hard to construct the past two days. God, he was a handsome guy, but she knew now that it was so much more than physical - precisely what defined him as dangerous goods.

At once, he took a right turn onto a well-maintained, gravel country lane. In the distance loomed a sprawling ranch house with stables and outbuildings in close proximity to the home. Grant maneuvered the SUV around the circular drive and parked in front of one of the buildings. Upon exiting the vehicle, they were immediately assaulted by two of the friendliest, hairiest, slobbery canines Marianna had ever chanced to meet.

"Watchdogs, they are not." Grant laughed heartily, watching the kids giggle delightfully while trying to fend off two monster tongues, that were threatening to give them an early bath.

"That one's name is Candy." Grant gestured to the lovable Heinz 57 mutt. Marianna's attention was drawn to an angelic little girl with a mop of curly dark hair and a smile straight from heaven. Katrina returned her grin as the little girl wrapped her arms around the huge bundle of fur.

"And this little minx here is Mindy." Grant introduced as he scooped up the child in his strong arms, giving her a bear hug and a kiss on the cheek.

Marianna couldn't take her eyes off this normally cool and collected man, whose love for his niece and nephew spilled out generously in lavish affection. Children were definitely his weak spot, she surmised, and this realization pleased her far more than she cared to admit. He thoroughly ruffled the hair of a young boy, who appeared to be about the same age as Denny. It was obvious, from the mass of curls on his head, that he was Mindy's brother.

"Meet Mark, the toughest ranch hand around these parts." Grant tweaked his nose, and Mark's little chest puffed out with pride.

"Hi there, I'm Terri - you must be Marianna!"

A tall, slender woman came rushing out of the house, wiping her hands on a towel, and Marianna caught her breath at the generous smile and gray eyes that were identical to Grant's. But where Grant's features were guarded and hard to interpret, Terri's smile was open and friendly, and her eyes shone with merriment. Marianna thought she had never met a more beautiful woman. Her regal features were framed by a mass of gorgeous black hair, which, even in its current state of disarray, glistened like spun silk. Marianna liked her immediately and held out her hand. Introductions were made with all the children.

"Sorry I'm such a mess right now, but to be honest, that's what life is often like around here – utter chaos!" She shrugged helplessly, and Marianna laughed. "I do clean up pretty good for dinner, though." She turned, laughing, and motioned for them to follow her into the house.

"Yes, you can dress her up, but you can't take her out." Grant teased as he poked his sister playfully in the ribs. She spun around and gave him a good whack in the gut in mock outrage.

"One thing about my bullheaded brother - you have to keep him in line at all times, or he'll wind up completely out of control. He's really just an overgrown kid, but I'm sure you've already figured that one out."

Marianna thought nothing could be further from the truth and met his gaze to find ironic amusement lurking behind those sexy gray eyes. Would she ever figure the man out? In another life, perhaps?

"Actually, we haven't known each other too long, only through our business dealings." Her voice trailed off as she met the questioning curiosity in Terri's eyes. Marianna knew it was better to set the record straight at the onset. The last thing she needed was another female misinterpreting their relationship and playing Cupid.

"I wanted to thank you for offering your home to us during our visit. I'm sure it will only be a few days." Marianna took note of the pointed glance Terri now bestowed upon her brother, with apprehensive suspicion. Just what had Grant told his sister? The dark beauty now turned her attention back to Marianna.

"You are welcome here as long as you like. It's great to have some female company around here for a change - of the adult variety, that is, and your children will keep mine out of my hair for a change, as they really don't get too many visitors their own age through the summer."

Marianna knew only too well what that was like.

"You will find the commute to L.A. pleasant and easily managed for a day trip."

So, Terri had been informed of the nature of her trip, at least.

"I do have a couple of friends I golf with – my sole weekly outing, and I'm counting on you to make it a foursome this week, so don't go rushing off too fast." Terri laughed at the anxious look on Marianna's face. "Oh, don't worry, we are anything but serious. I have to buy a dozen or so balls every time we go out - some young kid has probably made a fortune on all the little white spheres I've whacked into the bush and water hazards." She giggled delightfully. "I suppose I'm just buying back my own balls."

Marianna smiled in spite of her growing apprehension. She did not want to get too cozy with Grant's sister.

"Well, lunch will be served in about an hour. What say I let Grant give you the grand tour of the ranch?"

Marianna would have rather cut off both her thumbs, but under the circumstances, it would hardly be polite to protest. She allowed Grant to take her elbow and lead her out into the yard. The children were off playing, and she was pleased that they'd hit it off so well. It would ease the stress of the next few days just a little.

Mercifully, Grant maintained a respectable distance from her through the entire tour, showing her the stables and introducing her to the five horses that were housed there. She chose to refrain from commenting on his suggestion that they take the horses out to explore the miles of pasture that seemed to carpet the glorious foothills, like rolling velvet, clear through to the mountains. It sounded like a heavenly adventure - one that she knew she could ill afford to embark upon, at least with the earthy, charismatic man who was now at her side.

They returned to the main house for lunch, which consisted of cold cuts; sliced Mozzarella, Swiss, and Cheddar cheese; fresh mouth-watering home-baked buns with butter; preserves; various homemade relishes, and canned pickles. The tomatoes and lettuce, Grant informed her, were freshly harvested from Terri's bountiful garden, and the fruit picked off the miniature orchard out back. It was a hearty feast fit for kings – or ranchers, she supposed, and just when Marianna was certain she'd burst, Terri served warm apple pie with homemade ice cream. It was delicious, and Marianna said as much.

"Lunch was marvelous, thank you, but if I continue to eat this way, I'll pack on ten pounds while I'm here." Marianna sat back with a cup of good, strong tea and was shocked at the sudden awareness, that she felt so comfortable in Terri's home, as if they'd been friends for years.

"Well, my family works up a pretty hearty appetite here on the ranch - you'll meet my husband, Derek, later, and we have two ranch hands living in the outbuildings who come up for meals too. So, as much as I love to get outdoors, I'm often imprisoned in my kitchen - slaving away over a hot stove like a pioneer wife." Marianna laughed as Grant rolled his eyes in mock exasperation. He sat with his arm resting casually on the back of Terri's chair.

"Now she's telling tales - I've never met a woman who loves cooking more than Terri." Grant's tone was light but serious. "But cleaning? Well, that's an entirely different matter!" Grant ducked as his sister threw her napkin at him playfully.

"OK, so perhaps I'm not a domestic goddess but have no fear - I do employ a housemaid who visits once a week to rescue us all from eternal filth." Her infectious grin had them all laughing heartily, and Marianna had to fight a powerful wave of disappointment, when Grant announced that he had to make a run into the studio and wouldn't be back until the following morning.

"Mari, you'll be in good hands here, I promise, and in truth, I'm hoping you'll convince my overworked sister to crash by the pool with you for an afternoon. She could seriously use the break." Grant threw Terri a severe warning look that enlightened Marianna about an ongoing battle surrounding the issue of Terri's busy routine.

Later, lounging around the pool, Terri provided further insight into the volatile discord surrounding the subject. "Grant is really just an overprotective bear." She grinned affectionately while smoothing sunscreen onto her long, lean legs and upper torso. They'd already applied it to one another's backs without hesitation. The ease with which Marianna related with Terri reminded her of Tess, and she suddenly felt a sharp pang of longing for her friend.

"I suppose he has good reason, it is incredibly chaotic around here, but we're not yet to the point where we can afford to hire help in the kitchen."

Marianna had threatened to leave, in a half-serious tone, if Terri didn't agree to allow her to help with the supper preparations for that evening. She had finally convinced her it would be fun and that she needed some good company around the pool - feeling a little out of sorts so far from home.

"The problem is, Grant, cannot forgive me for refusing to allow him to pay off our mortgage. There was a time when I may have agreed to a loan of sorts, but Derek would not hear of it. You know, it's a guy thing."

Terri threw her a conspiring grin, and Marianna knew full well about male egos. Jeff had been consumed with pride, causing some pretty serious tiffs between them over the issue of her staying home with the children. Not that she regretted it - it was a gift she'd treasure forever.

"And he has very little room to talk," Terri continued with a grin. "Grant gets his digs in with Derek by helping out on the ranch and refusing payment. Truthfully though, I think Grant finds that the physical demands of ranch work provide him with a fairly effective outlet for the stress of his career." Terri's soft, affectionate look spoke volumes about the love she harbored for her brother. "Grant has not led an easy life."

Marianna had learned a little about that from Benny and Jerry but declined mentioning this insight to Terri.

"He's done well for himself over the years - one of the few rockers to hit fame, I suppose, and chose not to party it all away. I'm really proud of him."

So, some of it may have just been a rumor after all? Certainly, not the pictures in the papers - hard evidence that he'd been out and about with a host of beautiful women, and photographs don't lie. Terri continued, unaware of the keen impact these revelations were having on her guest.

"I'm not sure why he never married - it's a shame, really. He'd have made a great father. But there have been women in his life who soured him, and I guess he just doesn't trust the female population, in general." She looked over at Marianna in thoughtful consideration.

"You are different, though, from anyone Grant's ever introduced to me before." She gave her a gentle smile. "I'm not sure what exactly is between you, and I don't want to pry, but I hope, for his sake, that you are at least a little interested - you are just the type of woman he needs. Someone down to earth, honest, and too smart to get caught up in all the glitz and glamour of his famous lifestyle."

Marianna was pleased with Terri's insightful appraisal of her character.

"Oh, I don't think Grant is interested in me, in any long-term sense, at least." To her surprise, Marianna found herself confiding in this warm, friendly woman, for whom she felt the same sense of instinctive trust in, as she had for Grant when she'd first met him - even though she'd fought it with a vengeance.

"To be honest, I'm confused about his attitude toward me. It seems sometimes that he is trying to decide on my trustworthiness, but he's never given me any indication that he wants anything more than a fleeting professional friendship with me." It was true - he hadn't even made a proper pass at her, despite the five-alarm fireworks.

Terri gazed into the sparkling blue water thoughtfully. Marianna watched the reflection of the sun-kissed water, rippled by a gentle breeze, play across her face.

"That's interesting," she said at last, "Grant doesn't usually waste any time letting a woman know of his attraction for her." Terri looked Marianna squarely in the eye. "I don't want you to get the wrong impression of Grant. He's not a heartless womanizer, no matter what you've heard - on the contrary, he's cautiously selective, but it's obvious to me that he's very attracted to you, so his hesitation, where you are concerned, is something to ponder." She chewed her lip in consternation.

Marianna was pretty much speechless but felt the inclination for some type of response. "There is a mutual attraction I can't deny, but I have no reason to believe it's anything more than an average healthy physical spark between a man and woman. Even if there were something more, it could never work. My kids will always come first, and I could never expose them to Grant's lifestyle."

*A Kiss to Die For*

Terri smiled gently and touched her arm. "It isn't impossible, you know, rock stars do get married and raise families, some very successfully."

"I don't mean to be judgmental, but it's not the life I want for my kids." Marianna needed to clear the air on this point.

"You know, Grant is not going to do this forever. Oh, sure, he'll always make music, but I don't think he'll be touring very often. In fact, I'd be willing to bet that if he met the right woman," her voice trailed off, effectively emphasizing the implication of her observation.

"I would never ask any man to give up something he loves for my sake," Marianna was adamant. "And I think we are getting way ahead of ourselves here - I'm quite sure there's nothing even worth consideration." She sprang up purposefully out of the lounge chair. "Come on. I'll race you to the end of the pool." The finality in Marianna's tone effectively ended the conversation, but had she turned back to witness the secret hopeful smile on Terri's face, she may well have abandoned her fear of water and been tempted to swim right off into the ocean, in rapid escape of a certain shark named Grant.

Although she was loath to admit it, her frank powwow with Grant's sister had awoken something deep inside her - a burning desire for fulfillment that could only be appeased with having a loving partner. Gone was the Marianna, who was perfectly content to live the rest of her days single, grateful for the freedom of complications that accompany a committed relationship. Now, she was acutely aware of an aching void and had no idea how to assuage the consuming emptiness to gain back her waning peace of mind.

~~~

Derek Hawthorne was your typical sturdy rancher of the strong, silent variety, and Marianna could see instantly, that he and Terri were madly in love with one another. It wasn't until after dinner, when the ranch hands had retired, and they were savoring a glass of wine on the huge veranda overlooking the rolling pasture, that provided a truly magnificent view, that Derek unearthed his unique sense of humor.

He was a man of few words but made each and every one of them count, and Marianna found herself gazing enviously at the two of them, catching the intimate glances between them, filled with the promise of passion. She was horrified, at the now familiar ache growing in her loins and was eternally grateful that Grant was in the city this night and would not pose any threat to her raging war with self-control. She bid them goodnight, smiling at the fading sounds of their banter.

# Chapter Eighteen

The little Cessna arrived promptly at 8:00 the next morning. Marianna, mouth agape and with wary reluctance, allowed Grant to hoist her up into the cockpit. The instant his large hands closed around her waist, warning bells clanked through her head. She felt thoroughly ditched when he broke the contact and climbed into the pilot seat. The flight to L.A. was uneventful, the noise of the twin engines eliminating any obligation for forced conversation. The vast skies and the flight instruments before him duly arrested Grant's attention. Every now and again, he pointed at something, drawing her attention to the breathtaking beauty surrounding them.

Exactly one hour later, Grant landed the plane with smooth precision at the small private airport just outside the city, and was soon negotiating city streets, in the now familiar SUV on their way to the studio. Marianna remained in awe at this man's ability as a pilot - the same guy who professed to be scared silly of airplanes. Would he never cease to amaze her?

"It was the most effective way to confront my fear," Grant had reasoned logically, when she'd shared her observations. "And I needed a speedier commute option to L.A. Besides," he'd added with a grin, "I'm only brave when I'm in the pilot's seat." She'd watched with interest as he shut down all the controls and gadgets that had her totally baffled, and she couldn't help but respect his courage and conviction.

"How was your evening?"

That dynamite smile assaulted her sense anew.

"Great, your sister is a wonderful person," she replied with earnest admiration. She had admitted to Grant the previous evening, by telephone, that she believed her children were quite unaffected at the notion of her visiting L.A. for a while, and told him she was ready to go whenever the band wished it. He had promised to collect her the following morning.

Truth be known, she was beginning to feel a strong bond with Terri and was assailed with a pressing urge to get this business done with so she could say her farewells with as little regret as possible.

"Yeah, she is, isn't she? But then, she had me for a role model."

There was no way she was stepping into that one, but she couldn't resist a quick smile in response to his teasing tone.

"So, are you ready for some hard work, Pretty Lady?"

Marianna blushed at the endearment, if that's what it was meant to be, and deftly averted her gaze, unwilling to meet those all-seeing gray eyes. She was further unnerved by his hearty chuckle as he helped her from the SUV into the studio, and more than a little puzzled by his light-hearted joviality.

A bright smile of genuine pleasure lit her face as Benny came over and gave her a warm hug.

"How've you been, Gorgeous?" He winked at her and narrowed his gaze in mock sternness at the glowering look on Grant's face.

"Seems as though I've lost the job of your devoted chauffeur this time around." Benny searched her eyes as if seeking some denial there and shrugged good-naturedly at Marianna's silent withdrawal.

"Come on over, Marianna, we'd like to get started right away if that's O.K."

Gary gave her a warm smile of welcome, but she could see in his demeanor that he was all business today. And that was exactly how she wanted it - complete their work together so she could return home as soon as possible. Marianna pulled out the four songs she had selected from her portfolio and handed them over to Gary.

"I have enough copies to go around if you need them," she offered modestly. Gary was already immersed in the first one and nodded absentmindedly, without looking up from the pages she'd so painstakingly edited on the computer. She placed the copies on a table nearby, and the other band members immediately reached for them. The ensuing silence was heavy in the air. She felt utterly exposed and was certain that her every heartbeat resounded off the studio walls - like a hammer banging a gong, in the deliverance of absolute judgment.

"Do you still have the originals?" Gary's tone was clipped, impatient.

"Well, y-yes," she stammered, uncertain what had provoked this change in his mood - was something wrong? What did the originals have to do with anything? Could he be insinuating plagiarism? Come on; they weren't that good.

"Great, are they with you?" He looked at her now and crossed his arms over his chest, seemingly pacified at her answer, but a controlled impatience was evident.

"Yes," she answered, rummaging through her briefcase to find them. "Do you mind if I ask why?"

Gary smiled indulgently, like a kid about to divulge a very important secret. In this mood, he was truly hard to resist, and she smiled back, awaiting his reply. A glance at Grant found him studying her with narrowed eyes, the hint of a smile playing around the incredibly sexy lines of his mouth. She returned her attention abruptly back to Gary.

"It's all in the emotion." He emitted a patient sigh, at her blank expression, as if about to explain something very elementary to a small child.

"Magic, Marianna - music is pure magic but is nothing without emotion. May I see it, please?"

"Of course." She handed him the worn sheets of paper and cleared her throat nervously, waiting for further clarification, more than a little curious about the theory Gary had put forth, as she was indeed beginning to grasp the flow of his reasoning.

All the while he was perusing her work, Gary nodded with increasing satisfaction, and when he finally looked up, she could see the creative light aglow in his eyes. It was much like the first time she had observed them in the studio - her attention had been mostly on Grant, and that same gleaming concentration had radiated from his face. He passed the papers over to Grant now.

"Do you get it yet?" Gary's eyebrow lifted toward her in a conspiring invitation.

In spite of the intimidating spotlight upon her, Marianna's fascination with the philosophy prompted her reply.

"The emotion flows through the original writing, in the shape of the letters, the pressure of the pen on the paper," Marianna began intuitively.

"Exactly!" Gary's emphatic qualification drew a round of relief on the faces of the other band members. Apparently, this was no novel process.

"The fact that you actually penned your work, rather than straight to the keyboard, is brilliant!"

She somehow knew that she'd just received a formidable compliment, normally very sparingly dished out by the likes of Gary Keller, and was both honored and touched.

"We pen all of our first drafts."

"I'm afraid I don't have any tunes for these ones." Marianna offered apologetically, thoroughly pleased, and more than a little reassured at Gary's reaction.

"Doesn't matter, we'll work with the emotion - just relax and enjoy."

She was gaining a new respect for the intense labor put forth by these incredibly talented artists and realized that they were driven souls, destined to play out their fate - like it or not, and clearly, the members of RedRock thoroughly enjoyed their calling. She was aware, too, of the special bond they shared that had kept them working together for decades.

Marianna spent the rest of that day in rapt observation, fascinated with the tedious process of creating music. By the end of the day, they'd finished a rough recording for one of her songs, and the same earth-shattering emotion gripped her when they played it, choking her up and rendering her speechless - tears streaming unchallenged down her face. She was amazingly unashamed; strangely, she knew somehow that her presence had formed an integral element of the creation. With each tear, she was aware of an immense release – a depletion of stagnant pools, a breakdown of defenses, a healing of long-buried pain. She gloried in the liberty and was humbled by this divine miracle.

As they were sitting around afterward, relaxing with a soda, Jerry pulled a chair up beside her.

"Hello, little lady! Have we completely scared you off yet?"

She smiled at the genuine concern in his expression and was quick to assure him that she had come through relatively intact.

Lord, she was exhausted, though.

"I have no makeup left, but what's a little mascara among musicians." He laughed out loud at her easy banter.

"Yeah, well, mascara is highly overrated anyway when it comes to feminine beauty, with which you are generously blessed." He smiled appreciatively into her eyes, and Marianna blushed furiously at the bold compliment.

"How long do you think you'll be staying?"

His tone held a note of curious interrogation, and she looked up at him, wondering what was on his mind.

"I'm not sure. I plan to leave as soon as you fellows decide my collaboration is no longer necessary on the songs."

"Oh, yes, the songs. Well, I guess that's what brought you here, right?" Again - that inquisitive prodding.

At her nod of assent, he continued. "It's just that our rare guest writers don't usually travel here for these initial sessions, and I'm a little curious why you are here today." His gaze was frank. "Don't get me wrong – I'm thoroughly delighted to be basking in your intoxicating company." He smiled broadly.

Marianna didn't know quite what to say, stunned into complete shock. She had assumed this to be normal procedure and felt more than a little conspicuous with the knowledge that her being here was out of the ordinary.

"I was under the impression that my presence was necessary here." Her voice sounded lame. She had thought that the band members were in agreement with this.

"Did you talk with the agency?" Jerry asked quietly.

"No, actually, Grant called me and insisted that my being here would save valuable time."

"Ah, Grant," he nodded speculatively as if perhaps, this might explain it all.

Well, she was certainly a blind woman in the dark and beginning to get thoroughly annoyed with feeling out of sorts.

"Jerry, if there's something you're getting at, I'd like to hear it." He considered her thoughtfully, and she knew he was weighing his words carefully.

"Grant seems very taken with you, and I pretty much figured that your presence here was his doing." He searched her eyes as if assuring himself that there was no hidden malice afoot. "He's been through hell with the few women he's taken into his heart to care about."

"There's nothing going on between us," her voice trailed off at the gentle, knowing look that Jerry threw her way. She suddenly realized, in retrospect, that her intuition had elicited a warning buzz. when Grant had called, hinting that something didn't ring true - and he had come to visit. What was he about then? She was pretty sure he wasn't after a serious relationship.

"So why are you here then?"

It was a soft-spoken query, aptly echoing her own troubled musings, but looking into his eyes now, she knew without a doubt that Jerry would go to any length to protect Grant, and she felt a growing respect for this man and the deep friendship he was so loyally determined to honor.

"I'm not after his fame and fortune if that's what you are worried about." She looked earnestly into his eyes and saw instantly that he believed her. "But I can't deny that the man has me upside down and sideways - entirely confused most of the time." She bit her lip in agitated concentration. "In any event, I came here wholly believing it was at the entire band's request."

"Do you love him?"

Marianna's mouth dropped open at the mere suggestion of something so intimately candid. Not to mention ridiculous! Wasn't it? Did she? Certainly, a girl couldn't fall in love with a man she hardly knew and didn't even pretend to understand. At the very least, her feelings for him were complicated and, in no terms, casual. Marianna's brows creased in thoughtful reflection.

"Jerry, to be honest, I've been running from the man, a hundred miles an hour - even when he's nowhere close. He hasn't uttered barely two words to me since we've arrived," Marianna told him about the ranch. Jerry's eyes opened wide at the substantial implications surrounding the fact that she had brought her children with her.

"And quite frankly, I have no idea what interest he holds in me, if any. Sometimes it feels like we simply share a mutual physical attraction, and I do know instinctively that he's a good-hearted man. But it's obvious that he doesn't trust me - any woman, from what I've heard. Besides, we are so very different," she paused, watching Grant across the room, thinking that he hadn't even looked her way for most of the day. Perhaps there was no interest, after all, on his part. So why, then, was she entertaining this ridiculous conversation with Jerry?

"You didn't answer my question."

It was a probing statement, but the earnest concern in his eyes stopped any protest she may have offered. Marianna painstakingly searched her soul, measuring her words, vowing that no matter where this all led, she didn't want anyone hurt. It was important to be brutally honest with herself right now - she knew without a doubt that Jerry had Grant's best interest at heart and she unquestioningly trusted that the conversation with him would remain confidential.

"Let me put it this way. I care about Grant in ways I haven't yet begun to understand."

She paused, her throat aching with the intensity of her emotions as she gazed with appreciation at Grant's rugged masculine profile, relaxed now, his head bent in deep discussion with Gary. She could see the shadow of the day's growth of whiskers framing his jaw, the shortly styled wisps of hair kissing his sturdy neckline, and swallowed hard, aching to caress him.

"And I am really trying to just emerge from this entire process in one piece and go back home to my safe, happy existence." She looked squarely at Jerry then, her heart in her eyes.

"But if he were to walk over here and so much as touch me right now - just one touch, I'd be toast."

The realization hit her square in the gut. Was it love? She didn't know, but her obsession with the man could no longer be denied - the feral excitement in his presence, her pounding heart, and errant loins. She had been around attractive men before and knew the drill - it was far more than hormones driving this deep passionate fixation.

Jerry pulled her head gently down to his shoulder and pressed a soft kiss against her hair. It never occurred to Marianna to question the level of comfort this brought to her bruised soul.

"OK, Kid, you've passed my test and answered my question. Don't be so downhearted. This could be the foundation of something really special. I won't pretend to know what's in Grant's mind right now, and I can't guarantee that he's interested in more than your lovely feminine attributes, though I'd be willing to bet my share of the proceeds from your song on it. I can tell you that no great love ever comes to fruition for those who abandon their hope and faith."

He gently turned her face up with a finger under her chin, and she met his gaze unflinchingly.

"And if Grant can't recognize the treasure right under his bullheaded nose, then he's a damned fool." Jerry looked up. "Don't look now, but here comes Prince Charming, and from his thoroughly bitchy expression, I'd say we've ruffled some feathers, you and I." He sat back in amused silence, waiting for the action to unfold.

Oh great, leave me to the wolf, Marianna thought, with increasing alarm, as she watched the angry emotions thundering across Grant's iron features.

"May I have a talk with you, Mari?" The words were clipped, and his eyes locked on Jerry, who bowed dramatically and left her to the beast. She swallowed nervously.

"I'd like to take you somewhere private to dine before we head back to the ranch." His harsh look was disconcerting. "Unless you've made other plans."

His eyes followed Jerry with a dark, brooding expression before his gaze settled unwavering on her own.

This was getting ridiculous. Not surprisingly, Marianna was emotionally drained after this long, confusing day and was about to refuse Grant's offer when he turned her gently to face him.

"Mari, you've had quite a day. Gary can be very intense - we're used to it, but it's not easy for those who don't know him well."

The change in his manner was almost more than she could bear, and she felt a sudden rush of anger at the way he seemed to be constantly toying with her feelings.

"Gary is nothing more than a dedicated professional, and I respect that. To be honest with you, I'm totally exhausted and wish nothing more than to get back and have a good night's rest if that's alright with you." His eyes narrowed at her scathing tone - her breasts heaving with short angry inhalations.

"No problem. Apparently, others hold more attraction for your precious company than I."

Grant stormed off, and Marianna was aghast at the threat of tears brimming in her eyes, her heart crushed as if in a vice, inflicting pain she could not escape. Well, it was what you wanted, wasn't it? She asked herself weakly. As she watched him grab his coat and crash through the door, all she really wanted was to rush after him and...and what? Marianna feared that she was forever doomed to a life of perplexity and uncertainty.

Grant burst back into the room and strode purposefully over to her. "We should get back to the plane before dark."

With that curt observation, he was gone once again, leaving her to trail after him like a disobedient puppy. She didn't give any real consideration to the fact that there were at least four hours of daylight remaining.

# Chapter Nineteen

The flight back seemed interminable, with Grant's sullen brooding permeating the cockpit like a seething black cloud. Well, if he chose to be miserable, so be it. She had done nothing to warrant this obnoxious behavior. He was, by far, the moodiest animal on the planet - of this, she was convinced!

Jumping down from the little plane, they were attacked by four highly energetic children. Denny and Katrina related a wealth of detail about their day, but Marianna caught very little of it, with all of them talking at once. She stole a look at Grant. His features were once again transformed, soft and affectionate. Both Mindy and Mark rode back to the house atop his broad shoulders, and Grant laughingly promised Katrina and Denny the next excursion.

Terri met them at the front door and pulled Marianna inside, insisting on hearing every grueling detail of her day.

"Did they like your songs? Well, of course, they did, but was Gary civil enough to at least give you some feedback?" Before she could form a reply, Grant curtly answered for her.

"It seems Marianna has earned Gary's favor - quite an honor indeed, as I can't bring to mind another who could lay claim to that achievement."

She was beginning to suspect that she'd not had a proper taste of Gary's notorious 'bad side' yet. The look of astonishment on Terri's face affirmed her suspicion.

"As a matter of fact, our Marianna seems to have charmed every member of the band completely under her spell." Grant's tone was harsh - accusatory.

Except for one band member, she mused dryly, knowing that there was likely not a female on the planet that could penetrate that crusty, thick barrier that Grant threw up at whim. There would be absolutely no determining where a girl stood with Grant Furman, she surmised, returning his sarcastic glare with a formidable haughty one of her own.

"Grant, Derek asked me to send you down to the stables when you got in," Terri firmly dismissed him. "Besides, I have a hankering for some girl talk." Marianna threw Terri a grateful look, and with one last murderous glance, Grant Furman stormed out of the house.

"So…care to tell me what that was about?" They were lounging on the oversized couch in the sitting room adjoining the kitchen, facing each other. "Of course, if I am prying into forbidden territory, feel free to tell me to mind my own beeswax."

Terri's sympathetic manner melted all of Marianna's remaining reservations, at least where the brute's sister was concerned.

"That is exactly the question I would love to pose to your arrogant mule-headed brother," Marianna sputtered her frustration. "Except what would be the point? He is the most egotistical, headstrong, moodiest man I have ever had the misfortune to meet." Terri listened in apathetic silence, allowing Marianna to vent her angry frustration.

"To be perfectly honest, I'm not altogether sure the exact source of his ire, but I may have some insight."

"Aww, Honey, I know all too well how difficult my brother can be to deal with. But I also know he has a true heart and would never do anything to intentionally hurt you. Tell me more."

"It seems that Grant has brought me here without the band's consensus." She was aware of a dawning light in Terri's eyes as she nodded. "Not that I felt unwelcome by any stretch of the imagination. I had a conversation with Jerry, and he implied that my coming here was perhaps Grant's choice and that it was not normal procedure to bring the songwriters in until they had already gone over the lyrics and made their decision."

A sudden realization of something Jerry had asked her, brought a thousand more questions to mind in a jumbled array. At Terri's questioning gaze, Marianna pressed on.

"Jerry asked me if I'd spoken with Vic, their agent. At the time, I didn't see the significance, but now I'm realizing that if the travel arrangements were not paid for through the agency, then who?" Her voice trailed off as Grant sauntered into the room, looking every inch in control once again.

"I did."

It was an admission of fact, but his severe tone indicated there would be no discussion around it. His gray eyes were positively smoking, paralyzing Marianna with the intensity of their challenging depths, as if daring her to make something of it and hoping, with a sadistic fervor, that, indeed, she may do just that. She gave herself a swift mental shake and broke the spell.

"Well, thank you then," Marianna's chin lifted in proud demure. Under no circumstances would she tumble too gullibly into that rogue's web. She had been tangled there before and was quite certain that it was only a matter of time before she would be consumed - a spider's dinner, as it were.

"You're welcome," Grant nodded derisively and slowly exited the room.

Marianna visibly slumped with a sigh of relief, and Terri slid over on the couch to give her a hug. She released her at once but stayed close as Marianna continued.

"Is it just me? Or is the man not totally baffling?" She looked imploringly into Terri's eyes.

"Oh, Mari, you need to know that my brother rarely loses his composure with anyone - not even Gary, the greatest challenge of all times. Not that they haven't had their issues over the years, but my point is," Terri looked directly into Marianna's eyes.

"Grant, for whatever reason, has allowed you to get thoroughly under his skin, and in my opinion," Terri smiled gently, "this is long overdue." She sat back and surveyed Marianna speculatively. "May I ask you something very personal?" Terri waited for Marianna to nod her assent. "Do you love my brother?"

Oh God, not again...but this time, the answer was in her eyes, and she knew from the satisfied grin on Terri's face that Grant's beautiful, brilliant sister had not missed it.

Why, then, until this very moment, had she herself been in the dark? She knew now, with a certainty that shook her to the very core, that she was absolutely, impossibly, ecstatically, hopelessly - and miserably in love with the infamous Grant Furman.

She groaned aloud. The one thing she had vowed to avoid at all costs had slammed into her world - rocked her foundation with a force that the fiercest storm could not hold a candle to.

And she wanted him - oh God, she wanted him badly, which was exactly why she knew at once that she could no longer stay here under his sister's roof.

It was impossible, with her newfound realization, to resist the man, and she knew that if she allowed any further intimacy between them - if they made love - if his passion came anywhere close to matching her own, there would be no turning back. She had to think about her children.

"Terri," her firm resolve was evident in her expression, "I need to talk to Derek. Do you mind?" Marianna was desperate now.

"No, of course not, but you will come back so we can finish our conversation, won't you?" Terri was understandably bewildered by this new twist of events.

"Of course, and thank you, Terri, you are an angel and a wonderful person." Marianna gave her a quick squeeze before heading out the door. She hoped, above all hopes, that she would find Derek alone at the stables. He was her only salvation now.

A half-hour later, feeling more in control of her destiny than she had, since that first trip to L.A., Marianna escaped to her room to freshen up before a late dinner. What she had to say to Terri was difficult at best, and she anticipated strong objections, but she held confidence that Terri would respect her decision and not stand in the way. She found her in her greenhouse, picking tomatoes for a fresh salad.

"Terri, I need your ear." She faced her new friend with an earnest plea written all over her face. "I am leaving here tonight, with your help, of course." Marianna let this sink in.

"Oh, Marianna, I think you need some time to think things through," Terri began to object.

"No, I have made up my mind." Though her firm resolve remained, Marianna's features softened with affection. It was important that she make the gravity of the situation clearly understood. "I cannot stay. As you well know, I love your brother with an intensity that could very well destroy me, and I won't take that risk for the sake of my children."

"But I know that Grant would never do anything to hurt you, Mari, and I firmly believe he loves you too."

Marianna had considered that titillating possibility as well.

"That may very well be, but he doesn't trust me, Terri, and perhaps never will. I cannot take the risk - will not place my children in the middle of a relationship that would be tumultuous at best." Tears glistened like crystals in her pretty blue eyes. "Please, Terri, you have to help me – I'm drowning here."

"Against all that I believe in right now, I will do so because I have come to care about you almost as much as Grant does." Tears were streaming down her face.

"And I feel the same about you - I'm so sorry, but I have to go," Marianna explained her plan. "Derek has agreed to allow Mike the use of your vehicle to drive me into Denver tonight." Mike was one of the ranch hands she had met at dinner the previous evening. Derek had voiced the same objections as Terri but had fully respected Marianna's decision.

"I have arranged a late flight out of Denver - we will be traveling most of the night and be home by morning. What I need from you," Marianna looked her square in the eye, "is to plead absolute ignorance until you know we are safely on that plane." She held her breath while waiting for Terri's answer, knowing the predicament that Terri was to face – she would ordinarily never lie to her brother and would be making an enormous sacrifice for Marianna if she agreed. Terri searched Marianna's face now for any sign that she may accept an alternative.

"OK." She finally replied with heavy resignation, "I'll do it, but only until the morning. I can promise only that." Marianna softly wept with relief.

"Thank you," was all she could manage to get past the aching lump in her throat.

Dinner was a boisterous affair, and Marianna had decided not to inform the kids of her plan until just before their departure. In this way, there was less chance of anything going awry. She caught Derek's speculative gaze on her a few times and noticed that Terri was keeping a tight rein on her own composure. It was, overall, a nightmare to endure. Grant seemed to sense that something was up and kept looking from Terri to Marianna in search of a clue. Marianna quite simply avoided his gaze, for fear her resolve would crumble to dust in the heat of those searching gray eyes.

Shortly after the kitchen was once again in order, Marianna took Denny and Katrina into her room and explained that they had to go home tonight. She was prepared for some resistance but was totally taken aback by the force of Denny's reaction.

"No, Mom, I won't go! We're going fishing in the trout pond tomorrow - Mr. Grant promised us. I always wanted to go fishing, so we can't leave tomorrow!" The tears burst through Denny's determined defiance, and Marianna gathered him to her breast.

"I'm so sorry, Bud," Now both her children were in tears, and she felt like a huge failure as a mom - a monster, for putting her children through this turmoil. However, this only strengthened her determination to go ahead with her plan. She had taken too much of a risk already and, as a result, had placed the children smack in the middle of it. Watching her daughter now, with tears streaming down her cherubic face and her arms securely wrapped around a hairy dog named Brutus, Marianna felt her heart break into a million tiny pieces.

They snuck out to the truck like war criminals, she thought glumly, not daring to allow goodbyes. Instead, she promised the kids they could email Mindy and Mark, and yes - Mr. Grant, as soon as possible. She knew they were totally confused and couldn't understand why it was all so secretive, but Marianna felt she simply had no choice but to carry through with her plan. Cowardly though it may seem, she knew Terri would explain it to Grant on her behalf.

By the time they arrived at the airport in Denver, she was exhausted from her warring emotions and from trying to cheer her children, to no avail. The usual temptations from home were having no effect on their morose mood, and after a hearty thank you to Mike, she herded them onto the plane, feeling a measure of reassurance once in the air that perhaps, after a long while, she would find her serenity once again.

It was an endless lengthy trip home, and Marianna couldn't help feeling a deep sense of loss, in addition to the devastation from leaving Grant behind forever. In this, she had unequivocally committed to sever all means of contact with him. This included her dreams to work with RedRock in bringing her songs alive. It seemed a minute sacrifice in comparison to forsaking the love that had captured her very essence, imprisoning her heart and soul forever.

Through the haze of her agony, she was acutely aware of profound regret for the loss of special friends she had bonded with on this incredible journey. It was with a heavy heart that she had imparted her goodbyes to Terri that evening, vowing to remember her always and keep in touch. Terri had felt compelled to communicate her concern in a few final words.

"Mari, you know that I firmly believe in sticking around to work things out. I do respect your feelings and reasons for leaving, but I need you to know that my brother has been deeply hurt and betrayed by more than one woman. Trust does not come easy for him, and he has constructed defenses strong enough to hold back all of Cupid's armies."

Terri held Marianna's face between her palms and gazed directly into her eyes.

"Mari, you are the only woman who has managed to penetrate those walls and crack his steel barrier. Grant is scrambling to keep that armor intact, but simultaneously, he is fighting to hold onto you. Sweetheart, you are the one! He knows it - just needs time to sort it all out so that it is safe for both of you to cross that line. Building trust takes time. Please promise me you will not give up on him forever."

Terri's heartfelt plea had solicited a fresh round of tears to Marianna's eyes - she could make no promises and offered a final embrace before fleeing the ranch she had come to love in a matter of hours.

# Chapter Twenty

Marianna had been corresponding by email with Tess and Dennis throughout their fantasy cruise, and now, as she swung into the parkade at the airport, she smiled, grateful that at least Tess had found her happily ever after. She'd spoken to both of them by telephone twice in the past week and was thrilled by the blissful happiness evident in their voices. The proposal had gone off without a hitch, and Tess promised to bring the video camera footage over for Marianna to see as soon as they got back. They were the first couple through the gate, and Tess ran ahead into Marianna's embrace, tearfully thanking her for the wonderful gift.

"I will exact my revenge. You know that" Tess teased Marianna, but her gaze turned somber as she searched her friend's face.

In truth, Marianna knew she looked like hell. In the past week, she had been unable to choke down anything beyond a piece of toast here and there - hadn't slept more than a couple of hours at a time, and then, only from sheer exhaustion. She had busied herself fussing over Denny and Katrina, making the most of what little time she had left with them before school started up again. They were her salvation - the light that kept her going through the long lonely days.

The nights were an entirely different matter. When she had fallen asleep, her dreams were haunted with images of steely gray eyes and a rugged, virile profile. She'd woken up a few times to the sound of her name, whispered huskily, only to realize it must have been part of a disturbed dream. Her body ached for his touch with an intensity that frightened her senseless. She wavered between gratitude that Grant had chosen not to follow her, and deep aching disappointment, that he hadn't even tried to contact her. It was best this way, she knew. Perhaps Terri had managed to clarify that for him, or maybe he hadn't cared about her that way after all. Terri could very well have been mistaken. In any event, she needed to get on with her life now.

Marianna put her hands up firmly. "Not now, Tess, please. We will get a chance to talk in the next day or two." She forced a bright smile. "You two look sinfully relaxed and ready to take on the world. Let me see that rock on your finger." Marianna grabbed Tess's left hand in admiration of the beautiful full-carat diamond engagement ring. Dennis had been correct - it looked absolutely stunning on her elegant finger. The two women strolled arm in arm while Dennis used a trolley to wheel their luggage out to the van. Marianna almost felt like a semblance of her former self while she listened raptly to the highlights of their cruise.

Tess had surrendered momentarily, but Marianna knew that tomorrow would be a day of reckoning. She drove home in a deep depression. While it was good to see her friend so happy with the man of her dreams, she couldn't help pining over what might have been, for her and Grant. She knew with absolute certainty now, that there would never be another man in her life - had not the heart remaining to give, having left it behind in L.A. forever.

The next day, Marianna drove to the elementary school to register Denny. He beamed with pride to be moving up to grade three. This was to be Katrina's last year in play school, and Marianna had the choice to allow her to start Kindergarten, as she was turning five before the New Year, but had opted to delay another year - give her a little time to mature and have fun.

Tess had rung earlier and arranged to meet Marianna at their pancake house at 10:00. Jen was delighted to come and watch the kids for a while, and Denny and Katrina were, of course, elated at the prospect. Marianna dreaded the upcoming confrontation and could only hope that Tess was sufficiently wrapped up in her newfound happiness, hence less observant than usual.

"Mari, I've missed the hell out of you," Tess hugged her fiercely as they took their places at the checker-clothed table. The waitress smiled as she poured the coffee and left them alone. "But Honey, I haven't been gone that long." Tess searched Marianna's face. "You've lost weight, and the sparkle in your eyes is AWOL." Tess squeezed her hand gently and waited for Marianna to enlighten her with a quick recap of her trip to L.A.

"I will be all right once I get my feet under me again, and we get back into a routine," Marianna assured herself, more than Tess. "I just need to put this whole business behind me." She looked pleadingly at Tess for understanding. "Denny and Katrina need me, and I can't let them down, Tess."

"I, of all people, am certain that will never happen," Tess replied, with a soft, comforting smile, giving Marianna's hand a supporting squeeze. "Whatever happened down there, you will tell me in your own time, but for now, you need to know that I am going to personally oversee your convalescence. Just because I'm the next best thing to an old married woman doesn't mean I've forgotten how to have fun." Marianna gave Tess a grateful smile, appreciating the space.

"However, there is one thing I need to know," Tess's expression was mockingly stern. "How did you make out with your songs? When will they be released?" Tess halted at the crestfallen look on Marianna's pretty face.

"Tess, I walked out on the entire deal, save for the first song, and there's no way I can go back there." Marianna was reassured by Tess's sympathetic expression and opened up to her friend. "I can't risk seeing Grant again - I won't jeopardize my future peace of mind or compromise the well-being of Den and Kat." Marianna looked up with her heart in her eyes.

"Tess, I love the man beyond measure, beyond any healthy definition. I've fallen for a complicated, bull-headed hunk of testosterone who will never be there for me emotionally." It felt good to voice all the thoughts that had been tormenting her nights since she'd been back home." At Tess's thoughtful gaze, she compromised.

"Oh, I know now, that he is not the womanizer the media has made him out to be, at least not anymore. His heart is true - I believe that, but through all that he and I have been through, never once has he spoken of his feelings, or lack thereof. I have come to terms with the fact that, in all likelihood, they do exist in some form - there can be no mistaking that," Marianna's eyes took on a faraway gleam at the painful memories - his scorching looks and touch had betrayed him. "But for Grant," she fixed an unwavering stare upon Tess, "there is no comfort or trust, and I just can't go there, Tess."

"You are right."

Marianna gaped at her friend, truly astonished by this reaction. She was fully expecting a battle of wills with her good friend and visibly relaxed at the unexpected concurrence.

"The man is an ass," Tess continued, "and an absolute idiot for letting you go," she finished vehemently. Marianna was so stunned at the passion with which Tess had delivered her judgment she burst out into sudden laughter.

"Oh, Tess, what would I ever do without you?" The two women giggled, and for the first time since meeting Grant Furman, Marianna could see a ray of hope at the end of her tunnel of torment. She felt a semblance of the familiar determination and drive flowing through her veins once again. Oh, she knew, without doubt, the road ahead would be bumpy, and it would be some time before her every waking moment would not include the haunting of Grant's powerful image in her mind's eye. But today seemed just a little less gloomy, and maybe taking it a step at a time would be the catalyst to her survival. She was pleasantly surprised that the anticipation of tomorrow was not quite so sad.

## Chapter Twenty-One

"So, how long will it take them to reply?" Tess inquired between mouthfuls of popcorn. They were seated at their favorite table at the Hard Rock Cafe, waiting on the men to bring back refreshments from the bar. "God, this stuff is good!" Tess licked the salty butter off her fingers, one by one. "Why can't I get it to taste like this at home?"

Marianna smiled at her friend's fixation with popcorn and admired how the overhead lights played upon Tess's solitary diamond, reflecting vibrant fiery sparkles. Now, there was a matching wedding band adorned with tiny rubies and diamonds, which had been lovingly placed upon her finger in a touching ceremony just three weeks ago.

"I don't know, but rumor has it, I could be on pins and needles for at least three months," Marianna smiled as if this didn't bother her in the least. She had spent the last week fairly well glued to her laptop, putting the finishing touches on her first manuscript, and had dropped it off at the publishing agent, who came highly recommended by a friend in her online writers' group.

It felt good to immerse herself in positive productivity, keeping her mind from wandering aimlessly into the well of pain she was at risk of drowning in, every time she thought of Grant. She shook it off now. "If it sells, that's a bonus because I've come to realize that, published or not, the accomplishment remains, and I get to own that."

Dennis deposited the drinks on the table and planted a soft peck on the back of Tess's neck. She, in turn, snaked her arms behind and pulled him down for a proper kiss. Marianna's heart burst with joy for these two lovers who, quite obviously, were ecstatic and destined to be together.

Her gaze shifted to the handsome man approaching the table, loaded down with more popcorn and beer nuts. Tom was even hotter eye candy than she had remembered. Tess had been thrilled at Marianna's agreement to join them tonight, fully convinced that this was the medicine Marianna needed to begin healing. Tom and Marianna had both been witnesses to the recent marriage vows.

"Here, let me help you with that," Marianna stood up and reached to relieve Tom of part of the burden. He flashed her a grateful boyish grin, and once again, she was aware of the lavish female attention he commanded from the surrounding tables.

She could do worse, Tess had gently prodded her, and she was well aware that Tom was quite taken with her, although he respected her strong position to remain platonic. So far, Marianna had found she could relax and enjoy his company. With this newfound self-awareness of her desire for love and possible marriage in her future, she had risked giving serious consideration to her feelings toward Tom. There was no denying a physical attraction between them, but in light of the fact she'd been celibate for almost 4 years, it seemed an extraneous aspect. Of more relevance was Tom's character - his goodhearted nature and strong ethics. She knew that he would provide a solid role model for Denny and Katrina, loved children, was financially well set, and, quite undeniably, the perfect catch.

What was her problem then? Marianna was aware of the answer but was powerless to think of a way to get past it. A haunting image of Grant floated into her consciousness. Even after all these weeks, her skin still tingled where he had touched her, and little flames of desire consumed her insides just remembering that kiss - and those eyes. Amidst these musings, passion flushed her face, and emotion radiated from her deep blue eyes, and though totally unaware of it herself, it did not go unnoticed by the virile man seated next to her.

"You do know how to steal a guy's breath away," Tom murmured appreciatively. Marianna snatched back her self-control with an iron will.

"I'm sorry, I'm afraid I was daydreaming," Marianna returned, "alternatively, I may have been simply mesmerized by your masculine charm." Marianna decided to keep it light between them as she did not feel it fair to encourage Tom in any way toward something she could not give one hundred percent to.

She wished fleetingly that she were content to date on a more casual basis - perhaps engage in a flirtatious, satisfying. lusty fling. God knows it would be beyond awesome to get laid! Instinctively, she knew that Tom would eagerly accept her on those terms, but in her heart, she believed it unfair to him - and to her children. Besides, she was terrified that in the heat of passion, another man's face would take control - with steely gray eyes that darkened arduously to unfathomable depths and strong, warm hands that were pure magic.

"Must have been one heck of a dream," Tom regarded her thoughtfully. "Take a walk with me?" Tom offered his hand. "I'm in need of some fresh air."

Marianna hesitated and glanced at Tess and Dennis, who were totally wrapped up in each other and hadn't heard an iota of the conversation thus far. What harm could a walk do? Marianna allowed Tom to guide her to her feet and through the café doors, out into the unusually warm autumn evening air. She breathed deeply, loving the feel of being under the open sky. It was reminiscent of another place and time, which she was quite unprepared to give thought to right now.

"Marianna," Tom began.

They were slowly ambling along the busy Whyte Avenue, well known for its eclectic shops and eateries that drew a unique and diverse crowd. A city of nearly two million, Edmonton had long ago passed a smoking ban in all public places, and Marianna was enjoying the clear, fresh air. Tom stopped and gently guided her to a park bench just off the sidewalk.

"There is something I need your feedback on," She regarded him expectantly, wondering how on earth her opinion could factor into anything he might be contemplating so seriously. "Please, hear me out before you say anything," he continued, obviously as nervous as a schoolboy. She felt an ominous sinking in the pit of her stomach.

"Tom, I..."

"Please," Tom asserted gently. Marianna closed her mouth, forcing back the words that would discourage Tom from continuing on the pathway she now recognized as futile where she was concerned.

"I have been offered an employment opportunity here in Edmonton," Tom went on. Marianna knew that he owned a beautiful home in Vancouver, one of the most desirable cities in Canada. "Yes, it would mean relocating on a permanent basis." Tom accurately read her expression. "Mari, I respect your feelings and would never do anything to compromise you," he hesitated, "I want you to trust me on this." The earnest solemn commitment was evident in his direct gaze. "I do, however, need to honor my own feelings and do not wish to leave anything unsaid between us. At the very least, I never want to lose your friendship." He smiled gently. "Now, just wait," Tom insisted when Marianna opened her mouth to speak.

"I think you know by now that I have come to care very deeply for you and, for my part, can see us sharing a future together - love, marriage, more children if you wished - the whole ball of wax." "Tom took a deep breath." "You are an incredible woman - someone I can talk to, dream with, and I know beyond a shadow of a doubt that the physical passion between would be a given." Tom gently brushed a lone tear from Marianna's blushing cheek with his thumb.

"Mari, I'm not asking that you give all that to me right now," he looked into her eyes imploringly, "only that you search your heart and tell me if you think you might someday envision wanting the same things - with me. I don't need promises - I know they are not within your power to give right now. I simply ask that you think about it and let me know."

Looking into his earnest warm eyes, Marianna wished more than anything, she could throw caution to the wind and sate her desire for this man, but she knew it was time for candor.

"Tom, there is something you need to know," she started, wiping away a tear. "First of all, I do find you attractive, and I have thought about you - given some consideration to a committed relationship with you." She held up her hand when she saw the hopeful expression on his face. "You are right, I am not ready to offer you these things, and I wish I could say it might come in time. But the truth is," Marianna straightened and looked him directly in the eye, "though I already feel many of these things for you, it is not the absence of reciprocated desires that is the problem." At Tom's baffled expression, she rushed on.

"I cannot return what you are offering to me because there is another man who holds that power." At his relieved look of understanding, she added, "No, not my husband. It is someone I met while I was in California." They both sank down on the bench, Marianna feeling guilty for being the cause of Tom's deflated look. Without naming Grant, she explained the situation to Tom, not stopping until she knew there were no stones left unturned. She waited while Tom collected his thoughts and finally spoke.

"He's a damn lucky man. I wish that I could be gracious and hope with sincerity that he figures this out," Tom's voice was soft and low. He looked deeply into her eyes now. "But I can't wish the treasure that you are on an unworthy man." His expression softened with the depth of his feelings. "I can, however, promise that I will never pressure you and will offer unconditional support as your friend, no matter what you decide." He squeezed her shoulder affectionately. "May I say this?" Marianna looked as though she couldn't take any more revelations at this point, and Tom laughed, "Allow me to keep just a tiny drop in a bucketful of optimism that someday you will come to your senses and fall at my feet in a bid to marry me?" There was a twinkle in his eye. "OK, OK, at the very least, jump my bones?" She jabbed him playfully in the ribs. Her expression at once turned serious.

"Thank you for understanding, Tom, and I'm so sorry." Caring and regret shone in a haze of unshed tears from her eyes, and he shook his head.

"No need for apologies, Mari. You can't help your feelings any more than I," he said reasonably. He took her hand, and they walked arm-in-arm back to the café. And in spite of the disappointment, Marianna knew a deep bond had been forged, and she thought herself a very lucky woman indeed to be blessed with a wealth of loving friends in her life.

# Chapter Twenty-Two

Marianna slammed the car door and rushed into the school, her long auburn waves trailing behind her. She was picking Denny up early and then racing over to Tess's to collect Katrina, as they both had dental appointments. She could feel the nip of frost in the air, though thus far, they had escaped it. Not too bad for the first week in October, she reflected - it had been an unusually warm September.

She was not normally in such a hurried frenzy, but for the past two weeks, Marianna had been writing - seizing every spare moment, and was well into the meat of her second novel. It never ceased to amaze her, when she would finally emerge from the well of creativity to discover how fast the hours flew by. Today she'd been pushing it, she admitted to herself - they would be lucky to make it on time.

Now, with Denny in tow, she mentally recited the golden rule; don't run in the hallways. Far be it for her to defy authority. Marianna smiled at her son now, who was remarkably well-behaved if his teacher's feedback was anything to go by. She did suspect, now and again, that they were dealing with two entirely different children.

In the waiting room, Marianna had just settled into a particularly interesting, albeit dated, article in a Time magazine, when her cell phone jingled. Scrambling to retrieve it from her purse, she was a tad breathless when she answered.

"Hey," it was all she could manage as she mournfully surveyed the nail she had just broken on some unknown object in her purse. "And the answer is a resounding no," she added before Tess could start in on her again. The woman had been unrelenting in her attempts to convince Marianna to join a singles club where she had first met Dennis. The organization was hosting a reunion of sorts and, true to their nature, had requested the successful couples to bring along as many single people as possible. Marianna was thoroughly determined to stand her ground.

"Hello, gorgeous girl," her jaw dropped, and she was momentarily frozen on the spot.

"Jerry," she half whispered his name, recovering quickly. "It's so good to hear your voice," Marianna was genuinely pleased, though she couldn't imagine why he had called. She was staggered by the dull ache in her heart that was instantly reawakened by the poignant memories flooding her senses.

"Hey Love, how have you been?"

It was a thousand questions rolled into one, and she knew that whatever the reason for his call, small talk would not cut it. She needed time to regain her composure and was grateful when Katrina came bounding into the waiting room.

"Mommy, Mommy, look!" Marianna laughed at the comical picture her daughter presented, with her fingers pulling apart her lips to reveal her meticulously clean teeth.

"Jerry, I'm sorry, I'm at the dentist with the kids - can we talk later?" Much later, she hoped.

"Tell you what, call me when you get home at this number," Marianna quickly glanced at her display. "Mari?" Jerry's voice was soft, and he didn't wait for her reply. "Please call. It's important." Fear for Grant's safety immediately crashed through her stupor.

"Is he OK?" Anxiety gripped her innards.

"Well now, that, you would have to ask him - I'm steering clear from his stormy weather these days," Jerry replied. "Talk soon."

He was gone before she had the chance to ponder the implication of his words, and her heart finally slowed to a normal pace. She knew if Grant were in physical danger, Jerry would have told her.

Once home, Marianna recalled that Jen was coming this afternoon to take the kids for ice cream and to the library. After scooting them all out the door, she couldn't decide if she was grateful or alarmed by this timely diversion. Alone in the house, she picked up her landline and, against her better judgment, dialed the number on the cell call display, her heart thundering in her ears. He picked up on the first ring.

"Hey, I apologize for calling your cell, I tried the house, but no one answered, and it's a bit of an emergency…Mari." Jerry wasted no time getting to the point.

"What's up?" she implored, with more than a little apprehension in her tone.

"We need you back here," Jerry started, "and before you say anything, you need to listen to what I have to say." His tone was firm. If it were anyone else, she'd not agree.

"OK, I'm all ears," she assented, steeling herself. Nothing Jerry imparted could be more of a shock to her system. Go back to L.A.? Not for all the tea in China, Marianna assured herself!

"We are stalled here - Gary and Grant are in discord over the final songs for the C.D., and bottom line," Jerry had chosen to skip all the juicy details, she presumed, "they had both agreed to work with a couple of your songs, but then you hightailed it out of here, and they haven't seen eye to eye on anything since," Jerry explained. "Mind you, Grant's mood would scare Attila the Hun into reclusion."

"Jerry, I can't do it," Marianna was certain she would not survive it. Besides, she had her kids in school now, and she refused to put them second to anything, even RedRock. Hell, they were all famous, seasoned musicians – they needed to get on with their magic.

"You guys have been writing music for almost 30 years now, Jerry. I cannot believe a small- town girl from Canada could suddenly hold that much weight in the successful release of yet another C.D." Marianna astutely assumed there was more to this.

"You don't know Grant and Gary – it's complicated," Jerry retorted. "There are things you don't understand. Honey, I'm going to ask you to trust me on this," Jerry asserted.

"Jerry, my kids are in school now!" Marianna objected.

"It can wait until Christmas break." He had certainly covered his bases. "We all agreed to chill for a while." A suspicion was beginning to take hold in the back of her mind.

"Do Gary and Grant know about this phone call?"

"Not yet," Jerry admitted, "I wanted to be certain you'd agree before I stirred the stew pot," he chuckled and quickly added, "Don't worry, Mari, please just trust me. And in case you are remotely interested, the monetary gain for you on these next songs will be significantly prettier." Oh, Lordy, did he really think that mattered to her? "OK, I didn't think that was a motivating carrot, but a has-been musician has to play all his aces, right?"

"Jerry, I won't survive it," A single tear slid down her cheek, and he interrupted her at once.

"Mari, you need to do this for both of you."

No, her inner voice screamed – it was the last thing she needed, and it may very likely destroy her - at least the confident, independent woman she was trying so desperately to preserve.

"You will never escape it until you face it," Jerry's softly spoken words pierced her heart, "And as long as you run, it will always hunt you down."

Tears were streaming down her face now, unchecked. The gut-wrenching thing about it all? Marianna knew - deep down, in the darkest recesses of her soul, that he was right. Damn him all to hell! She had tried to push it away - told herself that time would heal someday, but no matter how much time passed, Marianna conceded now, she could not ever be the same person she had been before Grant - before Jeff's death. She, of all people, had learned that one could never go back to a better day. She bit her lip in agitated contemplation. Jerry, apparently wiser than she, gave her space and said nothing on the other end of the line. Finally, she found her voice.

"Jerry, I just need a bit of time to figure this out - I'll call you back within a day or so, OK?" Her voice was broken and husky with emotion.

"Thanks, Honey," he said gently and let her go.

She needed the breathing space to sort out the jumbled muddle of her thoughts and emotions.

Well, perhaps she would have to abandon the latter.

After dropping Katrina off the following morning at preschool, Marianna dialed Jerry's number. The answering service clicked in she and left a brief but thorough message letting him know that an email was forthcoming advising of her travel arrangements. This trip, Marianna vowed, would unfold on her terms - at her own expense and within her complete control. Thanks to the earnings she'd recently received from the contract, she had plenty of resources to see it through. She arranged to fly them all down directly after Christmas - for a week at the most. The tickets were open-ended so that she could opt to return home earlier if all went well – or in self- preservation if it came to that.

She had discussed it at length with Jen and her parents the previous evening, as she would require a sitter for the kids while she was at the studio, and they had all agreed that it would be the chance of a lifetime for Jen. Her parents trusted implicitly that Marianna would never allow their daughter to come to any harm. It was all set. All that remained was the interminable wait.

# Chapter Twenty-Three

She needn't have worried as the next few weeks flew by in a haze. The literary agent had called her three days later with the news that she had found a publisher that wanted her novel. Marianna was flabbergasted but immensely thrilled at this turn of events. Several steps of protocol were to be followed now, and she was thrown into working with the publisher on edits and deletions. That the changes were relatively minor, shocked Marianna - it was easier than she had dreamed possible.

~~~

The morning of their departure dawned bright and sunny, the snow crystals gleaming like sparkling diamonds as they gazed from the tiny window of the plane. Marianna's nerves were scraped raw, and there was a permanent hollow in the pit of her stomach. She was unable to manage the simple breakfast provided by the airline, but with a smile, gratefully accepted a steaming cup of tea. Denny and Katrina were in the seats across the aisle from her, with Jen wedged firmly in between. There was no hope for that poor girl, Marianna determined with amused affection.

~~~

Once she had settled Jen and the kids in their suite at the Travel Lodge Motor Inn, Marianna stepped outside for a breath of fresh air in a valiant attempt to revive her failing bravado. All too soon, someone would be there to collect her, and her stomach was tied up in a mass of knots. She glanced around, thinking it was a far cry from the accommodations she'd enjoyed on her previous visits. However, the price was right, and it was impeccably clean. The sudden honk of a car horn startled her. Marianna fairly well slid to the pavement with relief at the sight of Jerry sauntering toward her. She hurried to meet him, and he caught her up in a warm embrace.

"God, you are a sight for sore eyes." Jerry stood back and studied her appreciatively. "I thought I'd come and snatch you to myself for at least a little while," Jerry teased her.

Marianna was amazed at how deeply she had come to care about this man, whose infectious goofy sense of humor kept the band on an even keel. She recognized that underneath, was a sensitive, caring man - an invaluable friend. She knew that he and Grant were particularly close and chewed her lip in consternation, wondering just what they had discussed about her visit, if anything.

"If I weren't such a poor, pitiful soul, I'd offer you a penny for your thoughts," Jerry searched her face. "For now, you'll just have to settle for a good ear and a broad shoulder."

"I'm a tad tense, I won't deny that," Marianna began. "Truthfully, I want nothing more than to get back on that plane, so I suppose it's lucky for you that my kids are determined to have a good holiday," she laughed nervously. "Does he know I'm here?"

"Yup," Jerry squeezed her hand when he caught her apprehensive, pleading gaze upon him. "Mari, try to relax. It's going to be fine. Trust me."

"You keep saying that - it's not you I don't trust," she mumbled, deciding she must have been insane to agree to this arrangement!

"Besides, if the man doesn't come to his senses," Jerry stated, "I plan to woo you myself. Hell, I'll even serenade you - with your own songs, if it helps!" Jerry added emphatically, and Marianna giggled aloud. He negotiated a corner expertly and parked in front of the familiar brick building she'd simultaneously come to love and fear.

She was petrified now, not trusting her reaction, when she would finally look at Grant for the first time since her hasty departure in the summer. Not to mention his reaction. In her mind's eye, she pictured his unforgiving stormy expression - the steely eyes, icy gray bolts of pure fire, impaling her on the spot. This was ridiculous. She chided herself! Marianna looked imploringly at Jerry now with her heart in her eyes.

"Damn, I have no chance in hell, do I?" He murmured softly as he kissed her lightly on the cheek and proceeded to escort her into the studio.

Marianna's knees wobbled and threatened to desert her entirely as her gaze immediately settled on Grant, perched lazily on his customary leather stool, plucking on his guitar. He looked up then, and their eyes met in a blaze of furious electrical energy, which struck her helpless and rooted on the spot. God help the poor soul who dared to cross its path at that moment. At once, he looked away, breaking the spell and leaving her gulping for air. She was vaguely aware of Jerry's firm hand at the small of her back, guiding her into the recording room.

"Marianna, it's good to see you again." Gary greeted her warmly, in thoughtful assessment - unusual for him, she reflected apprehensively, feeling a twinge of guilt for having left them in a lurch in the summer.

"May we assume you are ready to work out some arrangements with your lyrics?"

Wasn't there a hint of amusement lurking in his eyes and the twitch of his lips? She may well have imagined it, as for the next hour or more, he was pure business. Damned men!

Marianna was ever aware of Grant, in brooding attendance, prowling silently in the shadows. If anyone were to ask, Marianna would be forced to admit that she hadn't absorbed an ounce of the entire discussion, her every nerve alive and raw to the man's mere presence. Oh God, what would she do if he touched her? She flushed hotly as blood fired through her veins at the alarming, delicious pleasures this thought evoked.

After several taxing hours, it was decided that the band would work with two of Marianna's songs. What Gary proposed next threw her into a stunned, paralyzing silence. It took her a moment to find her voice, and she cleared her throat.

"Let me get this straight," she began. "You would like me to provide backup vocals on the recordings?" Though she absolutely loved the tunes they had put to her lyrics, the thought of singing alongside them in this studio, threw her into a raging panic, and she felt lightheaded, suddenly horrified at the fear that she may just faint right on the spot.

At this moment, she was quite certain such a bold undertaking was not within her capabilities. Under normal circumstances, she would be hard-pressed to squelch nervous jitters, but singing with Grant - crooning love songs? She couldn't see how she would possibly endure it – it was out of the question. The very source of her frustrated agony spoke now.

"We need the softer, emotional mix that your feminine vocals will provide."

The rich huskiness in Grant's voice was a potent tonic, rendering her wanting and senseless.

God, how she had missed that sound!

"Your songs deserve it, Mari. Every now and again, this happens, except in this case, we have the unique magic of our vocalist and writer being one and the same. For us, the opportunity is golden." He was studying her thoughtfully, and she could detect no sign of anger or malice, no hidden agenda.

"It's backup vocals Marianna, harmony," Gary added. "You will be amazed at the flow." At her look of uncertainty, he continued, "Tell you what, let's try it and see how it goes."

She looked around and registered the expectancy on the faces of these incredibly talented musicians and caught Jerry's gentle, encouraging nod. If she weren't so damned fond of the guy, she'd rip a strip off him right then and there for dragging her into this intolerable mess.

"We've had enough for today, agreed?"

Gary put an arm around her shoulder, leading her out of the recording room. She fairly much dropped with the physical relief this respite was affording her. They all followed and grabbed refreshments from the wet bar refrigerator. Marianna sank gratefully down into the comfy leather chair, still in a state of shock. How long would it take to make the recording, she wondered? As if on cue, Gary spoke.

"We know you have only a few days to spend with us, Mari, as you will need to settle your kids back into their school routine," he spoke lightly while devouring a granola bar. "Just leave it to us. This will be a piece of cake." He flashed her the infamous gleaming-eyed, devilish grin that had turned many women to mush.

Marianna's eyes immediately flew to Grant, whose gorgeous orbs were fixated hotly somewhere between her lips and nose. She snapped her gaze away, trying to catch the precious breath he had so easily stolen from her with just a look. There was only one man who could melt her heart, and at the moment, he was much too close. As she stole another glance, the sardonic grin on his handsome features mocked her in an unspoken challenge. She desperately required deliverance.

"If that's all for today, I think I'll head back to my hotel and relax awhile." Marianna stood up stiffly and smoothed her jean skirt. With her promise to return promptly at 9:00 the following morning, she hastily made a beeline for the hallway leading to blessed freedom out on the street.

"Mari, wait," she halted reluctantly as Jerry quickly caught up with her. "I'll take you back to the inn." He chuckled tolerantly, brushing off her firm assurances that she was, indeed, capable of hailing her own damned cab, to get around this town.

She was royally pissed at him but, in truth, felt a little guilty about commandeering Jerry's time and ruefully admitted to herself she needed the feeling of self-control that the independence would provide for her. She attempted to explain it to him now, but he was insistent.

"Jerry, I am so completely out of my element here," Marianna smiled gently at him now. "Don't get me wrong, I love it here, and you have been amazing to me. I hope you know how much I appreciate it."

"My pleasure entirely - don't even go there," Jerry shot her a warning look of mock sternness. "Darlin'," he continued in a more serious tone, "I know that you are floundering here like a fish out of water, trying in vain to avoid that one deadly bite - the hook that could write your fate in a heartbeat." Jerry paused. "Trouble is, my love, you are swimming upstream here and, in my opinion, need a friend to lean on - either give you that final shove, or be there to catch you when you fall." He gave her hand a long gentle squeeze. "And dear lady, just know you can count me in." He parked the car now in front of the inn lobby and gathered her to him for a comforting hug.

"You are such a good friend - I could not survive this without you." Marianna pulled back gently and sniffed through her tears. "I will promise to do my utmost to endure this, if you agree to something in return." At his raised eyebrow, she laughed. "Please, please, if I suddenly lose all of my wits and begin making an absolute utter fool of myself, drag me back here, pack up my stuff, and herd me and my entourage onto that plane home."

Though spoken with a degree of mirth, Marianna knew by the reassuring warmth in Jerry's eyes that he understood exactly where she was coming from. If she really needed to go, he would be there for her. She felt immensely reassured as she made her way, exhausted beyond belief, up to her room.

# Chapter Twenty-Four

"**M**ommy, Mommy, can we go now, please, please?" Katrina was weary of being patient while Marianna had indulged in a much-needed nap and shower.

Now, gazing down at the expectancy on the tiny cherub face of her daughter, she knew she could put it off no longer. The children were set on going to the beach, as they had not the opportunity on their last trip to California. She could no more deny them this, than cut off her right arm.

"All right, Kat, go collect your brother and make sure you both bring your sunhats," Marianna instructed her firmly. The little girl tore through the connecting door to their suites and remembered to call for her brother, more or less, in her hotel voice.

"I'll get the beach bag then. It's been packed and ready for hours," Jen rolled her eyes dramatically as she laughed affectionately. She reported that they had all ventured out eagerly that morning for a quick walk down the street, past the many motor inns and restaurants along the drag that embodied a popular, affordable tourist area.

Situated in the busy Santa Monica district, it was relatively close to the airport and provided a reasonable drive - by taxi, to the heart of Los Angeles. Marianna had considered renting a car but dismissed that as folly, given the hefty case of nerves she was battling. Under the circumstances, she decided the less stress, the better. There were several shuttles coming and going, to and from various locations, and the four of them boarded one now, off for a relaxing afternoon at a popular beach. Mari smiled at the animated excitement on her children's faces as they strained their necks to gawk out of the windows, determined not to miss a single thing about L.A.

"Before I forget, Jen, I made reservations for you on the Long Beach Tour shuttle tomorrow morning." Marianna took the reservation slips from her purse and handed them to Jen. She hoped the unusually warm weather would hold out, this being the cooler rainy season in California.

"Den and Kat will be in Heaven," Jen knew the kids were dying to see the Aquarium of the Pacific and take a guided tour of the infamous Queen Mary. Marianna knew these tourist attractions were right up Jen's alley as well and was genuinely pleased to be able to treat her to this excursion, as Jen's parents were ill-equipped to afford her such luxuries.

The ride to the beach lasted mere minutes, and before they could say sunburn, the kids were gazing around them in wonder at the broad expanse of pure white sand, framing an endless sparkling blue horizon. It was breathtaking and a bit overwhelming, Marianna realized. Denny had been very little the only time she and Jeff had taken a Pacific holiday on Vancouver Island. They had driven the windy, mountain switch-back, stomach-churning four-hour highway trek to Tofino and, once there, breathed in pure delight - the raging open ocean that literally enveloped them from all directions. Marianna took on a wistful expression - Jeff had been taken from them all before they'd had the opportunity to return with Katrina.

Ushering the kids over to an area seemingly less populated - for the moment at least, she set up the beach umbrella, rented from a tiny kiosk just down from the bus parking lot. She had also included two small collapsible beach chairs that she and Jen arranged in the sand now. The kids were happy to lay out their beach towels and, for once, were not chomping at the bit for permission to run into the water, being slightly intimidated by the glorious sweep of the magnificent beach and ocean before them.

"There are a few things we need to discuss," Marianna turned both children firmly to face her, making sure she had their full attention before continuing. "These are the rules." Denny and Katrina nodded obediently. "The ocean can be very dangerous, and you are not - under any circumstances, allowed to even set foot in the water without either Jen or myself beside you." She paused to ensure this sank in. "Second, you are not to wander off from us, not even to find shells and other sand treasures. This is a huge expanse of shoreline - there are many people, and it would be very easy to lose each other."

As she spoke, she gazed around and was amazed at the sparse population on the beach. She supposed it would seem a bit cooler in December for California residents. even if it were downright balmy by Alberta standards, and the desk clerk had informed her that the temperature was above average today. In further consideration, she decided that there were actually more people here than it appeared – the area was simply immense!

She turned her attention back to the children and insisted that they repeat the rules. Marianna gave them the bucket and toys she had purchased, and mapped out the boundary perimeters between the water and their current location. She wanted them within her vision at all times and had positioned their chairs and belongings as close to the water as possible.

"Let's go for a walk," she'd taken note of the longing on the kids' faces as they gazed in wonder at huge waves crashing against the shore. "Jen, please relax for a bit - stay with the stuff, and we'll be back shortly." Marianna smiled - she knew Jen was dying to get into the latest Harry Potter book she'd brought on the trip. She'd bet her lunch that even that wizard couldn't hold a candle to the magnificence of the Pacific Ocean at its finest on this glorious day.

"Hey, Mom, look!" Denny pointed to a strange-looking object lying on the sand, and Marianna couldn't decide if it was a plant or animal in origin. She surmised it was no longer alive, suppressed a shudder, and warned the kids against touching it, as they continued picking up shells along the way.

"Mommy, can we go in the water, please?" Katrina drew out the last word with such earnest pleading that Marianna laughed, and they sauntered merrily over to the shore, the warm sand massaging their feet delightfully. She suspected that by late afternoon, it might be a bit too warm to traverse without sandals. Now their feet were immersed - the wet sand squishing deliciously between their toes.

"Now remember, we need to be careful wading in," she'd barely had the cautionary words out when a huge wave broke over them, gliding powerfully up their legs. Katrina giggled delightfully as the bottom of her bathing suit was instantly soaked with the foaming salt water, and then she was literally bounced on her bottom as the powerful drag from the receding wave pulled the sand out from under their feet.

"See?" Marianna laughed heartily at the shocked expression on Katrina's face, as she peered up at her mother in awe. "We cannot underestimate these waves. If they drag us too far in, the ground can literally disappear from underneath us, and the wave may take us out - we might not be able to get back to shore." She was serious once again, and Katrina and Denny both nodded vigorously, thoroughly humbled to submission by the tremendous force they had just experienced for themselves.

"Oh, Jen, isn't this beautiful?" Marianna was sinfully relaxed, her long legs stretched out luxuriously before her on the sand. The children were thoroughly engrossed in constructing sand castles directly in front of them, and Marianna was hard-pressed to believe the extent of calm she had managed to achieve here on the beach. This was exactly the medicine she needed!

"Mari, go ahead and take a nap if you want. I'll watch the kids," Jen had observed Marianna's lazy yawn as she stretched like a contented feline, basking in the heat of the sun. "As a matter of fact..." Jen let the sentence trail as she got up and joined the kids in their sand play. Marianna smiled affectionately at the wonderful picture the three of them made against the backdrop of the deep blue ocean and hauled out her camera to capture it.

~~~

"You are going to turn into a lobster if you're not careful," a deep, caressing male voice drawled at her ear, seducing her from slumber.

She knew that voice well. Her stomach lurched, and she felt faint - oh God, what was he doing here? Marianna shot up in her chair, trying to sort out the muddled confusion of her sleep-clogged brain, while scrambling frantically to drape the towel around her, oblivious to the erotic vision she made as her breasts gently bounced invitingly in her haste.

"H-how did you find us here?" She still couldn't fathom his presence. Could she never escape the dang man? How long had she been sleeping? Minutes, hours? No, it couldn't have been very long, she decided foggily as she eyed Jen and the children still laboring on the sand castle. All semblance of relaxation fled her body as she locked gazes now with Grant - his dark and smoky, as he calmly surveyed her from head to toe. She gasped at the raw hunger evident in the depth of his stare. and started as the children flung themselves upon him, mercifully breaking the spell that had bound them both.

"Mr. Grant, Mr. Grant!" Katrina had him in a fierce hold, her little arms squeezed tightly around his leg as Denny gazed up at him with adoration.

Traitors! Grant now swung both children up in his strong arms and hugged them warmly. Marianna was amazed at Denny's emphatic return of physical affection, as he had recently adopted the cliché that 'big boys' don't necessarily give out hugs so freely. She was pleased that, for now, he had jumped off that fence.

"Hey, you two monster children, why didn't you tell me you were hopping in your mom's suitcase for a vacation too?"

She literally cowered under the murderous glance Grant pinned on her, inferring that she apparently should have informed him that she had brought them along. She cringed at Denny's innocent explanation.

"Mom said you'd probably be much too busy to visit us this time."

Jen moved in to shake Grant's hand politely, and Marianna suppressed an amused giggle at the moonstruck expression on her face. She supposed no earthly female could be held accountable for falling under the spell of one Grant Furman - she herself, Marianna thought with trepidation, was clearly no exception. Some of her worried musings must have shown on her features as Grant murmured huskily in her ear.

"There is no need to panic, Mari. Den and Kat provide the perfect tempering chaperones."

If this was meant to reassure her to any degree, it failed miserably, as the blood flowed hot in her veins and her heart thundered in her breast wildly, with the sweet caress of his words on her senses.

"For now," the veiled threat of what was to come trailed off his sensuous lips and nearly sent her fleeing for her life, across the busy L.A. street - traffic be damned, to the sanctuary of her room at the inn. But no, she would not afford him that power over her! She needed to secure a firm grip on herself. Marianna cleared her throat and, with false bravado, placed her sunglasses on her face and peered up at Grant with apparent nonchalance.

"Well, it was nice of you to come and visit us at the beach, a pleasant surprise for the kids," Marianna offered generously. Be damned if she'd show him how his very presence was chafing her every nerve. She bestowed a dazzling smile upon him as she settled back down in the lounger. She felt decidedly less vulnerable with the sunglasses firmly perched in place - concealing the chaotic emotions sparking from her eyes. Grant reached out and slowly eased the armor off the bridge of her nose. With a crooked and purely evil grin, Marianna thought crossly.

"No need to hide your pretty eyes under those things when your beach umbrella is now doing the job quite effectively," Grant reasoned infuriatingly. "Besides, they were upside down."

Marianna wanted to slap that smug expression right off his handsome face, but no, she would remain tranquil - at all costs, she reminded herself with a deep, steadying breath.

"Actually, I came to invite you all over to my place in Malibu, which is also oceanfront." His gray eyes darkened at the objection he could see forming on Marianna's lips, and then the scheming lecher stole the remaining influencing power she had over her children with his next words.

"I have an oceanfront pool, which will be much safer for the kids to swim in." Denny's eyes nearly popped out, and Katrina looked up at Marianna imploringly.

She heaved a resigned sigh – knew she was hooped.

"All right, give us a minute to pack up." Still, Grant had arrogantly assumed her assent - or didn't give a damn if he got it, she fumed resentfully as he was already at the sand castle with the kids, helping them put finishing touches on it before they had to surrender their magnificent creation to the great Pacific.

# Chapter Twenty-Five

Marianna was immensely grateful for the children's lively chatter on the way to Grant's home. She wasn't altogether comfortable at the prospect of entering the residence - his personal space. It somehow seemed too intimate, and she vowed to stay at the poolside, close to the kids, for the duration of the time spent there.

When Grant turned into the attractive cobblestone drive and parked the SUV in the large garage at the front of the house, Marianna was taken aback at the lack of opulence his home presented - annoyed at the sense of pleasure this awarded her, to think that it mattered very little to Grant, to flaunt his material wealth to the world. The lawn was well-manicured, and the exterior of the house was obviously maintained, but aside from this, it looked like every other home in the area - upscale certainly but otherwise unassuming.

Now Grant opened the hatch and handed some grocery bags to Denny and Katrina, gaining their collaboration for a poolside barbecue that he later planned to treat them to. The children, quite predictably, basked warmly in this revered attention and followed him like adoring puppies into the house.

Entering the foyer, she was struck by the grand, yet simple elegance of his home. Immediately past the foyer and hallway that led to laundry, storage, and a half bath, the space opened up in splendid bright glory. The great sunken room boasted a huge stone floor-to-ceiling fireplace, and the entire south wall of the room was a mass of sparkling glass, affording a view to die for. A cedar deck, complete with a built-in brick barbecue, spanned the length of the home, and there were gardens leading to the ocean-side pool and patio to the right. Eclipsing all of this was the magnificence of the open Pacific - wild and powerful, very much like the home's owner, Marianna speculated.

As Grant busied himself with putting groceries away and directing the children with small chores to assist him, Marianna took the opportunity to survey her surroundings in further detail. The great room was simply furnished with no sign of ostentatious belongings. In contrast, the room had a warm, cozy feel - inviting one to a lengthy stay. This further insight into Grant's complex personality should not have surprised Marianna, in retrospect. She had come to know him as a deep, caring man with strong values and opinions. Of course, he would not give a care about what others may think of him or his home. It was obvious by the surroundings that everything here was placed and selected specifically for comfort, creating a haven, that she suspected he was fiercely drawn to.

"Can I offer you a lemonade?"

He was standing before her now, and she flinched nervously as his hand brushed hers when she took the frosty glass from him. She knew her edginess was not lost on Grant, but he mercifully chose not to comment upon it and guided her through the kitchen to the huge sliding glass doors, opening onto the deck and poolside.

Jen and the kids were already settled into beach chairs, and Marianna watched as the teenager she'd come to love as her own, took her kids by the hand and guided them into the shallow end of the pool – she'd resourcefully already found a lifejacket for Katrina. They began to splash and play enthusiastically.

Grant settled himself easily beside Marianna as she tried in vain to ignore the deafening drumming of her heart and the glorious sexual energy singing merrily through her veins. Her gaze was involuntarily drawn to his long, well-muscled legs, deeply tanned from the California sun. Then – quite without her permission - traveled upward in a natural progression to the tight abdomen and narrow waist - generously sprinkled with soft dark hair. By the time she reached the rippling muscles in his chest, the desire to curl her fingers into the swirling mass was nearly more than she could resist, and in a sudden panic – lest she might do just that, she tore her gaze away and looked helplessly into his eyes.

OK, well, that was a fatal mistake - those dark pools of mystery were hot upon her now, and she felt she could very nearly drown within the steely gray depths – she blushed furiously. At once, Grant seemed to overcome a fierce inner struggle and began to speak.

"What do you think of my humble abode?" The words were spoken casually, but she sensed a strained tension as if her opinion held a certain power. He studied her closely.

"It's beautiful," Marianna whispered softly as she gazed around her at the splendid view in every direction.

"It's not much by L.A. standards, but on the upside, it keeps the piranhas at bay," Grant quipped, with a hint of apology in his voice.

She knew, without question, that he would make no sacrifices on this issue, and warmth suffused her heart. It was one of the things she loved about him, she acknowledged ruefully. Grant made no contrition to anyone when it came to his standards and beliefs.

"Well, it far surpasses glitz and glamour any day, in my opinion. It's comfortable and inviting, Grant - I'm very impressed," she stated truthfully. His eyes brightened now as they caressed the features of her face, taking her breath away for the zillionth time, she figured.

"It's not the same anymore, Mari." It was a husky whisper, and her heart flew to her throat.

"T-the house?" she stammered stupidly.

"Without you," he stated simply.

The longing in his eyes was more than she could bear, and in sudden panic, she looked away. He may very well have mistaken her reaction for unreturned feelings, if his next words were any indication.

"I know you are avoiding me - I've no wish to make you feel uncomfortable." Grant pinned her with his heated gaze. She looked at him now, unable to restrain her own yearning that shone from her eyes in a radiant glow.

"I," she began, but he silenced her effectively with a gentle caress of fingertips over her lips, lingering there for a moment.

"I tried to fight it, Mari - I love my life, damn it!"

His frustration pulled at her heartstrings. Oh Lord. She knew exactly how he felt and sighed shakily, reminding herself sorrowfully that she loved him. For his part...well, she didn't know what it was. She had admittedly conceded that he did care for her - there could be no mistaking that - but love? Even if it could be labeled such, the quality of love without mutual trust was flawed, at best. And hadn't he just now professed his aversion to his feelings for her?

"I have it all, Mari. I've worked incredibly hard to establish peace in my life – this harmony. I've been through hell and back with the media, the band, and yes, with women," he added brusquely. "I lead a comfortable life. The guys and I are at a point now where we no longer need the money. We have the luxury of pure creation - fame be damned. I've never enjoyed being in the public eye." His tone was gentle now, confiding.

"Sure, we still want to sell our music - success remains a noble goal. It's our audience who really determines where it will take us." Grant closed his eyes and leaned his head back, stretching the taught muscles in his neck.

"If all I ever accomplish from this moment forward is to create music - forget the CDs, the recordings, and the fans," he paused and looked directly into her eyes. "It would be enough - I've known that for some time now. I owe everything to the fans - no room for doubt there," he acknowledged with a smile, "and so I've come to accept that one of the strongest motivators for me to continue in this business — in a sense, is payment toward that debt." He cradled her hand within his own, in reverence, it seemed. His eyes shot back up to hers, which were luminous with unshed tears, so moved was she by his candor.

"But more important is the bond between the guys and I. We are kin. Hell, we have been through more together than most families weather in a lifetime." Marianna could feel the driving force of his devotion within his firm but gentle grasp. "Quite frankly, I love making music with them - I'm not ready for that to end yet." He pinned her now with a heated gaze.

"And then you come along," his thumb began a slow sensual caress on her inner wrist, sending shivers of pure electric sensation racing through her being, ending in a throbbing ache at the core of her womanhood. He lifted her chin up, and she froze, unable to resist any part of him, powerless to change a thing.

"Woman, it is a damn lucky thing your precious children are within our sights at this moment."

Marianna watched in fascination, the play of hot fire in the depths of his pupils and the slow motion of his Adam's apple, the defined swallow, betraying the crack in his iron self-control. He closed his eyes and heaved a deep sigh of resignation.

"You and I are not finished with this conversation - not by a long shot." His look of pure determination sent a foreboding quiver down her spine. Murmuring something about a barbecue, he left her there, and she couldn't quite fathom what that had to do with anything at this precise moment.

"Last one to the kitchen loads the dishwasher," Grant laughed deeply as the children giggled and flung water at him from the pool, in their effort to scramble out and grab their towels. When Marianna swiftly rose to follow, Grant put up his hand to halt her progress. "Mari, you and Jen stay here.

We are going to give you ladies the royal treatment." He threw Denny and Katrina a conspiring wink, which they returned in kind, giggling gleefully. Marianna could not suppress her own laughter and halted at the sudden intensity of Grant's gaze.

"You really should do that more often," his throaty whisper pretty much melted her limbs, and with a shake of his head, he disappeared inside in hot pursuit of the kids, bellowing like some huge beast on the pretense of trying to beat them to the kitchen.

Their raucous laughter was music to her ears. Oh, how they needed a man like Grant in their lives. The meal was delicious, and Marianna, in spite of all the fears and reservations, found herself relaxing easily, joining in the cheerful banter. Denny and Katrina were so happy it made her heart ache. For now, she was determined to let them all savor the moment. There would be time enough for reflection later.

Grant insisted on driving them all back to the inn and took her hand gently within his own, as they cruised the ocean highway. She was lulled by the beauty of the city lights reflected on the waters of the bay. As he steered the car into the parking lot of the inn, something she'd forgotten to address sprang to mind.

"You never did tell me how you found us," she looked inquiringly into his rugged features and watched the play of emotions cross his face. She waved to Jen and the kids as they scooted on ahead into the inn.

"Well, no thanks to you, I managed it," Grant replied silkily. "Suffice it to say, I threatened a mutual acquaintance with his very life, once I realized that you were not staying at Shutters. The inn had a record of your departure shuttle."

His gentle smile caressed her. She fought off a primal urge to reach up and kiss the sexy lines around his mouth.

"Why didn't you let the agency book your accommodations?" he queried with deceptive lightness. When she said nothing, he continued, "It doesn't matter, though. I've decided this will be your last night in this inn." As her bewildered expression turned to one of alarm, he chuckled softly.

"I want you all to pack up first thing in the morning - be ready about 8ish - I'm moving you all to my place in Malibu," Marianna sputtered as he infuriatingly ignored her stormy expression, "even if I have to drag you kicking and screaming."

His resolute air brooked no argument, but still, she resisted. She might just as well throw herself in with a pack of wolves, and so seal her fate, as to stay with Grant - in his home. That would surely mark her demise.

"Grant, I cannot do that," she was deathly afraid to look at him directly and struggled to maintain an air of rigid determination, as she busied herself fiddling with an imaginary tangle in the seatbelt.

"You can and you will," he challenged her with galling arrogance as he deftly reached across and unclasped her belt.

What a damn bully! He was insufferable!

"Besides, your children will never forgive you, and you know it. What reason will you give them, I can't imagine, to deny the use of my comfortable, private home while you are at the studio?"

He had her there and knew it. She glared at him, shooting daggers into his very soul. Their faces were illuminated by the glow from the inn lobby, and she was incensed by the hint of a smirk lurking on his lips. His expression suddenly softened.

"Come on, Mari, Jen, and the kids deserve it, and you will be perfectly safe as long as they are with us."

It was true, she admitted grudgingly, even he wouldn't stoop so low as forcible molestation, with her children under the same roof. Would he? The trouble was, she mused, as she bit her lip indecisively, that just one touch from him might put the shoes on the other foot.

"Oh, and another thing," Grant imparted with the twinkle of a delicious secret dancing in his eyes. "My sister is coming into town tomorrow and will be dropping by the studio." Grant chuckled softly at the genuine pleasure radiating from her face at this news. "Would it make you feel better to know that she is staying with us too, at least for tomorrow night?"

Marianna's entire body visibly relaxed with the knowledge that Terri would be there, and she couldn't wait to see her friend again.

"I thought as much," Grant mumbled with a shake of his head.

Marianna was gratified, albeit more than a little surprised, when Grant merely brought her hand up to his lips and whispered a final farewell before coming around to escort her safely into the inn. As she made her way up to her room, the kiss lingered on her fingers, searing her body and mind with unspoken, forbidden promises of greater pleasures to come.

## Chapter Twenty-Six

The children were fairly exploding with excitement the following morning, in anticipation of their tour date with Jen, and moving into Grant's house - Marianna had a difficult time keeping them respectfully quiet. At the same time, they hurriedly finished their continental breakfast.

She was actually relieved, despite the Olympic somersaults in her stomach, at the sight of Grant sauntering over to their table. He warmly accepted Katrina's exuberant leg hug and went to pour himself a cup of steaming coffee from the small complimentary buffet.

Marianna nearly jumped out of her bones when he flung the chair around and straddled it easily, resting his chin on his muscular arms, folded casually along the back of the chair. The look he bestowed upon her was sheer devilry, turning her insides to pure mush. It just wasn't proper – in fact, it should be declared a mortal sin, that any one man be blessed with such rugged, virile superiority, Marianna decided heatedly. She couldn't determine which was worse - the sexy fire in his gray eyes, or the pure promise of sensuality in his perfectly formed lips, which were, at this moment, quirked with some private merriment she assumed. It was the combination, she supposed.

At the pointed rise in his brow, she realized she'd been caught ogling, and color suffused her face. She immediately shot up out of her chair, hustled the kids, and gathered all their belongings. With a throaty chuckle, Grant picked up their suitcases effortlessly and led them out to his waiting car as Jen and the kids boarded the bus.

Heading to the studio in a thick silence, crackling with electric currents, Marianna wished that Grant would at least say anything to break this tortuous spell he seemed to have woven around every fiber of her being. Worse, she suspected that the man was well aware of his effect.

She wanted to scream obscenities at him, pummel him wildly with her fists, and beg him to kiss her silly, all at the same time. She groaned inwardly, saying a silent prayer for these next few days to pass by quickly. Immediately upon entering the studio, she heard Terri's melodic laughter fill the air, and her spirits soared. Her new friend rushed over, and the two women embraced affectionately.

"Shoot, you just get more beautiful each time I see you," Terri teased her, with a sexy feminine version of the same southern drawl that her brother possessed, as she looked Marianna over with genuine appreciation. "It is so good to lay eyes on you."

"When I heard you were going to be here, the day brightened considerably," Marianna confided easily. "I feel significantly stronger now that I have a fellow female in my court." Terri chuckled at her friend's obvious distress.

"Well, you have me for at least another day, so relax. I won't let that big lug of a brother bully you," Terri stuck her tongue out at Grant, who responded with a mocking raise of his brow. "Nor any of these other rakes," she teased as they moved closer to the men she'd come to know and love over the years.

Marianna was feeling decidedly more in control but froze in place, when she saw the beautiful redhead dramatically enter the room, and immediately sensed intense disapproval from Terri. The fiery flaming beauty glared openly at Marianna and addressed her with a sulky expression.

"Well, well, if it isn't the illustrious novice songwriter." Shauna's silky voice dripped with honey. "I have heard rumors about you of late. Apparently, congratulations are in order?" She declined to await a response and sidled directly over to Grant, flashing him a slow sexy smile. Linking her arm through his, she leaned up enticingly and whispered something in his ear. He chuckled softly, and Shauna fixed her petulant gaze upon Marianna with a self-satisfied smirk.

Marianna could not believe how gullible and naïve she had been, to entertain that she might even have a hope of competing against the likes of the smooth sophistication that was Shauna. She felt the humiliation of tears threatening to spill as she watched them - Grant seemingly content with this bold intimacy, as Shauna fairly molded herself to his hard virile frame.

Well, to hell with Grant Furman! She should have listened to her voice of reason all along. She'd known better, damn it, and would really do well to be thankful for this fresh perspective. Tearing her gaze away from the pair, who were behaving disgustedly like wanton lovers - in her opinion, she whirled around to speak with Grant's sister. The murderous daggers shooting from Terri's eyes, aimed directly at the cozy couple, would have rendered Marianna to giggles if she weren't feeling so damned weepy.

"Well now, Shauna, we'd all love to sit and visit with you, but we have work to do," Marianna was gratified at the silky dismissive tone in Jerry's voice, and he threw her a conspiring wink.

"Yes, I'm sure it isn't easy working with an amateur, slowing up progress." Shauna glanced pointedly at Marianna, who couldn't suppress a tiny smile at the goofy face Jerry made behind the beautiful redhead's back. Shauna stiffened, her eyes hurling poisonous darts at Marianna, in reaction to the apparent slight, and turned her attention back to Grant, reaching up to kiss him full on the mouth. "I will see you later," she murmured throatily as she slithered silkily off his body and sauntered toward the exit - hips swaying seductively.

Marianna felt bile rise from her stomach and wished she were anywhere else at that moment. In a desperate need for escape, she hastily excused herself to the washroom. Once there, she splashed cool water on her face and gulped in blessed air.

Her first instinct was to charge straight out the doors and never come back, but Marianna knew that wasn't an equitable option this time. RedRock deserved more than this from her. She had left them hanging once and would not do so again. The door swung open, and Terri leaned against the frame with folded arms, watching Marianna with concern.

"You OK, Sweetie?" She opened her arms, and Marianna accepted the comforting embrace. "Don't let that bitch get under your skin - that's exactly what she wants!"

In spite of herself, Marianna laughed at the viperous curse Terri had sputtered - quite out of character, and she marveled at the true friend she knew she had found in Grant's sister. Now that was inequitable. Her tear-streaked expression softened.

"Thank you, Terri. I don't know what I would have done without you here," she hugged her affectionately and heaved a determined sigh. "I need to get out there and get this done," she resolved, "And then I can go home." Marianna puzzled, as to why this did not provide the comforting reassurance it should have. She wondered in dull contemplation, if — as with Grant, things were no longer the same, and somehow, all that she had worked so hard to achieve was crumbling to ruins at her feet.

Returning to the recording room, with Terri firmly by her side, she mustered all the bravado she possessed, offering a shaky smile to Jerry and the rest of the band members in general, making sure, at all costs, to avoid eye contact with Grant. Marianna figured if she could just keep her distance, she would make it through this horrendous experience - only needing to focus on her obligation to the band.

As she moved over to sit by Gary, she felt the burning scorch of Grant's glowering glare, clear through to her soul. Well, to heck with him - it would be a cold day in hell before she'd allow him to browbeat her any further! Marianna clung to the granite wall of frigid anger building within her, a much-welcome defense to help her focus on the task at hand.

Mercifully, Gary was to provide the lead vocals to the two remaining songs the band had chosen. She would ask for nothing more, if she could just weather this atrocity - insanity, and flee home to lick her wounds in peace.

She should have realized, she admonished herself again. There had only ever been one true love in her life - one man she could trust, and he was gone. She supposed this experience, in some wicked Freudian fashion, was part of the process of acceptance and letting go. But she'd been doing so well - a fresh wave of ire crashed to the surface, and if looks could kill, one Grant Furman would be pushing up daisies in no time flat. Mess with her emotions, would he?

Marianna was astonished to find that once her and Gary got to work on the recordings, she became completely absorbed in the music - in the flow and creation of what she could clearly see were damned good songs. In spite of her grievous state of mind, a well of elation built deep within her, and she was truly humbled to be a part of the conception - though under no illusions where credit was due. If not for these talented musicians, the lyrics would remain simple words, scrawled on loose-leaf paper, buried eternally in a file folder in her desk drawer at home. As it was, her poignant vocals emerged from somewhere deep within, complementing Gary's stronger lead, as if it were a part of him. Marianna was shocked at how quickly it all unfolded.

"Well, Mari, you are one amazing lady," She blushed furiously at Gary's rare gift of praise, but her mouth fell open at his next words. "We are finished." He grinned from ear to ear, clearly pleased with the outcome. "It was perfect!"

"When should I," Marianna was about to ask what time she should return in the morning.

"We are done like dinner. You are free to go now," Gary eyed her thoughtfully, "but you are quite welcome to hang with us for another day or two - we certainly won't complain about a beautiful woman gracing our studio."

Marianna struggled to wrap her head around the fact that she was actually free to go home - so why wasn't she bouncing madly with enthusiasm at the prospect? Why did her heart feel so heavy, and what was this sudden veil of depression that seemed to be descending gloomily over her?

"On one condition," Gary added, throwing her a stern look as he put his drum set in order. "Your presence will be required at our official celebration of the CD's release," he smiled warmly.

"I will do my best to be there," she responded with sincerity, though Marianna knew in her heart she wouldn't - couldn't come back again. She was touched at their easy acceptance of her presence within their ranks. She knew instinctively that it was rare and special, and felt honored at their reception. When the time came, she knew Jerry would explain on her behalf.

"Well," Terri, who had sat in silent observation in the corner of the room, now hooked her arm with Marianna's. "One thing for sure, you men have monopolized far too much of Mari's time, and we," she looked pointedly at her, "are going to spend at least one full day shopping in L.A. "Oh yes," she continued with a no-nonsense grin, "you are not getting away with this, Mari - this girl doesn't get off the ranch very often," Terri thrust her pointer finger back at herself dramatically, and Marianna laughed with affection, "and she's not about to waste this opportunity."

"There's a good reason they don't let her out much," the rich timbre of Grant's voice filled the room, and Marianna's knees threatened to buckle. "To be honest," he continued wryly, "I'm a tad concerned about this fair city, with you two lovely ladies on the loose."

"Be afraid - be very afraid," Terri stuck her tongue out at him emphatically as she delivered this warning.

Marianna resigned herself to spending at least one more bittersweet day in L.A. with Terri. Besides, how much trouble could she get into as long as she was busy shopping? Tomorrow night, she resolved, she would pack the kids up and head back to the inn to finalize their travel plans for home. With that determination, she said her emotional goodbyes to all the guys, hugging Jerry warmly, and asked him to please give her regards to Benny, who was apparently out of town at this time.

"Farewell, dear lady," Jerry kissed her cheek, "but we will meet again soon," he promised prophetically and gently released her.

"I will drive you home," Grant insisted, with his usual annoying arrogance.

Who did he think he was, daring to assume that she would just fall into step behind him like an obedient canine? She would have indeed insisted emphatically upon walking the fourteen miles or so to the inn, but as it was, Terri grabbed her arm and dragged her off to trail hurriedly behind Grant's long strides.

# Chapter Twenty-Seven

Feeling significantly refreshed after a long leisurely soak in the Jacuzzi tub that was cozily nestled in the ensuite adjoining her bedroom, she took a moment to gaze around her. The guest room was tastefully furnished with traditional Californian simplicity - one wall was entirely glass, affording her a magnificent view of the ocean.

She stood now, gazing down affectionately at Denny and Katrina, who were splashing playfully in the pool with Jen. All three of them were sporting the beginnings of a beautiful suntan, and they looked healthy and happy. She sighed heavily, knowing that their imminent departure from this wonderful paradise wasn't going to be easy for them.

Denny and Katrina's reunion with Grant had served to strengthen the bond between them, and this caused her grave concern. She stepped out onto the little balcony to breathe deeply of the exhilarating sea air. Somehow, she always gained a measure of peace in the ocean's presence. Her problems seemed minutely insignificant in comparison. She knew this to be an illusion, though. The hurdles before her now weighed heavily, and she anticipated a rough road ahead.

His sudden appearance on the patio provided a vision of male splendor, as he dove expertly into the pool and swam smoothly over to the children, joining enthusiastically in the frolic. Their squeals of delight at this unexpected diversion brought a smile to Marianna's lips, even as the rest of her body screamed for mercy - deliverance from the magnetic effect the man had on her senses.

"Mommy, Mommy,"

Katrina had spotted her from below, and she managed to tear her eyes off his rugged male form - bronzed skin glistening from sparkling sunshine reflecting off the water. She was shocked at her strong compulsion to lick every droplet clear. She looked at her daughter now, clinging to this lifeline and smiling shakily. Where the hell was her anger with the rake, when she needed it most?

"Mommy, you have to come down to the pool with us, please?" Katrina begged, appealed, and Marianna felt her heart melting in spite of the dangerous folly that would pose. No one, Marianna reflected, could plead more sweetly or effectively than her beautiful daughter.

"Yeah, Mom, you promised," Denny reminded her reasonably.

The traitor! Her mind buzzed wildly as she tried to conjure a viable excuse for why she could not, at this moment, honor that vow. Suddenly she had it! Where was Terri?

"Well, actually, I was just going to see Terri," she faltered as the woman herself materialized on the patio, dressed in a bright yellow one-piece bathing suit that left no doubt as to her intentions for the next little while. Good grief, was no one fated to be on her side of the court?

"Hey Mari, I thought you'd be down here by now," Terri flashed her a sunny grin, and though Marianna would have loved to resent her vehemently for foiling her only escape route, she couldn't stifle the affectionate response to Grant's sister, who, in Marianna's opinion, was a great lady, who had been a source of loving support, on more than one occasion through this crazy, outlandish adventure.

Marianna's eyes slid, of their own volition, to Grant, who was staring at her intently - their gazes locked. The fiery heat in those smoky gray orbs ignited a primal response within her, which threatened to consume her where she stood. With a strength she did not know she possessed, she tore her gaze away and mumbled her intention to join them shortly, but not before the man below had caught - just for an instant, the parting of her lips and the glaze of desire shining brightly in her eyes.

A few moments later, she emerged from the kitchen sliders, clad in the most conservative swimsuit in her collection – but if anything, the soft silky fabric molded to her curves and hinted at unseen delights much more effectively than any revealing bikini could have done. Her ample breasts, though mostly concealed, provided enticing cleavage, and the deep blue hue of the fabric mirrored the startling color of her eyes. She settled self-consciously into the lounge chair beside Terri, hastily draping the towel across her lap, in response to Grant's frank appraisal.

"Come on in, Mom," Denny pleaded, "the water is awesome!" Marianna could have cheerfully strangled her son at that moment, but Katrina instantly echoed his sentiments, and she knew they would not let up until she acquiesced.

What objection could she possibly throw at them, after all? Under normal circumstances, she was the first one in the water. She would not allow her wayward feelings for the presence of one oversexed bundle of testosterone in that pool, to affect her rock-solid relationship with her children. She jumped up and scampered her way as quickly as possible to the water, in firm avoidance of Grant's fiery gaze, which burned through her skin as sure as a flaming arrow.

Denny and Katrina were on top of her instantly, splashing and insisting on piggybacks that were her trademark aquatic antic, at least where her children were concerned. Marianna soon found herself thoroughly immersed in their happy water sport, and gloried in the pleasure of cavorting playfully with her children. Her features softened, and her body relaxed, resembling a young water nymph - the dazzling smile and mischievous sparkle in her eyes radiating luminous energy from within.

For the moment, she was blissfully unaware of her effect on the man, who was intensely fixated from the sidelines of the pool. She looked up with pleasure as a giggling Terri joined them in the water.

"OK, who wants to get wetter?" she taunted them, holding a hot pink Frisbee she had somewhere discovered, and at once hurled it deftly at her brother, catching him unawares and slicing him square in the midsection.

Marianna caught her breath as his sleek abdomen muscles tautened with the instinctive reaction, but mercifully, the moment was brief, and they all engaged in a vigorous game of skirmish as they attempted to catch the flying missile before it hit the water. Before long, they were all thoroughly drenched, and Marianna smoothed wet auburn tresses back from her face, laughing heartily - mirth dancing merrily in her eyes.

"I declare lunch break!" Terri bellowed her departure from the pool as she grabbed a towel and swiftly disappeared into the house.

Marianna was about to follow suit when Denny sent the Frisbee hurling just above her head. Laughing, she leaped up and missed, whirling around to swim after it, only to find herself flat up against Grant's firm, unyielding chest as he neatly reached up and caught the toy. Momentarily stunned, Marianna took a split second too long to react, and was promptly wrapped securely in his steely arms. He held her there in an iron vice, as his smoky eyes caressed every feature on her face and then some.

She snatched onto her wits and struggled to escape, hissing a reminder to him about the children. With an arch of his brow, he looked over at them, and she craned her neck around to witness, with vast alarm, that her treasonous children were paying absolutely no attention to their compromising position – indeed, were exiting the pool at a dead run into the house, after Terri and Jen. Oh, Lordy!

The alluring caress of his warm breath in her hair, snapped her attention back to Grant, and the instant she turned her head, his mouth expertly captured hers in a gentle, persuasive kiss. Already lubricated from pool water, their lips slid and slipped smoothly together like pure silk – the softest, most erotic physical touch Marianna had ever experienced.

Seductively slow and languorous, that kiss was stealing every ounce of sense she possessed and was most certainly responsible for the dense fogginess in her brain - the wayward feeling of belonging in his arms.

She was shocked at her inability - OK, face it, lack of desire, to fight her way out of his tantalizing embrace, and to her horrific astonishment, her body was, instead, moving sensuously against him, her feminine curves melting wantonly into his rock-hard body.

At once, the kiss altered, fiercely demanding, and she feverishly responded with an unleashed passion, that she had been bottling up until she'd nearly exploded with it. Now, under the spell of his charismatic male virility, she was unable to conquer it and protested with a mewing cry. Grant pushed her firmly from him with a deep groan, his chest heaving - desire burning in his dark blazing eyes. Marianna recognized the tenuous leash he held on his self-control and was immensely grateful for it because hers was most definitely AWOL.

"We need to talk, Mari," his voice was strained as he gently urged her out of the pool. "The kids will be fine with Terri and Jen. Let's go for a drive – we can grab a bite on the way."

Marianna swallowed nervously as she gazed into his eyes, the intensity of their shared passion still burning there. But there was something else in those gray depths - vulnerable, intense, honest, and caring. She nodded slowly and went to change. It was time to have it out, once and for all.

Terri met her at the bottom of the stairs. "Don't worry about a thing Hon," she gave Marianna an encouraging hug. "They are completely immersed in the Wii right now and likely won't even notice you are gone. I'm throwing mini pizzas in the oven to go with the salad." She gently shoved Marianna toward the door. "And Mari," Terri smiled warmly, "There is absolutely nothing between Shauna and Grant - I guarantee you that."

Marianna stepped outside to find Grant flexing his shoulder muscles, as he waited for her beside the car. As long as she lived, she would never grow tired of watching this man - the physical beauty and strength - both inner and outer, which radiated from him.

He looked up now, and his burning gaze captured her senses, sending her heart to flip-flops. Holding open the car door, he maneuvered his large frame to settle in beside her and took her small hand into his larger one, caressing her slender fingers sensuously with his thumb. The touch was purely electric, and Marianna thought that she'd surely die from it. At once, he lifted her hand to his lips for a gentle, chivalrous kiss before placing it back on her lap, his gaze smoldering into hers, and then turned his attention to driving. They traveled silently along the Pacific Coast Highway, leading them south of L.A. Grant pulled into an oceanside café and threw her a crooked grin.

"Hungry?"

She was madly ravenous all right, but the food was surely not going to cut it. In truth, Marianna didn't believe that she could manage even one bite. She was too wound up with emotional anticipation. Her heart sank low with the knowledge of what she knew must come. It was imperative that she make it crystal clear - her unwillingness to sacrifice the well-being of her children, in favor of her own selfish interests, particularly for a romance that seemed doomed from the get-go.

She frowned miserably as she mused on the odds stacked against them - their lifestyles, for one thing, not to mention the fact that Grant was terminally mistrusting and emotionally unavailable. As a cincher, there was the ever-present redheaded bombshell looming in the dark shadows. No matter what Terri imparted, she and Grant had a history - a particularly intimate history, which Marianna knew she could never hope to compete with. What she needed now was a whole lot of strength and mercy.

Grant, on the other hand, seemed relaxed - content with casual safe conversation for the time being, as they munched on a basket of delicious fish and chips he had ordered, at the waiter's strong recommendation.

Marianna's gaze was soft and luminous upon him now, as she listened raptly to him chat about the many issues surrounding the release of the upcoming CD. Apparently, Gary had not changed over all these years, ever battling for the controlling influence, and Grant admitted that it no longer bothered him the way it used to. Grant had ventured out on a solo career for a bit, quite successfully, and was comfortable with his decision to reunite and remain with the band now. They were his family, and he cared for each of them deeply.

Grant expertly linked his fingers with hers as they strolled along the beach after their delicious meal, and she was content to indulge in the pleasure of his touch, treasuring his nearness for at least a little longer. He stopped and pulled her down onto a piece of driftwood for a rest, pulling her head onto his shoulder and gently kissing her hair. The exhilarating ocean breeze stimulated her senses - the salty freshness of the sea air tingling her nostrils.

Marianna knew she would gladly remain forever with him here, if only circumstances were different. She sighed heavily and put some distance between them.

"Grant, I," her voice trailed off as he reached up and caressed the outline of her mouth with his thumb, followed by his lips. "No!" She pulled away and stood abruptly, forcing herself to confront the instantly heated anger in his gaze. "I can't do this with you." Tell him now, Mari, she ordered herself.

"Do what?" Grant's words were clipped. "Kiss me? Drive me half-crazy and then push me away?" Marianna caught her breath at the dangerous glint of steel in his dark gray eyes. "Well, for once," he continued, advancing upon her slowly, "we are in complete agreement. You cannot do this anymore." He soon had her backed up helplessly against a huge pile of driftwood. "I won't let you."

She panicked at his deceptive silky tone - the raw lust burning in his eyes.

"As a matter of fact, I have decided that you will not get away from me this time."

His words were ominous, and she frantically pushed past him and ran blindly. It was futile, she knew, and soon registered his footfall gaining swiftly upon her. Oh God…

He caught her and pulled her roughly down onto the sand with him, rolling swiftly atop of her, capturing her arms above her head with his steely grip. His head dipped down, and she groaned aloud as his lips skillfully captured hers in a searing kiss.

But even as she whimpered in protest, her body sensuously molded hotly to his, as if it was created solely for this purpose. The kiss was at once gentle, probing - his tongue sampling the sweet honey of her mouth. He raised his head, and his gaze softened. With one calloused thumb, he brushed the tears from her cheeks.

When had she stopped struggling? Her thoughts were jumbled and confused. Where was that damn redhead now, to douse the raging inferno that seemed to be drowning her?

He followed each salty trace of her tears with his liquid-warm lips, and she surrendered to his magic. He scooped her effortlessly up in his arms and held her close to his body, murmuring sweet words of comfort and adoration into her hair — the sleek column of her neck. She wept softly, agonizing over the injustice of her predicament. At that precise moment, she knew that she could no longer deny herself this yearning. She would have the pleasure of knowing his love this one time and treasure the memory forever.

Her body was singing, alive with unbridled desire, and she raised her smoldering gaze to meet his smoky one, all the passion and longing aglow on her face. He picked her up easily and gently lowered her to a sheltered patch of sand, conveniently hidden from the public eye, but it would not have mattered to her at that moment. There was no one else but Grant — his essence and pure masculinity.

His look scorched her, and flickering flames of desire engulfed her body, enslaving her senses. She had never felt more alive. At once, his kisses were searing - lips and hands hungrily everywhere. So smooth and practiced was his touch - she felt the wild thrill of the ocean air caressing her bare skin and was foggily unaware of the exact moment he had peeled off her tank top — wantonly grateful for it. Her nipples hardened, reaching up for his attention, and he did not disappoint, rolling each one lovingly with his thumb, murmuring how beautiful her breasts were.

When he copied the taunting action with his lips, she gasped as shooting bolts of white-hot desire licked the center of her sex, rendering her helpless, as his mouth continued its lazy suckle - expertly, turning her loins to liquid fire. He gently massaged the swollen generous mounds, then silkily caressed her belly, her hips - smoothly tugging her skirt off, then her – oh sweet mercy – saturated panties. She lay gloriously naked before him, panting with anticipation, aflame with raging lust.

"Please," she whimpered, throwing her head from side to side in frustrated need. His eyes were on fire, and he groaned his agonized need for her, then ever so gently slid his hand between her thighs, a tantalizing soft, feather-like caress, slowly gliding higher and higher. He moaned and caught his breath in torment, as his fingers slid silkily along the sweet, slick, hot moisture there. She cried out and writhed wantonly beneath him, thrusting her hips up for more. Oh God!

"Oh yes," he teasingly whispered, "just a touch," and watched her face intently as he worked his way up her thighs once more, for another mind-numbing caress.

Marianna was half insane with need and pleaded for more, spreading her long beautiful thighs with invitation, while reaching out to frantically unbuckle his belt. He laughed throatily and deftly shed himself of his clothing, flinging it violently in the sand behind them. Marianna groaned at the sight of his manhood, hard and thick, thrusting proudly and powerfully toward her as he knelt between her aching thighs. She arched her hips up to receive him, but he was determined to prolong the sweet agony.

"I knew it would be like this with you," he whispered hoarsely and teased her with the light slick sliding of his fingers against the silky velvet wetness of her engorged genitals. He increased the pressure ever so slowly, and she moaned her pleasure. "I knew you would be deliciously hot and wet for me."

The sweet slippery sounds of his loving added to her writhing agony. He groaned and whispered wild, erotic delights into her neck, and through a thick haze of desire, she knew a sudden victory, as his loss of control became evident. She reached between their bodies to caress his throbbing member, and he moaned in bliss.

She needed him inside of her now, but still, he denied her - sliding slowly down the length of her body, depositing a trail of torturous kisses all the way. When he reached the seductive vee of soft curls, he sucked in his breath and gently spread the folds of her womanhood – blowing softly upon the center of her pleasure.

It was mad torment, and she whimpered with aching, raging need. He teased her with the tip of his nose as he breathed in the heady, musky scent of her sex. First, his fingers and then his tongue tasted and explored every crevice there, massaging and flicking the sweet swollen nub – a tantalizing game of cat and mouse as he repeatedly stopped to gaze at her glazed pleading expression.

She begged him aloud for release, and he slowly slid back up to capture her mouth in a mind- blowing kiss that imitated the love play her body craved so furiously. The taste of her own passion on his lips nearly drove her mad. At once, his pulsating maleness was hot between her thighs, sliding huge and snugly inside of her, with one swift movement. Marianna nearly fainted with the pleasure of his shaft stretching and throbbing deep within her. She wiggled her hips enticingly in a desperate attempt to initiate the carnal mating thrusts.

But Grant was determined to take it slow and whispered, "Just stay still for a moment, feel me inside you," as he kissed her neck, ears, and eyes – swollen lips and breasts. "This has to be perfect." She could feel him trembling with the effort for control, and once more wriggled beneath him. "Oh God, let me savor you, Mari. It has been a long while for me, and I don't wish to end this prematurely."

"I don't care," she groaned in her frustration, "please, please, take me now," and with those erotic words, he began to move, penetrating sensuously in and out of her silky moist sheath, slowly building her to a crescendo, that rocked her to the very core of her being. Her body was a quivering mass of sensation as Grant deepened his thrusts harder and faster.

"God, I love the way you take me all in - so tight," he murmured, and she surrendered completely to the sweet rapture of release, as wave after satisfying wave of pure ecstasy engulfed her. The force of her orgasm sent Grant spiraling to his own, taking his pleasure with hard steely abandon deep within her - and then they lay still for a long time, holding onto each other tightly as their breathing calmed.

"Sweet Jesus, the things you do to me," Grant whispered into her hair. "So incredibly intoxicating," he continued, stroking her soft tresses.

You're not so bad yourself," Marianna stirred drunkenly in his arms, snuggling closer. "As a matter of fact," she reached for his once again swollen member, and he moaned with pleasure.

"Once could never be enough, you know that." His words were serious, as he nipped her earlobe gently. "But I think unless we wish to risk being caught in our present attire, or lack thereof, we had better take this to a more private venue," Grant's words threw an intrusive dose of reality on Marianna. She sat up abruptly, blushing at Grant's bold, appreciative gaze upon her naked form.

"Damn, woman, you have mighty fine breasts," he breathed out the words in a caressing sigh, and she jumped up as those ample soft mounds bounced enticingly – erect nipples flaunting her renewed aching desire, as she attempted to brush the granules of sand off her buttocks and legs. When Grant rose to eagerly assist, they very nearly ended up back on the sand once again.

Back in the car, Marianna could not help but bask in the glow of happiness that seemed to envelope every fiber of her being. She accepted that it was temporary and would necessarily end - that there would be no seconds. But she also knew that this amazing memory would be hers alone to harbor and treasure forever, to pull out whenever she wanted the ultimate perfect dream - her personal fantasy. And yes, she also conceded, it would be her cross to bear, a forever throbbing ache. Through the haze of acute pain that this reality evoked, she decided right then and there, that it was worth every erotic second of it.

# Chapter Twenty-Eight

When Marianna and Grant strolled into the kitchen, Terri looked up cheerfully from her dinner preparations and smiled warmly at the two of them, a twinkle evident in her eye. Marianna supposed even the most chaste nun would recognize the satiated bliss still radiating from her face.

"The kids are with Jen at the pool," Terri informed them unnecessarily, as the entire city of Malibu could surely hear their shrieks and frolicking antics. "And I am treating you all to barbecued wild Pacific salmon shish kabobs tonight," she continued. "So, really, there's nothing for you two to do here. Grant, why don't you take Mari for a stroll along the beach?"

Oh Lord, if she only knew what soul-devouring dangers lurk on the beach, Marianna thought hysterically.

"Actually, I think I'm going to lure her into my den," Grant countered mysteriously, "there is something I wish to show Marianna." He took her hand and led her down the spacious hallway and through some elegant French doors leading to what she suspected was the coziest room on the planet.

Once again, huge windows afforded an incredible ocean view, but the remaining three walls were adorned with shelf after shelf of glorious books. Marianna's mouth hung open in astonishment. She had dreamed all of her life of owning a library such as this. One corner boasted a stone fireplace with a huge hunter-green leather couch facing it – Mari presumed one could sink into it forever. Grant's mahogany desk faced the windows, and two comfortable leather chairs were backed up against the glass. There were also two very cozy reading chairs on either side of the fireplace, perpendicular to the couch.

"I see you approve of my den," Grant's gaze was warm upon her face. "This is, by far, my favorite room, and you are welcome here at any time, Mari."

She knew there was an unspoken message here, and it touched her heart. Grant walked slowly over and grasped her hand, leading her to the couch. As they sunk into it, side by side, she wrung her hands nervously together, not sure where to go from here. Grant's massive hand closed over hers, effectively stilling the movement.

"Something is bothering you," Grant began. "I'm damned out of my element here and entirely unsure of your thoughts." He caressed her cheek, "Mari, I could use your help - tell me what you need."

She looked imploringly into his gorgeous eyes, wondering how on earth she could ever hope to find words to explain her excruciating turmoil. She could feel the sweet bruising ache, still throbbing between her thighs - evidence of his intoxicating and very thorough possession.

"This afternoon," Grant paused and took a deep breath - the fiery depth of his gaze mesmerized her, "was damned truly amazing." His eyes caressed her features, and she flushed with the memory of their shared passion.

"Incredible," she murmured and sighed deeply. "Grant, I will never regret what has come to pass, though I am deeply disturbed by the irresponsibility of my actions. I have always put my children first, and now..." her voice trailed off - the agony apparent on her beautiful flushed features.

*A Kiss to Die For*

"And now," Grant persisted gently, "you are still the same awesome mother you were before. One exceptionally beautiful lady, who has just embraced her amazingly passionate sensuality." He lifted her chin to look deeply into her eyes. "You shared that passion naturally and freely with me today, and I am honored, to say the least. You are one remarkable woman – all woman," Grant's voice was husky with renewed desire. Marianna shuffled slightly away from him on the couch.

"Grant, I will never forget you," her heart shone in her eyes.

"Wait a minute here," Grant fixed her with a determined look. "After all that we have shared this day, please tell me that you are not going to turn tail and run again." At her crestfallen expression, Grant railed. "No, Mari! We have unfinished business here, and I won't let you go until we've talked this through."

At once, Marianna realized that she had been selfishly unjust to Grant. After all, he had not made any promises to her or she to him. But she knew that he had been deeply hurt by others before her, and the last thing she wanted now was to cause him pain.

"Grant, I need you to know that I would never embark on such an intimate relationship lightly." At his narrowed look, she hastily continued. "I tried to fight this - to stop it, truly, but I lost the battle and am deeply sorry." She flinched at the raw flash of pain she witnessed across his features, realizing how this heartfelt confession must sound. "Grant, you are the only one - since my husband, I mean."

"And that is supposed to make me feel better?" he hissed at her. "You assure me backhandedly that I am special enough to crack your ridiculous thick resolve, and that makes it OK for you to leave now?"

His stormy expression sliced any further response she could muster, and the force of his fierce anger had her just a little worried for her physical safety.

"I'm so sorry," she mumbled ineffectively.

"And what am I supposed to do with this now?" he demanded hotly. "This unmerciful hellish ache that holds me, hostage, whether you are here or three thousand bloody miles away? I didn't take you for the love, 'em and leave 'em type, Mari," Grant sneered. She knew that it was hurt driving his tirade. "I should have listened to my better judgment from the beginning. You are, so it turns out, no different from all the rest!"

And with that, Grant stormed from the room, leaving a gaping chasm where her heart should have been. Marianna hung her head and cried softly, sinking to the floor in a heap of despair. It was there that Terri found her, gathered her up, and led Marianna quietly up to her room.

As she lay on the big bed, feeling more utterly miserable than she'd believed possible, she heard the roar of his vehicle exit the garage and peel off down the road. Every cell in her body screamed to take immediate advantage and make good her escape before his imminent return.

Oh, Mari, you stupid fool! Why had she come back? What had she expected? But she knew the answer. It was all for the glory of love. It was the reason she'd come and, ironically, why she now had to leave. Grant was simply unable to give her what she needed, and this girl could unquestionably accept nothing less. Terri knocked softly on the door and peeked in. Marianna gestured her to enter - she had nothing to hide from this remarkable friend.

"I told Jen and the kids you were suffering from a monster headache and needed some rest," Terri sat down on the side of the bed and patted Marianna's hand. "I have no right to ask what happened, but I can harbor a pretty good guess," she bestowed a gentle smile.

"It doesn't matter now, Terri. I need to leave as soon as possible and just let Grant be," Marianna sniffed through her tears, peering up woefully, "but I will take that shopping day with you first and leave tomorrow night," she assured her. Marianna knew she had to do this for the sake of her children. She would not force them into another traumatic escape.

"You surely don't have to do anything on my account, but I do believe in my heart that it would be better for you to take a day to let the proverbial dust settle before you make any rash decisions." Terri squeezed her hand gently. "Why don't you wash up and come down for a bite with us? Then if you wish, you can retire early, and I'll have you whisked out of this house in the morning, before anyone else has a chance to open even one eyelid," she promised with an understanding grin. Marianna's expression softened.

"OK, it's a deal. I'll be down in a few minutes."

They spent the evening in companionable silence, Marianna declaring the shish kebobs to be the best she'd ever tasted. However, Grant's continuing absence was a burning ache for which there was no medicinal relief.

They took a hike along the beach and watched a movie together with Jen and the kids, before regretfully retiring for the night. Marianna was thoroughly fatigued - yet her nerves sparked every time she heard a car motor, simultaneously praying and dreading, that it would be Grant. In spite of it all, within a short time, she plunged into a deep, exhausted slumber.

Terri, true to her word, hurriedly bustled Marianna out of the house and into a waiting cab, very early the next morning. Jen and the kids were planning on enjoying every final second of their last day poolside, and Terri assured her that Grant had indeed arrived home the night before and was all set to spend the day watching over them all.

Shopping with Terri was akin to taking an exuberant child to a candy store. She ogled all of the treasures she rarely got a chance to feast her eyes upon, tucked away on her hectic, remote ranch. Marianna knew, though, that as a kindred spirit, Terri wouldn't trade it, for all the shopping in the world.

"You need to come and visit me in Edmonton," Marianna mumbled through a bite of delicious stone-baked pizza they had ordered at a quaint little Italian diner. "I can promise you shopping to die for, all under one roof!" she declared with a laugh, surveying the mountain of bags at Terri's feet.

"I would love to do that someday," Terri returned with an affectionate smile. "The kids would love it too, and I can't wait to meet Tess in the flesh," Terri laughed aloud. She had spent more than a half hour chatting easily with her on the phone the previous evening, much to Marianna's delight.

Marianna's pretty features clouded now as she realized that in a few short hours, she would be homebound, and Tess would be awaiting them at the airport this evening. Seeing the haunted look on her face, Terri's heart went out to Marianna.

"Well, I hate to say this, Hon, but we'd better head back if you are to make that dreaded flight."

Her regretful look almost reduced Marianna to the tears that had been threatening to overwhelm her all day, but she managed to keep them at bay, so determined was she to relish the remaining time left with her good friend.

"Are you sure you won't spend a few days at the ranch?" Terri had made the offer earlier when she'd realized that Marianna's schedule now allowed her a few extra days. "The kids would be ecstatic."

"I really couldn't. I need to get home," Marianna squeezed Terri's hand affectionately. She knew that as long as she was in close proximity to Grant, there would be no peace for her, and she desperately needed some semblance of normalcy right now.

Terri had provided further insight into Grant's personality, as they'd stopped earlier for an iced tea and pastry, and Marianna pondered on it now. Her heart ached when Terri divulged the nature of his distrust - the only three women Grant had ever really been seriously involved with over all these years. All of them were motivated by money and the status that came with being on the arm of Grant Furman.

He had mistakenly believed that one in particular, Shauna, had deeply cared for him and to his credit, the act she'd put on would have won an Oscar. Then, when the band experienced an inspirational lull, and Gary and Grant had ventured their separate ways to pursue solo careers, the limelight fell away from them for a time. That is when Shauna's true colors emerged, and she began taking up with other men. Grant had stubbornly refused to believe the rumors and steadfastly stood by her until, one day, he was confronted by Jerry.

Along with a healthy dose of tough love, he informed Grant that Shauna had tried to seduce him into her bed. Grant had raged at Jerry, socking him squarely in the jaw before storming out – he later returned with a remorseful apology and cried like a baby on Jerry's shoulder. Marianna hungered, with a vengeance, to hunt down and strangle the treacherous redhead before she left town.

She now understood, with certainty, that Grant would never have ventured into the intimacy they had shared, without some form of deep caring. Though this warmed her heart considerably, it didn't alter the fact that a long-term relationship between them was simply impossible. Bottom line - he had really not given her even one ounce of encouragement toward that end. She had no doubt that her leaving was best for everyone. But damn, she was depressed!

~~~

At the airport, Terri hugged Marianna fiercely and each of the kids in turn. Grant had hung back, keeping his distance, and only now moved toward her.

"Mr. Grant, are you going to come and live with us again?" Katrina's innocent question clearly stunned them all, but Marianna was the first to recover.

"No, Honey, Mr. Grant has a home here, and he works here too," she explained patiently, fervently hoping that the violent thumping of her heart was not outwardly detectable. Mercifully, the loudspeaker announced that it was time for boarding. She and Grant shared a look of longing that spoke volumes and cut to the very core of her being.

"Goodbye, Grant," Marianna whispered hoarsely, as she fought valiantly to hold back her tears. She tore herself away and whisked the kids through the line-up, not daring to look back.

Grant Furman stood watching them leave, his forlorn expression dark and filled with pain. Terri grabbed his arm and pulled him away, her heart breaking for her big brother, whom she loved beyond measure. There would be time for a talk later. Now, she needed to get him home.

# Chapter Twenty-Nine

The shrill ringing of the phone rudely awakened Marianna.

"Hello," she mumbled groggily. They had been three hours delayed on arriving home the night prior, and she had slept very poorly.

"Hi, Hon," Tess's tone was gentle. She knew that Marianna was hurting deeply and was determined to see her through this. "You up for some company? I've got Danishes," Tess knew Marianna could ill resist such a treat, especially when she was bone-weary and depressed. Normally Tess avoided tempting her, but today was a day built for comfort.

"Sure, give me half an hour," Marianna crawled out of bed and groggily replaced the receiver on the phone. After a long shower, she felt decidedly close to human again, and hurried to let Tess in the door.

They spent the next two hours talking, with Marianna pouring her heart out to her friend. Tess listened without comment, concern etched on her features. Marianna felt a sense of relief at having shared her grief, and was grateful that the children had slept on through half the morning. Now, watching them get reacquainted with their Christmas toys, that had been abandoned when they had all rushed off to L.A., Marianna was confident that her early return home was the right move. Another incoming call interrupted her thoughts.

"Hello," She listened intently as her literary agent informed her that she had arranged a book signing with the release of her first novel at a local bookstore in West Edmonton Mall. Marianna knew this would provide excellent exposure - an opportunity that didn't often come around and was normally reserved for accomplished authors. She gave her head a firm shake, to stave off the shock.

"Sure, I can be there," she scribbled down the details and stared at Tess in wonderment. Life just goes on, even when it hurts like hell, she thought blankly.

~~~

January brought extreme cold, and Marianna and the children spent most of their time indoors, venturing out only when absolutely necessary. Two days this week, the school bus service had been cancelled. When Marianna had checked the thermometer that morning, it read minus forty-four degrees Celsius, and she knew from hard experience that, coupled with the wind chill, it was actually much colder.

She cooked porridge, toast, and hot chocolate - her trademark wild winter breakfast fare, and when the kids settled in to watch a movie, Marianna immersed herself in writing. She had difficulty concentrating, and her mind inevitably strayed to L.A., where she knew the weather would still be balmy enough for a light jacket - her heart ached mournfully. This, of course, had very little to do with meteorology and everything to do with one Grant Furman and the cold, empty void he'd left in her existence.

She got up to stretch and make herself a cup of tea. There was always a sense of urgency - a restlessness, that came with the cold weather. It was not an option to just pop out the door for a breath of fresh air, to clear one's mind. The skin froze in a matter of mere minutes. Still, it never usually bothered her to this extent. Marianna reminded herself that it was bound to warm up a little in the next few days. Soon, she hoped, fretting that the colder weather may diminish the crowds for the book signing, which was to be held on Friday and Saturday.

Tess had insisted on taking the kids off her hands for those days, and Marianna smiled warmly, thinking of her best friend now. A week ago, Tess had invited them all over for dinner on the premise that she had some grand news to share. Denny and Katrina were beside themselves, as nothing excited them more than a big, fat juicy secret. They didn't have long to wait, as Tess was fairly bursting with the need to spill the beans - she was pregnant. The kids exploded with questions about the baby, and Katrina informed them all, in no uncertain terms, that she would be the first to hold "her." Marianna had laughed and hugged Tess fiercely.

"Oh, Tess, this is so wonderful!" Both women had tears streaming down their cheeks. A year ago, Marianna could not have imagined this scene, but now, it seemed so right. She was extremely happy for Tess and couldn't wait to return some of the "auntie" favors. She knew, without question, she would love this baby just like her own.

Later that night, Marianna lay in bed, mourning what might have been for she and Grant. She'd had a few anxious days, a couple of weeks prior, when her period had been uncharacteristically late. Though it was unlikely she was pregnant with Grant's baby, it was a definite possibility, as she hadn't the need for birth control since Jeff had died - it had, quite frankly, been the furthest thing from her mind, while lost in those glorious strong arms on that sexy, sandy beach. Safe sex had been recklessly abandoned, but she knew he'd been honest about his lengthy celibacy; thus, she wasn't worried.

She had spent those days anxiously fretting over her options. Keeping it from him was out of the question, but alternatively, she was certainly not prepared to base a long-term commitment around the existence of a baby, conceived from an irresponsible act. Even so, the thought of having Grant's baby brought a thrilling warmth and excitement, and when her period finally arrived three days later, she was taken aback by the deep sense of loss and disappointment that permeated her spirit.

Marianna now shook off her wayward thoughts and realized she had some pressing tasks to accomplish, in preparation for their upcoming visit to Tess's. She reflected with wonder on the profound life changes that both her and Tess had encountered during the past six months. Never in a million years, would she have predicted it. And now, though she continued to survive through the hazy pain of missing Grant, she had much to be thankful for, certainly with exciting things on the horizon - Tess's baby, her book, and her children. Yes, she'd had her share of profound growth experiences, thank you very much. Her life was where it needed to be right now.

~~~

"Go get him, Tigress!" Tess hugged her warmly and, none too gently shoved Marianna toward the door. Marianna marveled at the twinkle in her friend's eye. If she didn't know any better, she'd swear Tess was up to some evil mischief, and had to admit to a fair degree of apprehension - in light of the fact that Tess *owed her one*, big time.

"For goodness' sake, Tess, it's just a book signing," Marianna declared lightly, "I've heard these things are rather boring. And this cold weather may keep the masses home." The temperature had continued plummeting into the danger zone, and she hoped this was not going to be a complete waste of her time.

"Oh, you never can tell," Tess replied merrily, and Marianna laughed, catching her enthusiasm.

"Are you sure you want my yard apes overnight, Tess?" She was considerably concerned for her friend, who, at this stage of the game, needed all the rest she could manage.

"Don't even go there, Missy," Tess admonished her. "You need a break, and just think of all the writing you'll accomplish this weekend."

Marianna was looking forward to the precious opportunity for uninterrupted creativity. And she could come to collect the kids at any time, if necessary. She hugged Tess gratefully again and rushed off.

The manager of the popular bookstore had set up a table just inside the doors, where a seasonal display normally stood. She was young, Marianna reflected, for such a responsible position, but it soon became apparent that she was highly skilled at her job. Marianna received strategic exposure to not only the bookstore traffic, but also the general mall stream as well, which was overwhelming at the best of times. Watching the milling crowds, she reasoned that, apparently, a warm shopping mall was perhaps more exciting than being cooped up inside a stuffy house on such a frigid day.

Many people stopped just to chat casually about what it was like to become a published author, and to grab a warm coffee and refreshments that Robyn, the manager, had so graciously provided. By the end of the day on Friday, Marianna had sold over thirty copies of her new book and was absolutely thrilled. It pleased her to learn that Robyn had taken the time to read her book before the signing and was, therefore, able to provide relevant testimonials to potential buyers.

Her mood light, she decided to treat herself to her favorite Japanese kiosk down from the bookstore, before heading home for a long leisurely soak in her jetted tub, complete with a glass of warm cider. Thoroughly relaxed, she plugged in a movie she'd been meaning to watch and headed to bed shortly thereafter. She drifted off to the thought that it was quite pathetic, really – the highlight of her night being a hot bath and movie – all by herself!

The next morning dawned bright and sunny. Marianna gloried in the sparkling expanse of snow crystals, gleaming like millions of jewels, over the sprawling rolling fields on either side of the highway, during her half-hour drive into the city. Thoroughly pleased with herself for the progress she'd made on the new novel after she'd arrived home, optimism reigned for the day ahead.

Saturday afternoon at the bookstore turned out to be even crazier than the previous day, and she lost count, after effortlessly selling another fifty copies. Robyn was delighted for her and, of course, took a healthy commission for the store. It was a win-win situation, and she promised that her book would be placed on the front display, for the next few weeks.

Marianna was chatting with a pretty young aspiring writer, encouraging her to follow that dream, when out of the corner of her eye, she noticed a figure lounging against the pillar, just outside the store. She said goodbye with a genuine smile and glanced up.

"Are there any copies left?"

The rich, husky voice assailed her senses. Her ears buzzed, and butterflies careened off the walls of her stomach - she thrilled at the sight of him standing there, watching her, with those incredibly sexy eyes.

"Grant," It was a whisper. She drank in the masculine glory of him, as he was obviously doing in kind with her. Their gazes were locked solid, and for the life of her, she couldn't move a muscle. He sauntered closer.

"When can you get out of here?" It was a feverish demand.

"I – I think anytime now," she tore her gaze away and looked at Robyn, who was watching them with considerable interest. She couldn't have missed the obvious electricity crackling between them. Marianna would not have been surprised to see lightning bolts flash around them, and her heart was certainly thundering in her ears. The fierce ache between her thighs rendered her pretty much helpless. How in God's name did the man do that?

"Why don't you two go on ahead? I'll pack up the table," Robyn smiled at them, her eyes appreciative, as they landed on Grant's virile physique. "Marianna, I would be honored to host your next book signing - have your agent give me a call, OK?"

"Thank you so much, Robyn, for all you've done," Marianna gave her a quick hug and turned to Grant. He placed his hand securely on the small of her back and guided her firmly through the throngs of people to the far end of the mall. He was on a mission she knew, and didn't bother to question him as to where they were going.

There was no illusion of her getting away, and his touch was firing warm, delightful shivers up her spine. She felt the sudden need to escape the crowds - they were boxed in, and she couldn't wait to get to their destination. His own impatience became apparent, as he literally growled, when a wall of human bodies momentarily stalled them. Finally, the crowd thinned, and he led her into the huge Fantasyland Hotel lobby, wasting no time in finding the elevators.

Marianna regarded him with growing enlightenment. He had planned this ahead of time! How had he known about the book signing? Tess? A million questions were bouncing around in her brain, but at last, alone in the elevator, Grant firmly gathered her up into his arms and planted a thoroughly wanton kiss on her astonished lips.

All conscious thought deserted her, as she thrilled to the feel and taste of this man, whom she loved completely with her heart and soul. He was her drug, and she was on one glorious high. The elevator doors opened and still kissing her passionately, he fairly much dragged her along the hall to an opulent room.

Once inside, the desperation lessened, and he altered the kiss to a slow, seductive pace. Marianna could barely breathe, much less think, and clung to him for all she was worth. Finally, he lifted his head and pulled her to a beautiful chaise, in the sitting area of the luxurious suite.

"Marianna, we need to talk," Grant's struggle for control glaringly mirrored her own. "We are not leaving this room until we sort this out."

His look was thunderous, and she swallowed nervously. The physical ache of wanting was almost more than she could bear.

"Grant, how…" Marianna stammered.

"I will explain everything to you," Grant assured her, "for now, I need you to listen to me." He took a deep breath, and Marianna sat back to allow him time to gather his thoughts. His eyes caressed her every feature, and finally, he began.

"This doesn't come easy for me. I have learned the hard way, to cement my defenses firmly in place, before ever allowing my emotions to come into play. I have cared deeply for women in the past, and each time, I've been disappointed and betrayed." He paused – vulnerability obvious on his face. "Please bear with me while I try to open these doors for us to go through, together." Marianna reached out and squeezed his hand, to assure him that she was right there.

"I promised myself never to allow any woman the leverage to destroy me again," Grant continued. "I told myself females were all the same, and the whole love and marriage thing was not fated for me."

He looked at her with his heart in his eyes. "Oh, I know it works for some people - my sisters and brother - each are shining examples of spousal bliss. But for me," Grant struggled to explain. "I decided the problem was entwined with my calling as a professional musician. It occurred to me, that I could abandon my career, in favor of a normal life, perhaps find a decent woman, who would love me for who I am inside, and not for my image.

The trouble was," Grant's warring emotions etched into the lines in his face. "My calling as a musician was - is - a huge part of me. To sacrifice that for a woman, would be like selling my soul to the devil. I knew I would never be happy, and so," Grant fixed Marianna with a soul-searching gaze. "I accepted my lot in life. I have kept my relationships with women light and breezy, and always make it very clear where we both stand." He took her hand gently into his own.

"Then you swept into my life," his smoky eyes devoured her features as he spoke, "Mari, I didn't know what the hell to do with you, and wanted - tried very hard, to keep you in that neat little compartment, that I have reserved especially for intoxicating females." He smiled at her gently.

"But you kept popping up everywhere in my life, even when you weren't there - it was insane! I decided you were an obsession, that I couldn't seem to escape, and suddenly, nothing was the same anymore. It was affecting - hell, still is, affecting my work, which you know I hold sacred." Marianna interrupted now.

"Grant, I would never ask you to choose between your work and me. I would not want you on those terms, because I know that your career is a huge part of you, just as my children are for me - that is why I had to leave." Tears were rolling unchecked down her cheeks.

"Mari," Grant held her small hands between his larger ones, "it has all changed now, don't you see? Because of you," he spoke emphatically.

"I've had hours and days and weeks to think about this, and it's clear to me now." He lovingly brushed a tear off her cheek. "Don't go getting that pained look on your face - hear me out," he pleaded gently.

This was definitely a different Grant, contrasting the old impatient, demanding bag of testosterone, who she knew without a doubt, still lurked in there. She meekly did as he asked.

"I love my music, no doubt - hands down," he continued. "That will never change. But my career has changed, even before you. I've explained some of this to you already." He looked deeply into her eyes, and she nodded.

"You," he smiled gently, "have given me a gift beyond measure."

Her heart melted with his soft chuckle.

"You are the only woman who has ever accepted the whole of me. I know now, without a doubt, that even if I abandoned my career tomorrow - became a damn rodeo clown or some fool thing, that nothing would change for us - for you." He held up his hand at her look of protest. "I know, I know, as long as I don't give it up for you."

"I would never allow that," Marianna sighed, her love shining through her tears.

"Mari," Grant forged on. "I love my music - it is my life," he took her face between his large hands. "But I love you more."

Marianna gasped at the words that she was sure she'd never hear Grant say. He shook her face ever so gently to gain her full attention.

"I cannot go on like this without you – not for another minute. At least not without laying it all on the table, clearing the air, so to speak - without knowing I've given it my all. You deserve that - we deserve that," his body visibly relaxed as he continued to pour out his heart to her, sensing her attempt to understand.

"I need you to know how very much you mean to me. I need you in my life - you, Denny, and Katrina, have captured my heart, and I know," he chuckled, "it will never be truly mine again. The best part of it all, is that I'm OK with that. Actually, I'm wonderful with it!" His smile beamed upon her, and she laughed with him, but instantly her face clouded.

"Grant, I love you too, more than I ever dreamed possible, but it doesn't change a thing, really." Grant had never seen her so beautiful as she gazed up at him, with her heart and soul shining from her eyes. "You still have your career - God, you need to make music, Grant," Marianna was certain that Grant's destiny was not complete to that end, "and I need to hold my children the number one priority in my life."

Marianna reached up and gently caressed his rugged cheek, loving the hint of stubble that was beginning to grow there, and her eyes glazed, remembering the feel of it in a more passionate moment, over every inch of her body. God, she ached for him now. It was a physical pain that she knew she would have to bear for a very long time, if not forever. Grant watched the play of emotions across her face and, once again, captured her hands within his.

"You are wrong, Love," Grant insisted, "it changes everything. You have enriched my life profoundly," he continued. "It is not about what you've done or what either of us has sacrificed or will do," he pinned her with a level gaze. "It is about who we are together and about destiny. You are my destiny, Mari. I know it, as sure as I'm breathing. Without you, nothing else matters."

Marianna felt a tinge of hope lifting her spirits, but still…

"Grant, how can we?"

"Hush," He placed his finger gently upon her lips, "Hell, I don't know how we'll manage it - that really isn't important to me right now. I only know we can't let this go - it's too special, too precious. I love you."

His heated gaze verified his words - she saw it, felt it, gloried in it.

"We just need to give it 100%. Have faith, my beautiful Mari." Seeing the doubt still clouding her eyes, he plunged on.

"I know how much Denny and Katrina mean to you - I already love them completely - I would protect them with my life." Marianna knew this was true. "I promise you that they will remain the number one priority in both of our lives. I will never ask you to compromise their safety and happiness." He kissed her forehead gently. "But I will ask you to trust me on this."

Grant leaned back, finally allowing and waiting for her response. Marianna allowed tears to stream down her face unchecked. He had asked her to trust him. How could she not, now that he had given his so freely to her?

She knew full well how much the sacrifice had cost him - the risk he was taking for her at this very moment. She began to understand, that she had held Grant responsible all this time, in a quest to avoid her own fears - her reluctance to give up control and independence, her fear of losing another love.

It was clear to her now, and laughing out loud, Marianna Jacobs ecstatically surrendered to her destiny, and fell into the solid embrace of the rogue, Grant Furman.

Much later, lying entwined with him in the ridiculously mammoth king-sized bed, Marianna placed a soft kiss on Grant's neck. Their lovemaking had been beyond her wildest imagination and memory – all consuming – at times, almost violent, and yet, so tender that she was reduced to tears. Their sole awareness had been for each other. It was all they had needed for many hours.

"I feel that I'm in a dream, floating on a cloud of pure, sinful ecstasy. Pinch me – quick!" Marianna demanded in a sudden need for reassurance.

"Mmm," Grant groaned low in his throat and gathered her close to his warm hard chest. "I was so damn scared I was going to lose you forever," he whispered fervently into her hair. "I was shaking, like a terrified little kid, when I approached you at the bookstore," he confided with a sheepish grin.

Marianna slowly lifted her head up and looked into his eyes with a disbelieving giggle. Passion once again flared, at the blissful memory of him trembling above her, just before he'd merged their bodies into the most incredible, sensual journey imaginable.

"The great Grant Furman? Afraid of little ol' me?" She teased him, jabbing him in the ribs with playful affection.

"Oh, you are one formidable lady," he murmured with feeling, "a force to be reckoned with," he good-humoredly smacked her delicious bare bottom. "But my dear lady," his hands slowly teased over her body, "I do believe you have met your match."

Marianna could only sigh her agreement, as she yielded to the magic of his love, to her destiny.

# Epilogue

One year later...

"Mommy, Mommy, come quick!"

Katrina's urgent tone brought Marianna waddling from the kitchen, like a fleeing penguin to see what was the matter. She followed her daughter's shouts of excitement into the nursery - about to admonish her strongly for waking the baby, and stopped short at the touching sight before her.

"Mommy, he's smiling!" Katrina looked up, excitement glowing in her sparkling blue eyes.

She was going to be such a wonderful big sister, Marianna thought with pride. She moved over to the crib and gazed down lovingly at Brice - Tess, and Dennis's three-month-old son. Perhaps he is smiling, she thought and made a mental note to relay this glorious milestone to Tess. She and Dennis had taken an overnight trip, to celebrate their first anniversary, at Marianna's insistence, and were due back at dinnertime.

Grant came up from behind and wrapped his arms securely around her midsection. "Hey, I can almost reach," he teased her, lovingly caressing her huge belly and nuzzling her neck.

Marianna marveled at the fevered passion Grant still harbored, despite her current beached whale state – and how he still had the power to reduce her to a quivering mass of wanton desire. She felt horribly large and unattractive, but, in truth, she loved being pregnant, and knew that Grant loved it too.

Now, her sexy he-man moved to pick Brice up and change him - they were learning about proactive parenting readiness, and Marianna went back to finishing dinner preparations. Life was grand!

~~~

Marianna lifted her head groggily from the pillow, smiling serenely as Grant deposited their newborn son, Dallas, in the bassinet. He gently tucked the blanket around him and returned to Marianna, gazing down in wonder.

"She's a typical woman - much greedier than her brother," Grant teased, and Marianna laughed as she lovingly caressed the soft, fuzzy head of their newborn daughter, Kirsten.

"No, he's just like a man, falling asleep as soon as he's satiated," Marianna quipped gleefully.

In truth, Grant did not remotely fit into that stereotype. Indeed, he was totally insatiable. Marianna matched him in that department - the grandmother of all headaches could never drag her away. Even after all this time, they were never able to get enough of one another. Of course, after her emergency C-section, they would need to employ resourcefulness for a time – even in this maternity bed – the thought fired her senses.

She smiled, thinking how smoothly everything had gone. Oh, it hurt like hell for sure - the first time she had to hoist herself out of bed, she thought she'd faint with the fiery pain from the incision. But each time, it got easier, and now Marianna was quite capable of fetching her babies, to nurse and change them, all by herself. Grant, however, was determined to maintain a firm claim to that task, intent on spoiling her silly.

Up until four days before the birth of their twins, they had believed Marianna was carrying only one chunky monkey. However, two weeks before the due date, during a routine doctor visit, it was discovered her blood pressure had skyrocketed, and Marianna was ordered into the hospital.

Grant was predictably frantic and worried sick. To the utter amazement of the expectant parents, the ultrasound had revealed two babies – how on earth did they miss that? The doctors insisted they needed to come out immediately.

Marianna entertained a fleeting moment of vanity, when she'd reflected on the potential length of the resulting C-section scar, but Grant had kissed her soundly and told her she could grow another nose, and he'd still lust after her. She had giggled out loud and fell promptly into a drugged sleep.

Marianna had been deeply touched, when all of the band members showed up at the hospital in Edmonton, to congratulate the proud parents and hold the tiny babies. Gary had handed her a huge bouquet of roses, kissed her soundly, and gave the new father a huge bear hug, admitting that Grant had finally bested him - eliciting a huge round of guffaws from his fellow musicians.

Jerry had stayed on an extra day to sign papers, which dubbed him the official Godparent to Dallas and Kirsten. It was the only time Marianna had seen him tearfully speechless. She had reached up and tenderly kissed him, gently wiping the solitary droplet, sliding down his cheek.

~~~

Now, comfortably nestled in their marriage bed, nursing her voracious daughter, Marianna pondered her incredible fortune. She was, without doubt, the happiest woman on the planet. Grant was a wonderful husband and father to all their children. They had managed to work out an arrangement for his recording schedule, which he insisted be interrupted for the birth. He would be home full-time now, for another six weeks, before reverting to the schedule they had settled upon.

Grant had persisted that Marianna be afforded the luxury of a housekeeper, twice per week, to help keep up, and readily agreed to her compromise, that she remain a full-time mother to their children, with no nannies in the picture. He wanted her to be able to continue her passion for writing – second, of course, to him and the children. Her financial consulting career was over, and she had no regrets there. She had published two more novels during the past six months, and Grant was immensely proud of her.

Marianna had been equally adamant about Grant's right to pursue his work with the band, and so they agreed that he would be in L.A. every second week, while they were recording. The other band members readily approved, as this really didn't lessen the amount of time they had previously spent in the studio. Marianna had also suggested that more time could be spent in L.A., during the holidays, when she and the kids could travel with him.

Terri was ecstatic, because Grant was building his family a new home, on the twenty-acre parcel, that he owned, adjacent to her and Derek's ranch. They could stay there whenever Marianna and the kids were able to make the trip. While still private, the two residences were within walking distance, and both Marianna and Terri were excited at the prospect of spending some quality time together. Terri had visited them in Edmonton, during the summer, and the kids bonded like glue. Both moms had set up email accounts to administer the kids' communication.

Grant had opted to keep the residence in Malibu as well, as they both loved the house, and he enjoyed the hour commute alongside the ocean to L.A. Marianna had finally met Grant's sister Lorna, and husband, Rick, and his brother Jake, and wife, Marlene. The kids suddenly acquired three new cousins, though they were already in their teens. Grant's siblings had welcomed Marianna into their family with open arms, and she was immeasurably touched. Although she had actively searched endlessly for her younger sister, through all the years since her mother's death, she'd never found her, and Grant's family meant the world to her.

Marianna acknowledged with a little painful reverie, that she was slowly letting go of her old life - her time with Jeff and all their dreams together. She would, of course, keep his memory alive, especially for Denny and Katrina. She still loved her property and, for now, was reluctant to uproot the kids from their schools. However, they were young and resilient, and she knew they would easily adapt – God knows they loved the Colorado ranch life and could never wait to get there!

Tess and Dennis had fallen in love with Terri and Derek's ranch and were making noises about picking up roots, and following Marianna and Grant, in building a second home there.

Grant, however, was perfectly content to leave things as they were, as the band did not record the entire year, and the schedule seemed to be working out for them. He knew how much Marianna would miss the crisp, clear Alberta winters, though Colorado was a fine match, albeit warmer and more humid.

Marianna was well aware, that he secretly, barely survived the plummeting temperatures in Alberta, and endured them solely for her. She'd been unable to stop her fits of laughter on that erotic blissful night, when he'd admitted to her, a serious fear that his lungs might completely freeze, from the airport to the mall.

"How in the hell do you people live in this weather?" he'd lamented.

Dreaming of their future now, she grinned, anticipating her special surprise for Grant - she was ready to make that move to Colorado permanently. However, she was determined to keep this secret until after the band's final farewell tour.

All the boys had agreed unanimously, that touring was just too hard on aging rockers, but wished to give their fans one last treat. It had almost not come to pass, as Grant firmly declared that he would steadfastly refuse to leave Marianna and the kids, for the length of time that touring demanded.

It had been a formidable battle of wills, as she would not hear of him staying behind, and had finally convinced him that she could quite capably home-school the kids for that one year, and so travel with him.

The kids were ecstatic about the upcoming adventure, and Marianna had conceded that they would hire a childcare companion to accompany them. It was all settled, and Marianna smiled affectionately, as she regarded her big, strong, virile husband, who was really nothing more than a huge mushy teddy bear, where his family was concerned.

~~~

Gently disentangling herself from her husband's firm embrace, Marianna leaned up on her elbow, watching his glorious chest rise and fall with deep breathing. Even in sleep, his features were rugged, masculine, and sexy. Familiar, hot moisture invaded her thighs. God, how she loved him!

Though she knew she would treasure Jeff's memory forever, she no longer suffered guilt at the mind-blowing, intense pleasure she enjoyed in Grant's arms. Not even Jeff had taken her to the heights this man was capable of. Their union was passionate in every possible facet – in the bedroom, they excelled, maintaining their mutual hunger for each other through exploration, romantic commitment, and a strong emotional connection. He still had the power to render her senseless with one dark scorching gaze.

She surveyed their fantasy hotel room now, on the morning of their first anniversary, and said a silent prayer to Tess for taking the children - yes, all four of them, for the night. Dennis insisted on helping, and Marianna knew that even though they adored the kids, they'd be two very grateful adults, when Grant and Marianna came to retrieve their offspring.

Her eyes wandered over to the huge soaker tub, set into the side of a synthetic volcanic mountain, which made up one wall of their theme room. The previous evening, delicate rose petals had been placed strategically along the floor, in an enticing path to the tub and around the edges, and from there, to the giant bed. Hot steamy, bubbly-scented water had threatened to overflow, cascading from a waterfall in the rock face, with non-alcoholic champagne on ice waiting by the side. Chocolate-covered strawberries had topped off the ambience.

Her eyes glazed over at the memory of the erotic delights she and Grant had shared in that tub, and in this huge bed. Would she never get enough of him? Not as long as she lived, she knew. He stirred beside her now and threw his arm over her, drawing her close to him.

"Come here, woman," he growled thickly and kissed her hair, spanning her abdomen with his large hand. He had lamented that he couldn't quite get over how her belly had regained its almost original flat trimness, after growing so huge with their twins, and he lowered his head to kiss the scar from her surgery.

She had to admit, she fully appreciated the way her body had bounced back, and felt much sexier for it. At Grant's eager exploration of her stark-naked state, she scrambled out of bed, and he groaned in protest.

"We have to get a move on Stud, or Tess and Dennis will send out a search party," she admonished him with mock severity. "Besides, we promised to bring brunch," she added as a reminder.

As they chowed down later on quiche and spinach salad, Tess and Dennis insisted that the kids were no trouble at all. Still, Marianna knew better, and thanked them both profusely for allowing her and Grant a romantic hiatus together.

"When do you leave?" Tess was thoroughly dreading an entire year without Marianna's company - not to mention the kids.

Marianna had arranged for Jen to stay on the property, as her parents lived on the neighboring acreage. This opportunity would provide Jen with a taste of independence, as she prepared to embark on her own young adult life, in a year's time. Denny and Katrina were embarking on their home-schooling adventure, with gusto – Marianna had already started the process.

"Early Monday morning," she offered, with a gentle smile, "but remember, I do plan to come back and haunt you a few times while we are away, so don't go getting too cozy without me." Tess laughed and told her she'd hold her to it.

In truth, Marianna knew that Tess wholly approved of her plan to travel with Grant on tour. The band put on a clean show, and she'd be able to take the kids to watch their dad in action for certain venues. Grant loved the idea that Marianna would be present in the audience, watching him perform. He was, however, still concerned about the strain this may place on them all, and vowed to leave the tour if it got too rough. Marianna adored him for it but knew that they would weather it well - see it through. She would do this, and more, for the man she loved.

"Finally, they are all down," Grant flopped onto the easy chair in the family room with a contented sigh. Marianna could hardly get a turn tucking Denny and Katrina in these days, partly because she was so busy with the twins, but mostly because Grant absolutely cherished it and was very greedy, she thought affectionately.

"Come on, old man, time for your beasty rest," she teased him, taking his hand and leading him into their bedroom. He stopped short, at the candles glowing romantically throughout the room.

"Whoa…I thought we did this last night?"

He wasn't complaining, she knew, but she had an agenda, and he was about to discover it. She moved seductively over to him and began to undress him slowly, running her hands over his broad chest and flat abdomen as she went, thrilled at the sight of his bulging manhood. Not yet, she giggled inwardly. Then Marianna threw back the covers on their bed, and waited for his reaction.

What's this?" Grant unfolded the piece of paper, looking up at her with a questioning glance.

She watched him peruse the document and suddenly wondered if she should have perhaps conferred with him beforehand.

"Mari, what's this about?" Grant sat down on the edge of the bed and patted the spot beside him. She joined him there with some trepidation.

"Grant, I've sold the acreage," she began, and cleared her throat, as she took in his rigid expression, which clearly spoke of a need for further explanation.

"I was going to wait to tell you, until after the tour, but for several reasons, I felt it best to clear it up before we left," Marianna faltered at his stricken expression. "Oh, Grant, perhaps I shouldn't have gone ahead without you. I'm so sorry."

She reached out to touch his arm, but he stood up and moved over to stand by the window. Her heart skipped a beat. She had truly not expected such a strong reaction from him. When he turned around to face her, she was alarmed at the sheen of unshed tears in his eyes. What on earth was wrong?

"Mari," he murmured so softly, she nearly missed it, "You did this for me?"

His look was incredulous, and she nodded dumbly, not quite knowing how to handle this giant of a man, whom she loved so deeply. He struggled to control his emotional reaction.

"I can't accept this gift from you - it's your independence, your roots," he continued. "I would never expect you to give this up - surely you know that." She stood up to face him.

"Of course, I know that," Marianna assured him gently. "I didn't do this for you. I did this for us," she smiled and tenderly reached for his hand. "Grant, I realize that our schedule has worked fairly well so far, but wouldn't you prefer to be within easier commuting time to your family while you are in L.A.?" She gently prodded him.

"Hell yes, in Colorado, I can fly home every night."

"And we could come to stay in the Malibu house sometimes," Marianna added brightly.

"But, Mari, what about your home here? Your friends, Tess..." he trailed off.

"What about Terri and Derek? I know you miss them, and the kids miss their cousins dreadfully." She moved into his arms and rested her head on his chest. "And what about us, and what we need?" She looked up into his eyes, still shining with emotion. "You know that Tess and Dennis have plans to build there too."

"Are you sure about this, Babe?"

Marianna knew that he needed to feel confident that this was the right move for her. "Absolutely," she assured him. "Besides, did you notice who the buyer is?" she didn't wait for his answer. "Jen's parents. They have always yearned to own a larger acreage, but can't afford it at today's prices. Now that dream is alive for them - I've arranged a very decent price and a suitable payment plan, interest-free. They are ecstatic." Marianna was truly pleased with herself. "Especially now that Jen will have the option to move into their smaller one - still live right beside them."

"On one condition," Grant's tone brooked no argument, and she waited to hear it out.

"I will pay off the mortgage on Jen's parents' place in full, and I know what you are thinking - hear me out. I have more than enough resources to handle this, Mari, and I know you would have done the same if it weren't for your commitment to Den and Katrina's inheritance from their father."

Marianna shed tears of gratitude as she kissed his cheek.

"Not to mention what's mine is yours." Grant studied her for a very long time. "How in the world did I get so lucky to have found you?" He brought her hands up to his lips and kissed each finger tenderly.

"You are beautiful, brilliant, a stellar mother, talented as all get out - incredible between the sheets - and outside of them," he smiled crookedly. "Most importantly, you are a woman with heart," he shook his head in wonder. "I will spend the rest of my life in humble service, doing my damnedest to deserve you." He gathered her close and held her as if he'd never let her go.

"Grant, my love," she whispered softly, "I am the fortunate one - you taught me about trust and faith," she sighed seductively, "you are, by far, the sexiest, surliest, most stubborn man a girl could ever sink her hooks into, and I am never letting you go."

Grant pulled her chin up and sealed the bargain, with a kiss to die for.